Last Surrender

Last Surrender

A Northstar Novel

SUZIE O'CONNELL

For my fellow "Spice Girls."
You gals inspire me.

Special thanks also to Kay Lowe
for sharing your medical knowledge.

One

JEREMIAH GRIPPED THE RUSTY NAIL with his pliers and yanked it out of the fence post, glancing at his Australian shepherd when the dog jumped to his feet with eyes and ears alert. Murph's tail stump wiggled, and when Jeremiah followed his dog's gaze, he spotted Aaron striding toward them from the back door of the main house. The older man would be heading in to work shortly, so he was dressed in his brown and tan uniform, and the sight of it brought a trickle of adrenaline. He set his pliers on top of the post and waited for the sheriff to stride across the snowy yard.

Snow. On the eighth of May.

It didn't seem to matter how long he lived in Northstar; its weather and beauty still left him with the same wonder and awe as it had that first year he'd worked for the

Hammonds.

As Aaron neared, the trickle of adrenaline increased to a stream. He didn't like the grim set of the sheriff's jaw.

When Aaron was a dozen yards away, Murph raced out to him, prancing around his legs until the man gave in and lavished him with pets. Satisfied, the dog trotted back to Jeremiah looking entirely too pleased with himself.

"Well?" Jeremiah asked when Aaron reached him.

"Zach got the early parole."

"Fuck." He winced, glancing at his companion. "Sorry."

Aaron's brows rose. "Been a long time since I've heard you use that particular word."

"Yeah." He raked his gloved hand through his hair and scowled. He needed a haircut. "When's he getting out?"

"Couple weeks."

"Great."

"I seriously doubt he'd throw away all his hard work to get the early release and risk his freedom to get back at you."

"You don't know him."

"You're right. I don't. But I know one thing." Aaron nudged him with his elbow and offered a teasing grin. "He's not a hothead like you were."

Jeremiah snorted and folded his arms on the top rail of the fence. He let his gaze wander over the snow-covered hayfields and pastures dotted with cattle and horses. Above the cacophony of his thoughts, the quiet, natural sounds of the Lazy H ranch—cows calling to their calves, the twittering of birds in the willows by the nearby creek, the sighing of the wind through the pines blanketing the foothills—were a soothing song, but even that couldn't ease the clawing anxiety.

Not today. Maybe, if Aaron had brought different news…. But not now.

"He'll never forgive what I did."

"Do you really believe he'd gamble his freedom for revenge?"

Jeremiah held his friend's gaze with brows lifted and his mouth pressed into a line. It was all the answer Aaron needed.

"I hope you're wrong," he said. "I need to head in to work. You gonna be all right?"

Jeremiah inhaled, held it, and frowned. As he let the breath out, he said, "I will be."

Aaron wrapped him in a strong hug and didn't let go for close to half a minute, and Jeremiah closed his eyes and took another deep breath as he hugged the man back. Where would he be right now if Aaron hadn't wrestled him into submission that day eleven years ago with every diner in the crowded restaurant trying hard to pretend they weren't watching? What would've happened to him if, after that, Aaron had rightly slapped cuffs on him for a third time as he had the second and sent him back to jail instead of offering him a job?

Aaron released him but didn't entirely let him go, gripping his shoulder tightly. "I know what you're thinking about," he said. "Knock it off. The past is the past and whatever might've been won't ever be."

Jeremiah only nodded.

"Try not to think about this too much, all right?"

"Can't make any promises."

"I know. But try."

He watched Aaron stride away. When the sheriff was a dozen paces from the fence, Jeremiah called after him. "Hey, Aaron?"

The older man stopped and turned around. "Yeah?"

"Thanks. For everything."

Aaron could have said something like *no thanks needed* or *my pleasure* or any other of a dozen polite phrases, but he only dipped his head once in acknowledgement, and that said more than words could. It said Jeremiah was valued, that he was part of the family. And that was something he'd lost the day his older brother had put a gun to his head. Zach might be his cousin, but he'd never been family. Nor would he ever be.

He dropped his head onto his arms and pinched his eyes closed.

Maybe he *was* wrong. Not about Zach forgiving what he'd done—there wasn't a snowball's chance in hell of that happening—but maybe about how important revenge was to him. Zach was a lifer, as addicted to the power and money of his illicit empire as his customers were to the drugs he sold them. He couldn't rebuild that empire from behind bars.

Lifting his head, Jeremiah shook it and let out a mirthless laugh.

He hadn't seen his cousin in almost sixteen years, but the last time he had, Zach hadn't needed to say the words for Jeremiah to get the message.

You're a dead man.

Abruptly, he straightened. Grabbing his pliers, he ripped out the last four nails left behind when the old rails had succumbed to rot this winter and made quick work of nailing the new rails in place. Then he yanked off his gloves and stared at his trembling hands. He jerked his hammer off the ground and whipped it back to hurl it across the yard but stopped himself. His whole body quivered as he fought the surge of anger. He was better than this. The Hammonds had helped him get better. He wasn't the young, dumb hothead who had twice assaulted Aaron. Not anymore.

Letting out a guttural sound as he overpowered the raging despair and frustration, he dropped his arm and slumped against the fence post, ignoring the knot digging into his back. The hammer slipped from his hand, and he sank to the ground, sitting on his heels to keep his butt out of the snow. Murphy wiggled into his lap with a low whine, and Jeremiah buried his fingers in the dog's soft, thick fur.

He tipped his head back with his eyes closed. He still had a lot more fence to fix today, but there was no way he'd be able to get it done without hurting himself or breaking something.

After giving himself a few minutes to fully regain his composure, he pushed to his feet and gathered his tools. He returned them to their homes in the shop, called to Murph, and headed to the main house. He commanded his dog to stay before he stepped inside the front door. He found Tracie Hammond enjoying a book in the living room with her lunch sitting half-eaten on the end table beside her recliner. She looked up with a smile when he entered.

"Finally decided to come in for lunch?" she inquired.

Crap. He'd forgotten lunch again. "Not exactly."

"You know, someday I'd love to not have to remind you to eat."

"Sorry. I get so focused on work…."

"I'm teasing, Jeremiah." She studied him with narrowed eyes. Tracie Hammond was a gracious and compassionate woman, and she undoubtedly had no trouble gauging his troubled thoughts as if they were as plain on his face as the words on the pages of her book. "So serious today. What do you need, honey?"

"I hate to ask because I still have a lot to do on the fence," Jeremiah began. "But—"

"Yes," she interrupted. Setting her book aside, she rose and walked over to hug him. "Take the afternoon off. That fence isn't going anywhere."

"Aaron already told you."

"I was standing right next to him when he made the call. Are you okay?"

He started to give the same answer he'd given her son—that he *would* be okay—but instead, he took a deep breath and went with complete honesty. "Not right at this moment. I need some time to… I don't know. Wrap my head around it? I thought I'd have a few more years before he got out."

"We all hoped you would, too. Take all the time you need. The work will wait."

"Thank you, Tracie."

"Try that again."

Chuckling, he corrected himself. "Thank you, *Mom*."

"That's better."

She hugged him again, holding him longer this time, and when she released him, she rested her hand briefly against his cheek like he imagined she'd done to her sons when they were younger. She must've sensed he was on the verge of losing it because she ruffled the mop that was his hair and shooed him away with a promise to give him a haircut tomorrow. He glanced back at her as he walked out of the living room to the entryway, and though she'd returned to her recliner, she watched him with a concerned frown. When their gazes met, she smiled reassuringly, and he nodded in acknowledgement before he slipped outside.

He owed Tracie and her family—especially Aaron—more than he could ever repay. Not that they'd ask him to. He'd've been lost without the Hammonds. Or dead. Did they understand that… *truly* understand it?

"Come on, Murph," he said to his dog. With a snap of his fingers, the blue-eyed Aussie jumped to his side. "Let's go for a ride."

Without a conscious thought about what he needed to do to calm his erratic thoughts, he opened the driver-side door of his old Ford pickup to let Murph in and climbed in after the dog. The truck wasn't much to look at with some rust here and there and a few more dents he still needed to pull—it was a ranch truck, after all—but thanks to many a late night in the shop with Henry, the old girl ran like a dream, and she'd never once let him down. He turned the key in the ignition and smiled when the engine growled to life.

"Atta girl," he murmured, patting the sun-faded dash.

Despite the snow on the ground, it was close to fifty degrees out, so he reached across the cab and rolled the passenger-side window down enough for Murph to window-surf.

He drove off the ranch and turned south on the Northstar Scenic Byway, not questioning the impulse guiding him. When he reached the main highway, he turned left, toward Devyn, driving slower than he normally did to take in the mountains and hills and the sweep of the valley, trying to remember when this landscape hadn't been as familiar as his own reflection.

The highway curved east and ran straight for a few miles before crossing Northstar Creek and starting the climb up Badger Pass. As he crossed the bridge, he noted the three crosses just beyond and gave a moment's thought to the intricacies of fate. One of those crosses was for Pat O'Neil's ex, and the crash that had ended her life had set him free just as hitting a deer sixteen years ago today had knocked Jeremiah off the path he'd been headed down.

As he crested the pass and started down the other side toward Devyn, he glanced in his rearview mirror and let the memories roll through him.

That night, he'd driven a BMW sedan instead of an old ranch truck. Narrowing his eyes, he scanned the right side of the road. There it was, at the top of the small rise before the highway began the long descent into the valley—the turnout by the shallow gravel pit. Panic had surged when he'd spotted the pickup marked with the county sheriff's department insignia. He'd been so close… so close to completing his run, but when Aaron had pulled onto the road and followed him, he'd been so anxious that he hadn't paid proper attention to the road in front of him. Eight miles down the pass, he'd been watching in his mirror, waiting for those red and blue lights to turn on, and he hadn't seen the deer.

He'd hit it full on at seventy miles an hour.

It was a miracle he hadn't been killed.

The BMW, spraying sparks that had glowed eerily in the dark night, had skidded into the ditch and up onto a pasture access approach, coming to an abrupt stop against a remarkably sturdy fence.

The deer had—mercifully—died instantly. It was a small consolation, and all these years later, Jeremiah still regretted that loss of life. And yet… he wouldn't have everything he did now if not for that deer.

He saw the spot where the BMW had ended up and pulled over. Shutting the truck down, he waited for a semi hauling cattle to pass by before he stepped outside and let his dog out. Walking around to the front of his truck, he propped his foot on the bumper and patted his leg. Murph leapt up to his thigh and then onto the wide hood of the old truck. Jeremiah joined him, leaning against the windshield.

The storm that had dumped six inches of wet snow in Northstar hadn't been cold enough to bring snow to the broad valley around Devyn, and a distinct snowline ringed the valley. Everything above six thousand feet was blanketed in white while everything below gleamed emerald.

It was gorgeous. He was lucky to be alive to appreciate it and the turn his life had taken.

He reached over to ruffle Murph's ears and was rewarded with enthusiastic kisses.

"Yeah, you're part of all the good things, too," he said, laughing. "One of the best, in fact. We're both pretty lucky, aren't we?"

He didn't give voice to the thought, but he couldn't stop it from resounding in his head.

How much longer would his luck last?

Because, no matter how much he hoped he was

wrong, he knew in his gut Zach wasn't going to let him off the hook for ratting him out.

* * *

Heather adjusted her grip on the steering wheel and scowled. She'd done it again—ruined her parents dreams of her marrying the perfect man and giving them three more perfect grandchildren. On her birthday, no less. And not just *any* birthday. Her thirtieth. The one that was supposed to be the transition into full, no-more-excuses, time-to-get-serious adulthood. Somehow, breaking up with her boyfriend seconds before he proposed because some stupid, childish voice in the back of her mind balked at the idea of being tied down—the same voice that nagged her about how temporary everything in her life felt even if it wasn't—didn't seem like a very adult thing to do.

Dinner with her family tonight was going to be oh-so-fun.

She flipped on her blinker as she reached the exit for the highway out to Northstar and swiped at the tears leaking down her cheeks. Why was she crying—or almost crying—anyhow? It wasn't like this was the first time she'd broken up with a great guy.

Oh, no.

She had quite the track record, stretching all the way back to Shane McGuire, her first serious boyfriend in high school. And every single one of the boys and men she'd dated—or, in the case of Luke Conner, had wanted to date—were now happily married to incredible, loving wives. Of them all, Shane was the only one not married, and that would change next summer when he and Becky Epperson finally tied the knot.

She didn't begrudge them their happily-ever-afters; they all deserved nothing less.

The fault wasn't with the men. It was with her.

Why did she keep doing shit like this? Giving up on a good thing because she was…. What? Stubborn? Overly picky? Afraid?

Dustin was a good man, like all the rest, if a little too set on the whole white-picket-fence dream for her tastes. He was kind and generous, tall, and good-looking, and he had a good job and a loving family who had accepted and adored her from the get go. He was—as far as she and the many, many women she'd caught eying him could tell—absolutely perfect.

That was the problem, and it was the same one she'd had with Ty Evans. And a dozen other men. He was *too* perfect, and she'd known from their first date that she would never be entirely comfortable with him. And the reason why had nothing to do with him. She couldn't imagine letting him see the cracks in her. Because, in his wonderful, compassionate perfection, he would try to help her heal them and only end up cracking himself.

Sure. She was going to go with that explanation. That way she sounded noble and selfless and not totally insane.

Of course, her mother's first words after Heather broke the devastating news were likely to agree with the latter explanation. Heather could almost hear the practiced balance of exasperation and disappointment in her mother's voice. *Are you crazy?*

"Plenty of evidence pointing in that direction," she murmured, glancing at the leather wrist band on her left arm.

Maybe Dustin wasn't so perfect after all. He'd never once asked why she always wore it, assuming, as everyone else did, that the band with its elegant Western tooling was a fashion statement. And she'd never felt the desire to explain it to him.

Tired of that depressing line of thought, she skipped through her playlist until she landed on Eminem's *The Way I am* and cranked the volume up.

Halfway between the interstate and the top of Badger Pass, she spotted a familiar 1978 Ford F-250 parked on an approach to a pasture on the other side of the highway. Its owner and his ever-present four-legged companion sat on the hood. At first glance, they looked rather comfortable, like they were taking in the scenery, but maybe the old truck had broken down and they were waiting for someone to stop. As far as she knew, the man didn't own a cell phone. She slowed and pulled over onto the approach across the highway from them. Leaving her truck running, she climbed out and waited for a car to pass.

"Need a ride, cowboy?" Heather called as she jogged across the road.

Jeremiah turned his head toward her, and she expected him to grin that shy, adorable grin he usually gave her, but his lips barely twitched, and his eyes remained distant.

Guess I'm not the only one having a shitty day. She rested her hand on the hood near his leg. "The ol' girl finally give up on you?"

"Not yet."

"Then… what are you doing here?"

"Retracing steps and pondering the quirks of life and

fate."

Heather's first instinct was to laugh at the turn of phrase, but his somber expression quieted the urge. "Want some company?"

He eyed her, and for a moment, she thought he was going to turn her down. Then he scooted over and patted the hood in invitation. She climbed up beside him without considering for even half a second why she hadn't just turned around and left him to his pondering. She might not have given him much thought, but that didn't mean she was oblivious to the way he'd always looked at her. And right now, with her heart and mind twisted into knots about Dustin, his quiet but obvious attraction to her was soothing.

"So, what quirks of life and fate are you pondering?" she asked, redirecting her thoughts before they spilled out her mouth and got her in trouble. She reached across him to let his dog sniff her hand, gauging his expression from the corner of her vision. When the Australian shepherd nudged her hand with his nose, she ruffled his ears.

Jeremiah didn't seem to notice. Man, he *was* caught up in his own thoughts.

"My cousin'll be out of prison in a couple weeks," he said quietly. "He got the early parole."

His cousin? Right. Zach Neely—sentenced to twenty years in prison for masterminding the biggest drug ring this county had ever seen. It had been all over the news when she and her family had first moved out here, but she'd been too young and having too much fun much exploring her new home to pay much attention to it. "Ah, I'd forgotten about him."

"Most days, I do, too. But not today." He leaned

forward with his forearms braced on his thighs and stared unseeing across the valley at the mountains. "I wish Aaron had waited to tell me."

"What's so special about today?"

"Today marks sixteen years since he arrested me. And Zach getting out early makes it difficult to celebrate that."

"You want to *celebrate* getting arrested?"

"That arrest started me on the *right* path even if it took me a few more years to see it." He shook his head. "I need to go back and remember it all today. To remember how far I've come."

Heather stared at him. This was *way* deeper than anything she'd expected. "Ah," was all she could say in response. Suddenly, agonizing over her breakup seemed pathetic.

Abruptly, he looked at her with a thoughtful frown. "Funny you of all people should pull over." Then his expression shifted into a glimmer of the smile she was most familiar with. "Happy birthday, by the way."

"How'd you…?" She held up her hands. "Never mind. Thank you. Some birthday it's turned out to be, but thank you."

She glanced over him. He was dressed in a plain gray long-sleeved T-shirt and straight-legged jeans rather than the button-up shirt and classic Wrangler jeans many of their Northstar neighbors preferred, and with his hair shaggier than he usually kept it, he didn't look much like a cowboy, but the stubble darkening his jaw added a hint of ruggedness to his otherwise boyish face.

A memory flashed across her mind—of the first time

she'd met him, shortly after the Hammonds had hired him. It wasn't a clear memory, but she recalled that he'd been even shaggier and a whole lot skinnier. Sometime between then and now, he'd added weight and muscle, and even that boring T-shirt of his couldn't hide it.

She cocked her head. Why hadn't she ever noticed what a cutie he was? Or that he was so sweet?

"Not having a good day?" he asked.

"Not particularly. And I'm on my way home to have dinner with my family, which is bound to make it worse."

He looked at her like a man teetering on the edge of indecision, working up the courage to speak. It took a while, but finally, he did.

"If you need a backup plan, I'd be happy to buy you a couple of drinks."

"Thank you. I mean that. And I will probably take you up on that." She offered her hand and he shook it. "I'll let you get back to pondering the quirks of life and fate. See you later."

"Sure," he replied in a way that said he didn't expect she'd be knocking on his door tonight.

Giving his dog another pat, she slid off the hood and crossed the highway. She climbed in behind the wheel of her truck and rolled the window down to wave as she drove away. He lifted his hand in farewell. As she watched his truck shrink in her rearview mirror, an idea blossomed with delightful brilliance.

In addition to being generally perfect, all the men she'd dated had one more thing in common—they all fit within her family's narrow definition of a "good man". With his criminal background, Jeremiah definitely would not.

Since she'd made a habit of bucking against her family's wishes most of her life, maybe it was time to apply that tradition to her love life as well.

By the time she reached Northstar, it was already after three. Everyone was supposed to gather at her parents' house at five, so she detoured to her cabin in the same subdivision where the Hammonds had their vacation rental just long enough to drop her overnight bag inside and run a brush through her hair. It probably wasn't a smart idea to head down early, but if things were going to go the way she was certain they would, she might as well get it over with and give herself more evening to enjoy with Jeremiah.

She wasn't entirely surprised that her mother, sister, and both sisters-in-law were in the kitchen when she arrived, decorating her cake at the island. Her father, brothers, and brother-in-law were certainly still out working somewhere on their small ranch. She leaned against the wall beside the kitchen door and watched as her mother's skilled hands turned white icing into delicate lace against a smooth chocolate backdrop. The cake would undoubtedly be a feminine work of art when she was done... and absolutely the opposite of what Heather liked.

Finally, the three younger women realized they had company and glanced in her direction. Her sister, Brianna, couldn't be troubled to give more than a nod in acknowledgement. Brock's wife, Anna, at least smiled, but she had her hands full scooping more icing into a piping bag for Lily, who was so focused on her task that she remained oblivious to everything else. Curtis's wife, Christina, was the only one who put down what she was working on and wiped her hands on the apron that did nothing to hide her gigantic belly. Heather took a step further into the kitchen, but Christina didn't wait for her to come to her. She greeted Heather at the door with a big hug and a laugh.

"Happy birthday, old woman!"

Heather gave a sniff of laughter. "Thanks."

"You're early," her mother remarked. "Where's Dustin?"

"In Bozeman."

This was a conversation they'd had so many times that she didn't need to spell it out for her mother, and she didn't expect she'd have to wait long for her mother to connect the dots.

Lily didn't disappoint. Without so much as a brief smile of welcome, her mother groaned. "Not again. What did you do?"

"I woulda thought that was obvious. I broke up with him."

"Oh, Heather…. *Why*? Dustin is such a wonderful man."

"Yes, he is."

Lily waited for her to elaborate with brows pinched together and an icing-spattered hand on her hip. Heather met her gaze head on and waited her out. For such a dainty and classically feminine woman, Lily Brown had a deceptively forceful nature, and Heather watched the practiced poise slide into scorn.

"When are you going to grow up and stop pushing good men away? Or do you *want* to be alone the rest of your life?"

"Somedays that's a rather appealing idea."

"What is *wrong* with you?"

Heather stared at her mother in stunned silence. Lily was strict and stern and rigid in her idea of what was and wasn't the proper way for a woman to behave, but she was rarely cruel. She glanced between her mother, Brianna, Christina, and Anna. They were all slight, delicate women, and Heather stood four inches higher than the tallest of them with a heavier frame toned by her highly physical job. She felt like an awkward giant standing next to them.

Her mother's words echoed in her mind. *What is wrong with you?*

She straightened her spine and glared down at her mother, meeting Lily's disgust with fire.

"A lot. Thanks, Mother. Happy fucking birthday to me." She stormed to the door and yanked it open.

"Heather Jade Brown, don't you dare—"

She slammed the door behind her.

She was halfway out to her truck when the door opened again and Christina jogged awkwardly out it. Heather winced, momentarily guilty for making her friend run when she was so close to her due date.

"Heather, wait! Please."

She stopped and waited for Christina to reach her. "I'm not going back in there."

"I didn't figure you would. I wasn't going to ask you to."

"Then what do you want?"

"I'll go out with you. We'll celebrate your birthday in town, away from all this. Sounds like you could use a couple drinks tonight."

Heather eyed her friend's pregnant belly and lifted a brow. "That's all right. I already have a backup plan."

"Oh?"

"Yeah. I bumped into Jeremiah a bit ago, and it turns out I'm not the only one who has something to drink about today."

"Jerry Mackey?"

"I'm pretty sure he prefers to be called Jeremiah."

"You can't be serious. You *just* broke up with Dustin, who was a great guy, and—"

"And Jeremiah's not?"

"Well…. Come on, Heather. He was arrested for running drugs, or did you forget that?"

"And one mistake—which he's paid for—should condemn him for the rest of his life?"

"But it wasn't just one mistake. Have you forgotten that he assaulted Aaron not once but twice?"

"And yet Aaron turned around and offered him a job on the Lazy H… a job he still has *eleven years later*. Seems you've forgotten *that*."

"The man has a temper, Heather."

"Maybe he *did*. Or maybe he was just a hurting kid lashing out. I don't know, and I'm not going to judge him for what happened over a decade ago until I *do* know."

Heather pressed her mouth into a flat line. Once upon a time, they'd been the best of friends, but that had changed when Christina had married Curtis, even though Curtis was easily Heather's favorite sibling. "I miss the days when you were still my friend first and my family second."

She'd said it gently, but that couldn't strip the bite from the words, and Christina stared at her for a moment with her eyes rounded with hurt. Then her friend spun on her heel and marched back to the house.

She should call her friend back and apologize, but right at that moment, she wasn't in the mood. There had been a time when such a thought would never have entered her mind let alone escaped her lips, and Heather missed it. She needed Christina's unconditional friendship today, and that comment about Jeremiah made it painfully obvious she didn't have it anymore.

Scowling, she jumped into her truck, started it, and slammed it in reverse, spraying slush and mud as she peeled away from her parents' house.

She wasn't sure if Jeremiah was even home yet, but if he wasn't, she'd wait on the porch of the bunkhouse he shared with Austin McGuire. Anything was better than sticking around to listen to her family deride her for breaking up with Dustin or going home to stew in the silence of her cabin.

She was in luck. His old Ford was parked beside the bunkhouse, and she pulled her three-year-old Silverado in beside it. The stark difference in their vehicles ignited her anger at Christina's remarks all over again. Whatever he might've done when he was young and stupid, Jeremiah had busted his ass to get to where he was now, and he'd done it with admirable humility. That said a lot more to her about his character than the choices he'd made as a dumb teenager.

He answered her knock with unveiled surprise. So he really *hadn't* believed she would take him up on his invitation.

The smile that spread slowly across his face was one she'd never seen before, and right then, it was exactly what she needed.

"That offer still open?" she asked.

That sweet, surprised smile widened into a beaming grin, like she'd just handed him the world. Euphoria swamped her.

It was nice to be wanted without conditions.

Two

"ALL RIGHT, KIDDIES," Henry quipped as he pulled up in front of the Hotel Sidney bar. "Don't have too much fun. And if you want to head home before Aaron gets off work, Linds and I will be in town until ten or so."

"I'm not going to call and interrupt your date, Hen," Jeremiah said.

The older man ignored that. "Lindsay gave you our cell numbers, right, Heather?"

Heather checked her phone and nodded. "Yep."

"We gotta get you a cell phone for nights like this," Henry said, meeting Jeremiah's gaze in the rearview mirror.

"This is the first time in eleven years that I *might* need a cell phone," Jeremiah retorted. He rocked forward to press a kiss to Lindsay's cheek. "Thanks for dragging us into town. Have fun on your date."

"You know we will," Henry's beautiful redheaded wife replied with a devious gleam in her eyes. It disappeared when she rotated in her seat, replaced by a gentle smile. "But seriously, call if you need to."

"Yes, ma'am."

He slipped out of the back seat of Henry's quad-cab truck and jogged around to open the door for Heather. They stood on the sidewalk and waited until Henry drove off before turning and heading into the crowded bar. At least two dozen men swiveled on their barstools or in their chairs to watch Heather saunter to an empty high-top table against the far wall. Jeremiah rolled his eyes, but he couldn't blame them. She'd gone home to change while he'd made arrangements with Henry and Aaron for their rides to and from town, and his jaw had nearly hit the floor when she'd stepped out onto her deck. In boot-cut jeans that hugged her shapely backside, hips, and thighs and a faux-leather halter top with a cutout that showed a hint of cleavage, she was devastatingly sexy... and by the confident set of her shoulders that was exactly what she'd intended. Her long, rich dark hair was pulled back into a high ponytail, and she'd added a hint of dark eye shadow that made the fire in her blue eyes blaze.

God help any man dumb enough to get in her way tonight.

Beside her, Jeremiah was invisible in his best jeans and a long-sleeved black T-shirt. Only a couple men spared him more than a fleeting glance. Not that he was surprised. He was only an inch taller than Heather, and despite eleven years of hard labor on the ranch, he had nothing on the bulkier men here—hardly competition to most of those ogling his companion.

They'd barely claimed their stools when a particularly brave man ambled over and leaned on the table between them with his back rudely to Jeremiah.

"You're going to give this whole place heat stroke, woman," the man said. "Let me buy you a drink to cool you off."

Heather laughed. "*Wow*, that was cheesy. Sorry, pal. I'm not interested in anything you have to offer. So, if you'd be so kind as to *piss off*…."

"You've got a smart mouth. You might want to shut it before it gets your friend here in trouble."

"You come on to her uninvited, and *she* has the smart mouth?" Jeremiah snorted. "Congratulations, dude. You are the jackass who gives the rest of us a bad name. I'd, uh, give you a prize, but I'm all out of Dickhead of the Week badges."

The man whirled around to face him. "You want to start something? Is that it, little man?"

"I don't… but she might. And if you're dumb enough to take her up on it, you'll find out quick that the phrase 'hits like a girl' ain't an insult."

The man glanced between them, then stalked away, muttering under his breath. Jeremiah bristled when the word *bitch* drifted back to him. He turned to Heather to apologize, but laughter danced in her eyes.

"Yeah, no shit!" she called after the man.

Without turning around, he flipped her off.

She laughed. "That was fun."

Jeremiah let out a breath. "It kinda was. But I'm beginning to question the wisdom of inviting you out for drinks tonight. I'd rather *not* get into a fist fight, thank you."

"Oh, come on. I know Henry taught you how to brawl properly. And I hear he was one of the best in his day."

"I can hold my own, but that doesn't mean I want to *have* to tonight. We're supposed to be celebrating, remember?"

"Or commiserating."

One of the waitresses came over to take their order, and while she was listing out the finger foods on special tonight, Jeremiah studied Heather. Earlier, when she'd stopped to see if he needed help, he'd thought she looked… troubled. With that and the aggression simmering just beneath the surface, she struck him as a woman fighting an internal battle. Since she'd made no mention of her boyfriend, he had a pretty good idea what it might be.

"You all right?" he asked when the waitress left to get their drinks.

"Not really."

She didn't elaborate, and he didn't press her. The waitress returned with their drinks, and after Heather had drained half her strawberry daiquiri, she sat back and offered him a smile.

"You haven't asked what my boyfriend will think of me going out with you," she said.

"Last time I checked, you didn't need anyone's permission to go out with a friend. And anyhow, I get the feeling he isn't in the picture anymore."

"Is that what this is? Just two friends out for drinks?"

He held her gaze for a moment, but then he had to look away. He took a sip of his rum and coke but almost choked on it; a lump had formed in his throat, and his heart raced erratically. He'd been waiting for this moment a long time. She hadn't confirmed that she was single, but a woman still happily in a committed relationship didn't go drinking with another man dressed like *that* with a look in her eyes like she wanted to make every man pay for what one had done to her. He opened his mouth to explain, then snapped it closed again.

Just go for it.

He dared to meet her eyes, and the brief flicker of vulnerability he saw in them gave him the courage to say what he needed to.

"If you really did break up with your boyfriend, I'm interested in applying for his position in your life—have been for a long time—but I'm not going to apply for it tonight. So yes, this is just two friends celebrating a birthday and the anniversary of an event that knocked a life onto the right track."

She studied him for a long time with her eyes narrowed, but the fact that she didn't immediately reject the idea of a possible future for them was encouraging.

Then, to his surprise, she raised her glass. "I'll drink to that."

"Just… do me a favor?"

"Okay. What?"

"Try not to get me killed or thrown in jail tonight. I get that you're pissed at men right now, but I'd rather not take the direct or indirect brunt of it. I have a full schedule tomorrow, and I don't think the Hammonds would appreciate me taking tomorrow off after I already took half of today off."

She nodded and toyed with her straw for a moment before taking a sip of her daiquiri. "Fair enough. I'd hate to be the reason you landed back in jail. What was it like?"

"Prison? I hated it. Concrete and cinderblock and steel, rigid schedules and routines, no privacy, no individuality, no sky…." He shuddered as the memories slunk out of the far reaches of his mind he'd banished them to. "I would honestly rather die than go back. It's five years of my life I'll never get back—five years I can't think about without my skin crawling."

"That bad, huh?"

"Worse."

"Okay. I promise I won't do anything tonight that'll get you sent back." Then she laughed. "We do make a pretty good team, though."

Quietly and methodically, Jeremiah locked those memories away again and chuckled. "We do, don't we."

"What made you think I can fight?"

"It's no secret that your dad is a Golden Gloves boxer."

"Yeah, but that doesn't mean he taught me."

"Didn't he?"

"No."

He opened his mouth to apologize, but she smiled, a silent statement that no apology was needed. Frowning, he sipped his rum and coke and waited, sensing that an explanation was forthcoming. He couldn't begin to clarify why he thought she knew how to fight; it was something he knew instinctively. She was too confident in her movements, and even face to face with a cringe-worthy display of macho bravado, she'd been entirely fearless.

"My father didn't—still doesn't—think girls need or should learn how to fight. But I taught myself anyhow with some help from my brother Curtis. It's come in handy a time or two."

"Might've come in handy tonight, too."

She shrugged. "Sorry about that. You're right. I'm in the mood for a brawl, and I shouldn't even be pissed at men right now. I'm not, really. Mostly, I'm pissed at myself."

"Why?"

"Because I broke up with a great guy. A perfect guy."

Jeremiah lowered his gaze to his nearly-full drink. What could he say to that? He was here as her friend, but dammit, he'd watched her date and love other men for so long that the last thing he wanted to hear about was how perfect her ex was. Because he'd met Dustin once or twice, and the guy *was* perfect, and if he wanted to fight to get Heather back, Jeremiah had no hope of competing for her affection.

"Doesn't matter how perfect he is if he isn't right for *you*," he heard himself say.

"Try telling that to my parents. They were hoping he'd be the one to finally make me settle down."

"*Make you* settle down?" Jeremiah shook his head, struck by the words she'd used and the hint of despair that edged the anger out of her voice when she said it. He wanted to explore the emotion behind it, but something in her demeanor stopped him, giving a clear impression that it was an off-limits topic. "Out of curiosity, if Dustin was so perfect, why wasn't he right for you?"

"Because I'm not."

He blinked at her. Surely she wasn't insinuating she

wasn't good enough for her ex. "Not what?"

"Perfect."

She'd said it so quietly that the din of the bar almost buried it.

He leaned back, stunned by the undisguised vulnerability etched into her face. "What does that matter?"

Her search for the right words played out across her face, but in the end, she couldn't find them and only shook her head. It might be a breach of etiquette, but he stood and walked around the table and held his arms out to her. She surprised him again when she didn't hesitate to slip into them. When she dropped her head onto his shoulder, he couldn't be sure which of them was more distraught—he'd never seen her like this, and he didn't like it. She was always so sure of herself.

But no one could be strong all the time.

"I'm sorry," he murmured. "That your family doesn't support your decision *and* that you aren't sure you made the right one."

She didn't respond immediately, and when she did, her words shocked him again.

"But I *did* make the right one," she murmured. "Even if I didn't want to admit it until just now."

The last she'd said in barely more than a whisper, and he wasn't sure if he was supposed to have heard it. If she'd had more than half a strawberry daiquiri, he might've thought it was the alcohol talking. Since he wasn't sure how to respond, he didn't say anything, and sooner than he was ready, the moment passed, and she slipped out of his arms and returned to her seat. She flagged the waitress down and asked for a shot of Captain Morgan. As soon as she had it in her hand, she tipped her head back and gulped the shot, twitching her fingers at the waitress to request another.

For the next hour, Jeremiah nursed his rum and Coke. As appealing as a nice buzz sounded tonight, his reason for drinking in the first place had long since faded into the background of his thoughts. He wanted to keep his conversation with Heather on less volatile subjects, and to do that, he needed a clear head.

When a Fallout Boy Song came on the stereo—*Thnks Fr Th Mmrs*, he thought—Heather jumped to her feet with a tipsy cheer and dragged him to the corner of the room that served as a dance floor. The people gathered there weren't dancing so much as bouncing in place to the beat with arms lifted and waving in sync. The surge of self-consciousness was drowned out by a rush of desire when she moved in so close that their bodies bumped frequently, and when the song ended, she draped her arms around his neck, and he saw the intent in her eyes with barely enough time to avoid the kiss.

It took every ounce of his will power to tilt his head back with her lips so close to his. Everything in him wanted to close the distance and see if she tasted as good as he thought she would.

Disappointment flickered across her expression, but after a moment, realization burned through it.

"Just friends tonight," he whispered near her ear. And even though it might kill him to resist if she tried again, he was determined to uphold that promise.

"Wow," she said. Something close to awe widened her eyes. "You meant it."

"Yes, I did."

"I guess I'm not used to that. I kinda like it." With her arms still locked loosely around his neck, she started swaying to the slow song now playing. A thoughtful frown drew her brows together. "How come you never asked me out before tonight?"

"A lack of opportunity," he replied.

She lifted a brow.

"And maybe I've always thought you were way out of my league."

"Huh. Here I thought you were just shy."

"That, too. Have I been that obvious?"

"Kinda, yeah. But in a sweet way."

Any other time, that reply might've come across as condescending, relegating him to the friend zone so many men dreaded, but tonight, sweet seemed to be exactly what she needed. Still, he couldn't help but ask, "What do you mean?"

"I don't know. I've always had this feeling that you liked me but you'd never make a move unless I wanted you to. It's refreshing. There's no pretense. Just…."

He waited what seemed like minutes for her to finish her thought, but then she only shook her head again. The song ended, and the one that came on after it was one neither of them cared much for, so they returned to their table. When the waitress stopped by to see if they wanted more drinks, Heather asked for another daiquiri and then turned back to Jeremiah.

"I thought you wanted to drink tonight," she remarked.

"Guess I didn't need to after all. To be honest, I never got much into the drinking scene, and the last time I was in a bar was… Christ, eleven years ago—with Joe's ex-girlfriend right before Aaron offered me the job on the ranch."

"Joe?"

"My brother."

She narrowed her eyes, trying to remember, and suddenly, she paled. "The one who…?"

"Killed Aaron's wife before killing himself? He's the only brother I had."

"Until you met the Hammonds."

Nodding, he let out a chuckle. "Until I met the Hammonds."

"I'm glad they offered you a job on the ranch. It's nice to hear a sad story turn in a happy direction for once."

"Yes, it is," he murmured. He flagged the waitress down and asked for a water. Lifting it in a toast, he said, "To us. And to finding peace and happiness from the chaos."

Grinning, she clinked her glass to his. "To us."

As he watched her sip her daiquiri, he wondered if this latest twist in his story was real. Was the woman he'd admired for so long really sitting across the high-top table from him, smiling with such sweet sympathy and warmth? This twist, like all the others, had a surreal quality, but the glass was too cold in his hand, the music too loud, and Heather's smile too beautiful to be nothing more than a creation of his imagination.

He took a long swallow of his water, glad he hadn't ordered another drink because he wanted to remember every vivid detail of this night.

Please, God, don't let this be a dream.

* * *

Heather opened her eyes and was disoriented for a moment. Other than the glowing dash lights and the bazillion stars, it was pitch black out. When had they left town? She must have dozed off at some point with her head on Jeremiah's shoulder, but she wasn't in any hurry to detach herself from him. There was something about him right now—a stillness or a quiet patience—that was incredibly soothing. And she *wasn't* drunk. A little buzzed, sure, and relaxed, but plenty sober enough to appreciate whatever quality he emanated that she needed.

"You seem to be in a much better mood," Aaron said quietly on her left. "I'm glad you decided to go out with Heather."

"Yeah. We had a good time."

They were silent for a moment, and she sensed an unspoken conversation passing between them.

Finally, Aaron let out a chuckle. "Took you long enough."

Jeremiah snorted. "Yeah, yeah. It was definitely worth the wait, though."

"The best things usually are."

They lapsed into silence again, and Heather couldn't help but smile at the confirmation that Jeremiah had indeed been hoping for a date with her for a long time. And yet he'd never acted on it. *A lack of opportunity*, he'd said earlier when she'd asked. But there had been times between boyfriends when he could've asked her out, and he hadn't. Why not? And what had changed?

Her mind was too lazy to bother trying to find an answer for that right now, but she couldn't deny that she was suddenly very curious to see where this would go. Some of the things he'd said today…. They made her want to know him better, to find out who he was beyond his reputation. Because she was damned sure after his comments on the side of the highway and then at the bar that his reputation was not a remotely accurate representation.

The quiet in the cab of Aaron's truck and the hum of the road beneath the tires lulled her into a blissful half-conscious state, and too quickly, it was all over. Aaron pulled up in front of her cabin and announced their arrival.

"Time to wake up," Jeremiah murmured close to her ear.

"Can't be," she mumbled. "I'm having too much fun."

"Me, too. But I'm also exhausted, and I know you are, too—you slept the whole way back. Besides, I'm sure Aaron wants to get home to his family even if he's too polite to say it."

He didn't give her the chance to come up with more excuses for why they needed to stay right where they were; he unbuckled himself, opened the door, and slid out. She shivered at the sudden loss of his body heat. She expected, since they'd gone out as friends, that he'd climb back into Aaron's truck as soon as she was out of it, but he walked her to her door.

"I didn't know you were such a gentleman."

"Tracie made sure of it."

"Thank her for me."

They stood on her deck for almost a minute, neither of them wanting to say goodbye, and Heather glanced over her companion. He stood with his hands in his pockets, rocking back on his heels a few times while he waited for her to head inside. Impulsively, she hugged him.

"Thank you for salvaging my birthday," she whispered.

"You're most welcome. And thank you for giving my crappy day a pretty fantastic ending."

This time when she leaned toward him, testing his decision to keep tonight in the realm of friendship, he didn't lean away. Emboldened, she touched her lips to his, and when he still didn't retreat, she deepened the kiss. Then he was kissing her back like he was trying to restrain himself but couldn't.

Her head spun, and it had nothing to do with the alcohol she'd consumed tonight.

Who knew Jeremiah could kiss like that?

When he pulled away, he rested his forehead against hers for a moment, and in the dim glow of her neighbor's porch light, she caught sight of a ghost of a smile on his lips.

"Can't wait to try that again when we're both totally sober and you aren't on the rebound," he murmured.

"Me, neither."

"Goodnight, Heather."

He turned away and trotted down the steps, and then he was gone.

She watched Aaron's truck all the way to the highway.

Whoa....

She'd thought only to enjoy a fun night with a friend to get Dustin off her mind. When she'd showed up at the bunkhouse to take Jeremiah up on his offer of mutual celebration and commiseration, kissing him had certainly *not* been part of the plan... but when they'd danced, she hadn't been able to get the idea of kissing him out of her head. It was *way* too early to be indulging in a physical attraction—she'd broken up with Dustin *just* this morning, for crying out loud. And besides, the problem was that her attraction to Jeremiah wasn't purely physical. Not even close. The way he'd stood up for her with that macho jackass without getting all macho and possessive himself…. She liked it and what it said about him. There was a lot more she liked, but thinking about it tonight wasn't going to do her any good. She needed to push Dustin the rest of the way out of her heart first.

Shaking her head, she headed into her house. She closed the door and frowned at her living room, unable to remember turning on the light beside her couch before Henry and Lindsay had arrived to drive her and Jeremiah into town.

"About time you showed up."

She jumped and turned toward his voice. With her hand over her pounding heart, she glared at her brother, who sat in her shadowed dining room at her table with a look on his face too dark to be explained away by the lack of light. "Fuck, Curtis. What the hell are you doing here?"

"What is wrong with you?"

Now, where had she heard that before? Right. Their mother had used those exact words only this afternoon. "If that's all you came to say, get out."

"You ditched your family to go out drinking?"

"Wouldn't be the first time my family drove me to drink," she snapped.

She wandered into her kitchen without bothering to turn on any more lights and yanked the water pitcher out of the fridge. Curtis followed her in, standing a few feet away with his arms folded tightly across his chest and a deep scowl contorting his handsome face.

"You made my wife cry, Heather."

"Maybe she should've kept her Brown family judgments to herself."

"She's your friend. How could you do that to your friend?"

"Guess she's not as much of a friend as she used to be."

"She says you went out with Jerry Mackey."

"Jeremiah," she corrected. "And so what?"

"For one, didn't you *just* break up with Dustin this morning?"

She glanced at the clock on her microwave. It was just after one. "Technically, it was yesterday morning. Besides, we went out as *friends*, so what does it matter if I just broke up with Dustin?"

"Fine, whatever. But *Jerry Mackey*?"

She met his gaze over the rim of her glass. "Jeremiah."

"He's a felon, Heather."

She set her glass on the counter hard enough to slosh water out of it and whirled on him. For half a minute she stared at him, seething and unable to put her anger into words. Once upon a time, Curtis had been the one member of her family she could count on to be reasonable. When had he turned into their parents?

"The Hammonds wouldn't have hired him let alone kept him on for over a decade if they had even the tiniest doubt about him," she snarled. "People make mistakes,

Curtis. And people change."

"Not that much."

"Sure they do. *You* have. You used to be the first in line to give someone a chance, but you've turned into a judgmental asshole just like the rest of our family." She shoved against his chest, herding him toward the front door. "Get out of my house."

He hesitated on the threshold of her home with his hand on the doorknob and the door opened a crack, letting in a draft of cold, damp spring air. The disdain in his sneer sickened her, and it took more strength than it should to keep her fist balled at her side.

"You're really going to let a felon come between us?" he asked.

It was amazing, the way disappointment dripped from his words. How did he *do* that?

"I needed a friend tonight, and that *felon* was a better one to me than my own family."

She shoved him out the door and slammed it behind him. Turning the latch on the dead bolt, she put her back to the door and slid down it. She pinched her eyes closed to stop the tears from coming, but they came anyhow. Fumbling with the laces, she loosened her wrist band, pulled it off and hurled it. Unable to stop herself from crying, she tipped her head back and let the tears roll silently down her cheeks.

The old doubts ratcheted up. Had she made a mistake going out with Jeremiah tonight... in kissing him? Compared to Dustin, what did he have going for him? He was a ranch hand driving a beat-up old truck living in a bunkhouse with another ranch hand. Even if he wanted to find another job, that felony would make it difficult; Devyn was a small town, and many people remembered the drug ring and Jeremiah's part in it far better than she did.

Heather sneered.

That was her family talking.

With the tears slowing, she massaged her wrist as if that alone could make the pain and anger go away.

To hell with them and what they wanted and what they expected of her. Every decision she'd made with a thought to gaining their acceptance hadn't been right for her. Dustin—as great as he was—wasn't right for her. What he wanted from life wasn't what she wanted. She wasn't even sure *what* she wanted, but she was certain Dustin and his dreams for the future weren't it.

Kissing Jeremiah tonight… that was the first thing she'd done in a long time that *had* felt right, and she would not apologize for it or regret it because her family thought it was wrong.

She pushed to her feet, swiped her tears from her face, and retrieved her wrist band. With jerky movements and a dark scowl, she stalked across the house and climbed the stairs to her room in the loft.

It didn't matter what her family thought. This was her life to live, not Curtis's or Brock's or Brianna's or their mother's or their father's.

It was easy enough to think it. The trick was remembering it.

Three

HEATHER WATCHED LUKE CONNER from the corner of her vision as he went over some Ramshorn business or other with his mother behind the log-slab counter, and he must've sensed her gaze because he glanced up and made his way to the table she shared with her two best friends.

"Can I bring you ladies anything else?" he asked.

"I'll take a refill," Heather replied, handing him her glass.

"I'm good. Thanks," Christina said.

"I'll have a refill, too," Ainsley added.

He took the two glasses behind the bar, refilled them with iced tea, and brought them back before laying the check face-down in the center of the table and striding away to greet the party of six walking in.

She didn't say it out loud, but the fact that so much of the smiling, charismatic boy she'd known in high school had returned gave her hope.

She glanced covertly at him again. It wasn't that she harbored any feelings for him anymore. She didn't. But she couldn't help but wonder from time to time what might've happened had he said yes when she'd asked him out at the Hayfever potluck that godawful summer. He and Shane McGuire were probably the two men of all she'd dated or hoped to date closest to what she needed.

They both knew what it was like to break.

Even Ty, as patient and compassionate as he was, couldn't truly understand that.

But they'd all been too young to be serious about anything, and by the time they were old enough to start thinking long term… JP's plot had taken its toll on them all. Still, Luke had found the love of his life, and Shane had reunited with his. They'd healed. And if they could come through everything they had to find love and happiness, anyone could. Even her.

"He's a totally different man since he married Ryan," Heather observed. "It's good to see that."

"All right, you opened the door with that comment," Ainsley said. "It's time to spill it. Have you talked to Dustin since you broke up with him?"

"No," she replied.

"Has he even tried to call you?" Christina asked.

"Once—a few days after. He left a message, and I haven't called him back."

"Are you going to?"

"Hadn't planned on it."

Ainsley's clear blue eyes twinkled mischievously. "You *do* tend to stick to it when you decide you're done with a man."

"Yeah," Christina replied with a brow lifted. "Even when she regrets it."

"Missing a man isn't the same thing as regretting breaking up with him," Heather retorted.

Christina stared at her, and Heather held her gaze defiantly. The woman had apologized for her judgmental comments about Jeremiah, and Heather had rescinded her hurtful claims that Christina wasn't as good a friend as she'd once been, but it was still true that their friendship was strained. And the way Christina's eyes narrowed, daring her to bring it up again, was *not* helping the situation.

"Hey, now," Ainsley said, glancing between them. "None of that. You've both made your apologies, so let's not create reasons to need more of them, all right?"

"Sorry," Heather muttered.

"Me, too," Christina murmured. "I didn't mean that how it sounded. It's just... I don't like that you and Curtis are angry with each other right now."

"I'm sorry you're stuck in the middle—I am—but as long as he refuses to admit that he was a dick, I have nothing to say to him. Or to the rest of my family."

She had no hope of explaining why she was so defensive of Jeremiah or why she was letting that come between her and her family, so she didn't try. Instead, she leaned back in her chair and let silence settle awkwardly over their table while she sipped her iced tea. When Luke neared their table on his way back from seating his new customers, she yanked her wallet out of her back pocket, dug out enough cash to cover their bill and his tip, and held it up.

"Need any change?" he asked as he snagged it on his way by.

"Nope. Don't need a receipt, either."

"It was my turn to get lunch," Christina said quietly.

"Call it my way of apologizing for being a bitch."

Nodding, Christina levered herself out of her chair. "I'd best get back to the ranch. Brianna's not feeling well today, so I need to help Lily cook dinner for the crew."

Heather wasn't feeling remotely charitable, but she made herself stand and embrace her friend. No matter how annoyed she might be, she wasn't willing to lose one of her best friends. That Christina hugged her as tightly and lingered as long as she did was a testament that she was just as aware of their weakened friendship and didn't like it.

"Don't let my mom work you too hard," Heather murmured.

"I won't."

Heather waited until Christina had slipped out the door before she sank into her chair, and she stared at the door for a long time after that with her brows drawn together. Christina had been married to Curtis for six years, so she and Heather should've had plenty of time to adjust to how that had affected their friendship, but instead, it was getting more difficult to find common ground. Between this third baby and Curtis's decision to retire from boxing after his upcoming match in July, this last few months had exacerbated the problem. As much as Curtis tried to pretend he was ready to retire and spend more time with his family, Heather wasn't blind. His pride was suffering; he'd failed to win any titles in his career, and being the son of a

Golden Gloves boxer, that surely stung. It didn't matter that Curtis hadn't had access to the same world-class training their father had.

"Does she seem happy to you?" Heather asked Ainsley.

"She's been under a lot of stress lately," her friend replied thoughtfully. "This pregnancy has been hard on her."

"The pregnancy or Curtis retiring from boxing?"

"Probably both."

Heather's frown deepened. "I wonder if this is the life she really wanted. I mean, come on. Three kids in six years, doing the stay-at-home-mom thing? It's not her. It's like she stopped being the Christina we knew when she married my brother. Whatever happened to the girl who partied it up in college, who dreamed of being an equine veterinarian, who said she'd never play the happy little housewife?"

Ainsley stared at her iced tea with her lips pinched between her teeth.

"What?" Heather asked.

"Dreams change. And Christina isn't you. So maybe cut her some slack, all right?"

"Yeah, sure. I could be reading too much into it."

"You probably are. But I will say this. I wholeheartedly disagree with what she said about Jeremiah. I don't know him well, but he's always struck me as a very sweet guy." Ainsley leaned over and hugged her. "Besides, you *do* have great taste in men, even if you always seem to pick the ones who fit your family's ideals and not yours. Maybe that's the problem."

Heather nodded. She'd thought the same thing on her birthday.

"It says a lot to me that you're so defensive of him. You've never defended any of your boyfriends before."

"I've never needed to."

"Maybe there's something here that's been missing before." Playfully, Ainsley nudged her. "And you can't tell me you aren't thinking about something more than friendship with him."

"I *did* kiss him on my birthday," Heather agreed slyly.

"What?! And on the day you broke up with Dustin?"

"I'd like to blame the alcohol, but I was barely tipsy."

"Gallus." Ainsley shook her head, grinning. "But that's so you."

She laughed at that. Glancing at her watch, she stood. "We'll have to continue this chat later. It's about time for me to head down to the Lazy H. Tracie called yesterday to ask if I could come by to give Jessie some barrel racing pointers."

"Well, she couldn't ask for a more talented teacher."

"Thanks, Ains. I'll talk to you later."

Heather left, lifting her hand in farewell to Luke and his mother as she stepped outside. She still had more than an hour before she needed to be down to the Lazy H to set up for her afternoon lessons with Aaron Hammond's fifteen-year-old daughter, but it was too nice a day to be indoors. Besides, if she headed down early, she might have a chance to watch Jeremiah at work, get a better feel for who he really was. He, the Hammonds, Austin McGuire, and Jake Stirling were branding today, and they'd be in the pen right next to the outdoor arena, so she'd have a perfect viewpoint to spy without being obvious. And maybe while she was at it, she'd give herself and her horse a workout in the arena to warm up before she had to focus on coaching Jessie.

She drove down to her family's small ranch, which sat across the road from the Lazy H, sandwiched between the much larger Circle S and C-Diamond ranches. Her father and brothers were in the pen beside the barn branding and vaccinating calves, and she hoped she'd be able to load her horse without them noticing she was there. She hooked up to her two-horse trailer, parked in front of the barn, and walked around it to the small pasture… but her horse wasn't there. With a growl, she strode over to the pen. So much for avoiding her family.

Sure enough, the younger of her two brothers was astride her stout blue roan mare.

"Hey, Brock!" she yelled over plaintive bawling of cows calling for their calves. "Why the hell do you have my horse?! I told you last night *and* this morning that I needed her today."

"Tubbs threw a shoe!" he yelled back.

"So use Hank."

"Why don't *you* use Hank?"

"Hank can't corner worth a shit, dumbass. I need Rain."

"Tough. I'm busy."

She climbed over the fence and dropped into the pen, startling a dozen calves. "Get off my horse, Brock, before I knock you off her."

"We've got work to do here, Heather," her father snapped.

"So do I. And Rain is *my* horse—chosen, paid for, and trained by *me*."

"And you agreed to let us use her from time to time in exchange for boarding her on this ranch."

"Excluding those times when I need her for my work. This is one of those times, and I made sure to let you all know last night."

"Just use Hank," her father said. "Come on, Brock, Curtis. Let's get back to work."

How could he have gone to all her rodeos, watched her compete and win all those ribbons and trophies, and not have learned enough to know why she couldn't *just use Hank*?

"No."

Her father spun on his heel. "Excuse me, little girl?"

"You heard me just fine. I need *my* horse for *my* job."

She stood nose to nose with her father, glaring up at him. The fury that snapped in those fierce blue eyes should've made her cower, but she *would not* be intimidated by him.

"Brock, give your sister her damned horse." To her, he added, "Don't expect me to be so forgiving the next time you—"

"Don't worry, Dad. I'll find somewhere else to board my horses so we won't have any problems in the future. And you can also expect to pay for my services like everyone else from this point forward."

"You are part of this family, young lady, and you are expected to contribute to it like the rest of us."

"When I start being treated like a full member of this family, maybe I will."

Seething, she took Rain's reins and turned away, barely biting back the insults gathering in her mind. Most days, it was hard to remember when they hadn't had this ranch—she, at least, had taken to it like a duck to water—but on days like today, it was all too obvious that her father had bought it sight unseen and moved his family from the Kansas plains to this secluded Montana valley without any clue how to run a ranch. Had she really been fourteen already when they'd moved out here?

She glanced back just in time to see Brock clumsily manhandle a calf to the ground and snorted. Some rancher he was. Sixteen years of branding, and he still hadn't figured it out.

She led Rain into the barn so she could unsaddle her and check her over before she loaded her. She hung Brock's saddle on the hitching post in front of the barn and loaded her horse in the trailer, glad she'd had the forethought to load all her tack in the trailer this morning before she'd gone out to lunch with Ainsley and Christina.

Since Tracie had told her Jessie would meet her at the outdoor arena at two, she headed straight there. The barrels were still set up from Jessie's frustrating practice yesterday—the one that had prompted Tracie to call her—so she unloaded Rain, saddled her, and walked the mare lazily through the course. Noting some resistance and stubbornness, Heather directed the mare around the barrels, switching up the distance from them and which barrel they turned around first.

It wasn't long before Rain was responding to even her slightest commands.

"That's my girl," she murmured. "Brock was plow

reining you again, wasn't he. Because he too dumb to know how smart you are."

She continued their workout, watching the goings-on in the pen next to the arena. Compared to her family's fumbling branding operation, the Hammonds and crew worked effortlessly together, like a well-oiled machine. Even Jeremiah. He wasn't much of a roper, but he had no trouble at all dropping the calves to the ground to be branded and vaccinated; every movement of his lean and deceptively powerful body was confident and fluid and incredibly fascinating. Even more intriguing was the way he stroked the calf's head, apologizing for the pain.

He might've been doing this five years less than Brock, but she couldn't tell watching him. Of course, he'd probably branded or helped brand easily five times as many calves in his career here on the Lazy H. But that wasn't the difference that struck her the most. It was his easy, open smile and the way he teased his companions and was teased in returned.

This wasn't just a job to him or a means to an end or a way to please his father like it was to Brock.

He loved this.

Like her, he hadn't been born to this life or even raised in it, but it suited him every bit as well as it suited her.

Henry caught her watching, nudged Jeremiah, and grinned. "Enjoying yourself?"

"I am," she replied. "Not much in this world more fun than watching an octet of sexy cowboys doing their thing."

"You need to have your eyes checked if you're including me, girl," Austin said gruffly.

"Mmm. You and John are the best looking of the bunch, Austin."

John snorted. "Then you need to have your head checked, too."

"Well, most of these boys here got their good looks from somewhere, didn't they?"

"Yeah—their mothers," Jake teased.

"Oooh!" the others crowed before breaking out in good-natured laughter.

"Come on, boys," Austin said. "These calves ain't gonna brand themselves."

Heather watched them as they got back to work, noting how they playfully bumped and prodded Jeremiah. She didn't have to hear them to know they were teasing him about her, and she liked that he took it with a smile.

He was part of their family and part of the Northstar family, she mused, glancing at Austin and Jake. She loved this community and all its residents, and she wished her family had put more effort into becoming a part of it when they'd moved here.

For a moment, she let her eyes drift closed to let the rest of her senses take over. The warmth and movement of her horse, the heat of the bright sun beating down on her, the scents of dirt churning beneath Rain's hooves and horse sweat melding with the crystalline air, and the steady, rocking rhythm as she nudged her mare into a walk toward the center of the arena....

Right here in the saddle with the towering mountains surrounding her, the sapphire sky above, and the freedom of wide open spaces filling her and driving out all the bad vibes—this was her home. This was where she belonged.

Opening her eyes, she turned Rain toward the gate, then pointed her at the barrels. Sensing what was coming, Rain quivered with excitement, her ears forward. With a deep breath, Heather leaned over Rain's withers and tapped her heels to the mare's flanks. Rain shot forward and Heather turned her toward the left barrel. They rounded it with just inches between her thigh and the barrel and raced toward the second barrel.

Thrill pumped through Heather's veins. Every fiber in her body was perfectly in tune with her horse. Time seemed to stop even as they flew through the course and sped back toward the gate. Sitting back in the saddle and loosening the grip of her legs, she slowed Rain to a walk, and she couldn't keep the triumphant grin from her face as she leaned over the mare's neck and scratched along her mane.

Claps and whistles came from behind her, and she wheeled Rain around to find John Hammond and his entire branding crew perched on the log rail fence of the arena.

"Don't you boys have calves to brand?" she called.

"We do," Nick replied. "But we're taking a break. That was some incredible riding."

"It was," Henry agreed. "I knew you were good, but *damn*, woman."

"No wonder Jess is so excited you agreed to coach her," Aaron added. "You should've seen her last night when Mom told her you'd give her some pointers. I thought she was going to hit the ceiling."

"Thanks." She beamed and tried not to wonder why it was so hard for her family to be complimentary of her skills when it came so naturally to the Hammond clan. She wondered…. "Um, John? I have an odd favor to ask."

"Shoot."

"I need a place to board Rain for a while. We're completely out of room over at the Bar E, and it's just not going to work out with her at my folks' ranch. Could I pay you to—"

"No, you can't," the rancher interrupted. "But she's welcome to stay here as long as you need. Since you'll be coaching Jess from here on out, it only makes sense to keep your horse here, right? When we're all done, Jeremiah can show you which pasture to put her in. Bring that racehorse of yours over, too, if you need to. We've got more than enough room for them both."

Well, hell. That was easy. She lowered her head with a grateful smile. "Thank you."

"You're welcome. All right, boys," John called. "Heather's here to work, and so are we, so let's get back to it."

As the men turned back to their task, Heather caught Jeremiah's gaze, and their lips curved at the same time. He hadn't said a word, but the way he watched her—with desire and a hint of reverence—spoke volumes. Maybe a week and a half wasn't enough time to get over her breakup, but it wasn't like she was pining over Dustin. And besides, Ainsley was right. Jeremiah was different than the others she'd dated, and if *he* was different, a relationship with him would be, too… and it might be the one to work out. Unless, of course, she just wasn't cut out for happily ever after.

* * *

"Hey, you guys need to see this," Henry called. "Especially you, Jeremiah."

"Especially me?" He released the calf and pushed to his feet. "Why especially…."

His voice trailed off when he saw what had distracted Henry, and he understood immediately why he'd be more interested than their companions. Heather was setting up for a run around the barrels. As if a magnet pulled him, he strode to the fence and climbed up it with his eyes locked on her.

The way she clung to her mount through those tight turns….

She was fierce and magnificent—strength and poise and grace embodied.

"I think our boy here is in love," Jake teased, perching beside him.

"He *does* have that starry-eyed look," Austin agreed.

"Shuddup," Jeremiah muttered without heat, still mesmerized.

"The way you're looking at her right now and that kiss on her birthday…." Aaron laughed. "It was a date."

"It wasn't a date," he corrected automatically for the hundredth time in the last week and a half. "We went out as friends."

"So you keep saying, but I'm not buying it," Henry remarked.

When Heather finished her run, his companions clapped and whistled, and she turned toward them with surprise edging the radiant joy from her face. She recovered in a heartbeat, and Jeremiah listened to the ensuing conversation, watching her expression carefully as his companions complimented her. For someone who had won multiple awards and who made her living training horses and their riders, there was a disconcerting amount of humility and even shyness in her eyes.

When John told them to get back to work, he lingered, unable to turn away from her, and when their gazes met and they smiled at the same time, his heart tripped over itself.

For years, he'd hoped to catch her attention, and now that he had it… it was incredible.

"Jere," Nick called. "Come on."

Reluctantly, he turned away and reclaimed his post near the fire where the brands—a simple H turned on its side—were waiting red hot for the next calves to be branded.

"Now I'm *positive* it was a date," Jake said. "Did you guys see that look just now?

"It wasn't a date," Jeremiah groaned.

"Then maybe you should ask her on one," Nick retorted. "Tonight would be good."

"Your mom cooked dinner for us."

"Yeah, and Heather's already here. And you know Mom made enough for her, too, just in case."

"I doubt she'll say yes."

"Jeremiah," Austin said quietly.

He turned his attention to his roommate.

"You've been waiting for *years* for a shot with her." The older man reached over and gripped his shoulder hard enough to make him wince. "This is your shot. Take it."

With his lips pressed into a line, he nodded, and gestured to the calves, hoping they would take the hint and let the matter drop. He didn't mind the teasing—their jesting was born of an easy camaraderie that had been missing from his life for a long time before the Hammonds had hired him and folded him into their family—but, as John had pointed out, they had work to do, and the sooner they finished it, the sooner he'd be able to focus on Heather.

Because Austin was right. For the first time, the door was open, and he'd waited too long to let his chance slip away.

Nick and Henry cut a calf from the small group left to be branded, working so seamlessly together that Jeremiah wondered if they'd developed telepathy after all their years working together. Nick roped the calf's head, Aaron hooked her heels, and without a word, they backed their horses to put tension on the ropes. Jeremiah stepped in and lifted the calf off her feet with Nick's son Will half a step behind him to help him pin her to the soft dirt of the pen while Austin pressed the brand to her flank and John administered the vaccines. The older men slipped the ropes off the calf, and in short order, she was up and racing across the pen to where her mother bellowed for her. Henry and Jake already had another calf roped, and the process was repeated for the three-hundredth time that day.

The team slipped back into their easy rhythm, and in less than an hour, the last calf of the day had been branded, vaccinated, and turned loose into the pasture with her mother. Since they'd finished early, Jeremiah leaned against the fence with John, Jake, Austin, and Will watched the three brothers practice heading and heeling on the male calves they would brand tomorrow.

There weren't many things he couldn't do around the ranch anymore, but he'd long ago accepted that he'd never be as good a roper as any of his companions. Not even seventeen-year-old Will.

Finally, John called an end to their frolicking, and he, Nick, Henry, and Jake led the horses into the barn to be unsaddled and brushed down while the rest of their crew set to work cleaning up.

"You all make that look so easy," he remarked to Aaron.

The older man shrugged that off. "You want to see someone make it look easy, you should watch Andy Epperson. He's truly gifted. In fact, if you ever want to learn from a master, I bet he'd show you a few tricks. Give him a few weeks, and you'd probably out-rope every one of us here."

"I doubt that."

"Why? You've taken to everything else about this life like you were born for it."

Jeremiah only nodded, wondering why he suddenly felt self-conscious. It wasn't often anymore that he doubted his ability to do anything that was asked of him in this job. Maybe it was nerves about the prospect of asking Heather on a real date. His heart skittered in confirmation.

"Ah," Aaron said, glancing to the arena where his daughter was currently circling her buckskin gelding around one of the barrels. "This doubt isn't about your roping skills. You've got a lot to offer, and now that you've got her attention, she'll see it. So make sure you invite her to dinner before you head back to the bunkhouse to get cleaned up."

He had every intention of doing exactly what Aaron suggested, but when they finished cleaning up, Heather was back on her horse and demonstrating some technique or other to Jessie, so he gave in to his nerves and walked up to the bunkhouse he shared with Austin. Murph trotted faithfully by his side.

The bunkhouse was small with two tiny bedrooms at the rear and a tinier bathroom between them, a kitchenette and dinky dining area to the right of the front room, and the living room with its worn couch and recliner to the left, but it was tidy and comfortable. More importantly, it was home. He kicked off his manure-encrusted boots just outside the front door and headed for his bedroom—the one behind the kitchen—and stripped out of his filthy clothes with an amused shake of his head.

"I'm covered in shit and grime, and I couldn't be happier about it," he laughed.

Murphy jumped up on the bed, and Jeremiah obliged, vigorously rubbing him all over. "You may not be much of a cow dog, but at least you stay out of the way."

Lifting his gaze to the only photo he had of his entire family, his amusement faded a little. Would any of them have believed the turns his life had taken? Would they be proud of what he'd become, or would they be too embarrassed and disappointed by the stupid choices he'd made that had brought him to this point to appreciate the hard work it had taken to get here? He hoped they'd be proud, but he'd never know.

He climbed into the shower and ran the water hot to stave off the aches he'd surely be feeling from today's branding, wondering as he washed his hair—now two-inches long instead of the four-inch mop it had been last week—if it was weird that he appreciated Tracie's haircuts so much. It wasn't the money she saved him, but rather the reminder of his mother cutting his hair in the kitchen of their house in California. He suspected Tracie's haircuts were the reason those memories were still clear when most of the rest were in danger of fading into oblivion.

That question was still on his mind when he stepped out of the shower and wrapped his towel around his waist. He paused in front of the mirror, noting the bruises that were beginning to form where a calf had kicked him. He was proud of the muscle definition working on the ranch had given him even if he still looked too short and skinny next to the Hammond brothers, who all stood three inches taller than him at an even six feet with heavier frames.

Frowning, he slid his fingers over the slash of puckered, shiny pink skin that curved around from the nape of his neck to the front of his right shoulder, then turned his left side to the mirror and traced the other, similar scars. There were three smaller ones on his left arm between his shoulder and bicep and a patchwork of half a dozen more on the left side of his back from the top of his shoulder blade to his lower ribs. The largest of them he could cover fully with his palm.

"You about done in there, kid?" Austin called. "Or do I need to go shower down at the main house?"

"I'm done," he replied and turned abruptly away from the mirror before the memories attached to his scars had a chance to take root.

As he passed Austin, the older man regarded him with a brow lifted.

"You didn't ask Heather to dinner before you came up here, did you."

Austin wasn't asking a question; he already knew.

"Well, it looked like she and Jess were getting ready

to call it quits when I left, so you might want to get your ass down there before she leaves. Unless you'd rather spend dinner getting harassed instead of getting to know that girl better."

"I think I'll get my ass down there."

Chuckling, Austin slapped him on the shoulder and ducked into the bathroom.

Jeremiah dressed quickly in his favorite pair of soft-worn straight-leg jeans and a plain gray-blue T-shirt that, he realized as he ran a comb through his damp hair, was the same color as Heather's pretty Silverado. Smiling at that, he trotted into the living room, yanked on his clean work boots, and laced them snuggly.

"Stay, Murph."

The dog grunted and gave him a look with his ears back and the whites of his eyes showing that said, *You're killing me.*

"See you down at the main house!" he called to Austin.

"Why are you still here?" his roommate replied.

He didn't bother responding. His old Ford started like a champ, as always, and when he parked it next to Heather's thirty-two-year-newer Silverado, he patted the hood on his way to the arena.

"You may not be as pretty, old girl," he said, "but I bet you'll be running long after that young thing is rusting in the junk yard."

"You're probably right about that," Heather remarked.

He froze mid-step and glanced up. He hadn't realized she'd been standing so close, just inside the fence of the arena. As he reached her, she glanced over him with a teasing smile that couldn't quite hide her appreciation of what she saw, and his neck heated uncomfortably.

"You clean up pretty nice, Mackey."

"Took some work to find me under all the grime," he remarked, "but I managed."

He ambled over to the gate and slipped into the arena to watch Jessie practice. As far as he could tell, she seemed like she had a good handle on her horse and how to run the course, and he knew she was a talented rider, so he didn't understand her breakdown yesterday.

"What's the deal?" he asked Heather. "I don't think I've ever seen this girl as frustrated as she was yesterday."

"For one, she just started working with Cisco a week ago, and he's a great horse—quick on his feet, athletic, and smart—but they're not used to each other yet, and when she fell off and hit the barrel first thing yesterday…." She shrugged. "It shook her confidence, and he sensed her tensing up and started shouldering the barrel."

"And that means…? Sorry, I don't know the terminology."

"He's dropping his shoulder to turn around the barrel and hitting it more often than not."

"And hitting the barrel adds time to the run."

"Exactly."

"So, how do you get her to stop tensing and him to stop shouldering the barrel?"

"A few different ways, but today we're working on stopping him when he starts to drop his shoulder and then turning him away from the barrel."

Jeremiah watched Aaron's daughter do exactly as

Heather described, and one corner of his mouth lifted. "Incredible."

"Not really. It's pretty basic."

"No, I mean you. What you know, how well you know it."

She ducked her gaze, but he caught the shy smile she tried to hide. "Thanks."

"Eleven years," he said, "and I still have a lot to learn about this life."

"You can't tell." Her eyes rounded like she hadn't meant to say that out loud. "I mean, you fit right in with the Hammonds and Austin and Jake. If I didn't know, I would think you've been doing this all your life. You've certainly picked it up faster than my dad and my brothers. Curtis and Dad are decent, and of course Todd knows what he's doing, but Brock's an idiot."

He stared at her with his head tilted and a frown drawing his brows together. "I don't understand."

"We haven't had the Rocking A all that long. Dad retired from boxing when I was fourteen and decided he wanted to be a rancher, so he bought it from my brother-in-law's parents when they were about to lose it to the bank."

"So… where are you from? I've always thought you were born and raised here."

"Nope. Dad didn't buy the Rocking A from Todd's family until I was fourteen—that birthday was my first day on the ranch. I was born in Kansas. Mom grew up on a dairy farm in the middle of nowhere."

His lips quirked. "You know, most people think Northstar is the middle of nowhere."

"Nah. Northstar's mountains make it feel like somewhere." She shuddered. "I can't stand the flatlands. Makes me feel like I'm at the edge of the world and about to fall off. Dad's a mountain boy—born and raised in Missoula—and I guess I inherited that from him. What about you? Where were you born?"

"Huntington Beach, California."

She gave a teasing groan. "Oh, God, you're a *Californian* transplant!"

"Maybe, but I've been in this county longer than you. I was eleven when I moved in with my grandparents after my parents died. They had a construction company in Devyn. Joe was already here, learning the trades with the idea that he'd take over from them some day."

He turned his gaze out across the pastures of the Lazy H, blindsided by the rush of grief. *Ah, Joe.*

He slammed the door on those thoughts. They had no place in his head anymore. Blaming himself for his older brother's death was useless and only cast a shadow over everything Aaron and the rest of the Hammonds had done for him, and he refused to repay their kindness with regret. Maybe Joe had confronted Aaron on his behalf, but it had been his choice to threaten Aaron and Erica with a gun. What had he hoped to accomplish?

That was a question Jeremiah would never find an answer to, so he let it slip away as he did every time it entered his mind.

Abruptly, he turned to Heather with a grin and changed the subject before she could probe into his past. "I'm supposed to invite you to join us all for dinner. Specifically, to join *me* for dinner."

"I'd love to."

The speed with which she replied stunned him. It was almost as if she'd known the invitation would come.

"All right, who was it?" he asked.

"What do you mean?" Her tone was just a little too sweet and innocent.

"Who told you I'd ask?"

She fought the smile, but it spread across her face all the brighter for the battle. "I think the list of who *didn't* tell me might be shorter. Aaron mentioned it first. Then Nick, then John, then Austin."

"Those buttheads," he said fondly. "I can't even be annoyed at them for their meddling."

"No, you really can't," she agreed. "They love you. And anyhow, I was going to ask if you wanted to go out tonight. I thought a swim at the Ramshorn sounded like fun, but maybe there'll still be time for that after dinner."

"Wait. You were going to ask me out?"

Without the slightest *hint* of hesitation, she nodded.

"You sure you're ready for that? It hasn't even been two weeks since you broke up with your boyfriend."

"I'm sure. It's like Ainsley said at lunch today—when I'm done, I'm done and ready to move on."

He stared at her with his mouth agape as the seconds ticked by. Was this conversation really happening? "I'm sorry to be dense, but I can't quite believe this is real. Does this mean we're exclusively dating, or are you thinking just a couple of dates first to see if you're interested in more?"

"It means we're exclusively dating, if you're on board with that. I've never been much for casual here-and-there dating."

He almost laughed. If the frank discussion wasn't so surreal, he would have. Figuring it would sound monumentally lame and pathetic, he refrained from admitting just how long he'd waited for this opportunity. "Sounds good to me."

"Good. Because I've been wanting to do this again since my birthday."

She slipped her arms around his neck and claimed his mouth with a dizzying confidence and quickness. Vaguely aware that Jessie was loping her horse around the arena and could be watching, he kept a tight rein on the desire raging through his veins. But good God. The way Heather angled her body against his was incredible, and when she broke away, he groaned low in his throat.

"Don't forget," she whispered, "John said you're supposed to show me where to put my horse when Jess and I are done."

"Uh-huh," he mumbled, dazed. "Whenever you're ready."

"Oh, I'm always ready."

The insinuation in her words was so blatant that he swore under his breath.

With a smug grin, she touched her lips lightly to his before slipping away to address her student. Feeling a little like the world was tilting beneath him, Jeremiah leaned against the fence and watched her saunter away.

One thought resounded in his head. Heather Brown was a wildfire, and if he managed to avoid getting burned, it would be a miracle.

Four

HEATHER TURNED HER CHAIR backwards and straddled it with her arms folded across its back, drumming her fingers on her forearm. Her mother regarded her with narrowed eyes and lips pressed into a thin line but said nothing about her daughter's casual posture. It was petty of her, but Heather was still mad at her family, and she wasn't about to sit down to a ridiculously formal family meeting without making sure they knew she was here on her terms. She'd been sorely tempted to ditch the planning session—she already knew what she needed to do to make sure the ranch ran smoothly while the rest of the family was away for a week for Curtis's last match—but Christina had begged her to come.

She glanced from one member of her family to the next. All the adults were present and accounted for—her mother and father, Curtis and Christina, Brock and his wife Anna, her younger sister Brianna and her husband Todd. Her herd of nieces and nephews were outside playing on the jungle gym in plain sight through the dining room's picture window. All these happy families and here she was, as usual, the odd one out.

When everyone was seated, Lily opened the binder she'd put together. It contained every list, ticket, receipt, agenda, and schedule; everything was planned down to the most minute detail, even the agenda for this meeting. Heather barely refrained from rolling her eyes as her mother read out the plans and checked with each member of the family to make sure they all knew what was expected of them. Thank God she wasn't going. There was a small prickle of guilt over missing the end of Curtis's career, but she'd gone to plenty of his other fights, and anyhow, *one* of them should stay home with Christina. The match was just a week before her due date, and they'd all agreed it would be foolish for her to go.

"Heather? Did you hear me?" Lily asked.

"Yes, Ty is fully aware of the schedule here, and we've worked our schedule at the Bar E around it."

"Good. Thank you."

"You really think you'll be able to handle this place by yourself while we're gone?" Brock asked.

"The first cut of hay will be baled before you leave, there's no feeding to be done, and arrangements have already been made for moving the irrigation. Even *you* could handle that on your own."

They stared at each other across the table, and it was a damned good thing they had all that oak between them.

"I suppose if you get into trouble, you could always call your new boyfriend. He's good for that at least."

"He's a better rancher than you are, that's for damned sure."

When Brock shot to his feet, Heather laughed.

"Sit down before you say something else stupid. I'm already far too tempted to break your nose again." She rose from the table. "If we're done here, I need to get going."

"Got a hot date?" Brock sneered.

"Not that it's any of your business, but yeah, I do."

"Heather," her mother sighed. "Couldn't you wait at least a couple months?"

"Why? To satisfy *your* opinion of what's proper? This is the twenty-first century, Mother."

"You know we don't approve," her father said quietly.

"I don't really give a damn if you do or not."

The phone rang then, interrupting what surely would've been another delightful Brown family war about how much she disappointed her old-fashioned and rigidly "proper" parents. Lily answered it, and Heather lifted her hand in farewell and turned toward the front door.

"Heather. It's for you."

Who would be calling her here? She hadn't lived in this house since she'd left for college twelve years ago. There was only one person she could think of, and she hoped she was wrong. She had no desire to put herself through the pain and doubt talking to him would surely bring. Her mother held the cordless out to her, and grudgingly, she took it.

"Hello?"

"Heather. I was beginning to wonder if I'd ever get to talk to you again."

Yep. Dustin.

Dammit.

"I thought you would've figured by now that there's a reason I haven't called you back."

"That's why I called your parents. I thought they might be able to convince you to talk to me."

Wow. He really *wasn't* right for her. "Looks like I made the right decision if you really believe that."

"Please, don't be like that, Heather. I love you. I want to marry you and make a family with you. Is that really so bad?"

She spared her family a scowl, then stepped into the kitchen. Leaning against the island, she pinched her eyes closed and massaged the bridge of her nose as if that could ease the sting of tears. Why was talking to him now so much harder than breaking up with him had been? The answer was obvious—because a part of her did love him—but grappling with that knowledge and the understanding that, even as wonderful and sweet and perfect as he was, there was and always had been something missing from their relationship. Something she absolutely needed in order to give herself fully. The worst part was that she had no idea exactly what it was or how to find it or if it was even possible *to* find.

"I'm sorry I wasted two years of your life."

"You didn't waste anything. Please, Heather. Give me another chance."

"I can't."

"Why not?"

"We don't want the same things out of life, and you can't build a life on a broken foundation."

"You might change your mind. If you'd just open yourself to the idea…."

It was so similar to what her mother always said that it triggered a rush of anger that burned away the grief. "I am so sick of people assuming they know me better than I know myself, and it's starting to seriously piss me off."

"Hey, easy. That's not what I'm trying to say. Not at all."

"Isn't it? I'm thirty years old. I'm pretty sure my maternal alarm would've gone off before now if it was going to."

Silence greeted her from the other end of the line. She could picture him so easily, sitting on the edge of a seat, his handsome face contorted in a frown of anguish and disappointment and his beautiful green eyes so sad. Maybe he'd rake his hand through his dark blond hair as the realization sank in that he wouldn't be able to convince her to give their relationship a second chance.

She sighed. "I'm not mad at you, and I love you, too—it'd be impossible not to because you're an amazing man—but I'm not going to change my mind. I'm sorry. Please don't call me again. Goodbye."

She pressed the call-end button, set the cordless handset gently on the counter, and snuck out the kitchen door before her family realized she was gone. Undoubtedly her mother, at least, had eavesdropped, and with her heart aching, Lily's attempts to convince her that she was making a mistake not reconciling with Dustin would force her to break the promise she'd made to herself the night she'd broken Brock's nose.

Never let them see you cry.

Somehow, she managed to slide in behind the wheel of her truck, start the engine, and drive away from her parents' house before the tears fell. Unlike the ones that had slipped silently and numbly down her cheeks on her birthday, these came with a swirl of razer-edged emotions.

Damn him. Why couldn't he just make it easy on them both and let her go?

Ty had. Maybe it had been easier for him because his real love had shown up in Northstar and because they hadn't been as involved as she and Dustin had been. But Ty also knew her well enough to understand that when her mind was made up, there was no changing it.

Abruptly, she realized she had parked beside Jeremiah's old Ford in front of the Lazy H's workshop with no memory of deciding to seek him out or of driving over here. She still had two hours before her date with him, so what was she doing here?

Shutting the engine down, she climbed out of her truck without questioning the subconscious compulsion that had drawn her to him. He was a good friend—he'd proved that on her birthday—and she needed a friend right now. Christina was too much her husband's wife these days, and Ainsley had her own family, which made spontaneous gab sessions a thing of the past.

As she approached the man door of the shop, she caught the sound of a drill. With her curiosity piqued, she slipped inside without knocking. The shop was well lit, and in the center of it was what appeared to be a shed on wheels. Jeremiah's blue merle Australian shepherd was sprawled beneath it on the cool concrete, and though he perked his ears when he spotted her, he couldn't be bothered to greet her. The man himself had his back to her, giving her ample opportunity to observe him. Despite her wrenching conversation with Dustin, she was captivated by the smooth, habitual motions of his body as he screwed a half sheet of corrugated metal siding in place. He wasn't a big man, but he was proportionally and gracefully built with undeniably masculine lines that made her pulse jump. Desire stretched and purred as she watched the flex and play of muscle beneath his black T-shirt—short-sleeved this time, she noted, realizing he usually wore long-sleeved shirts, even in the heat of summer.

Spying an odd mark peeking from just below the hem of the sleeve on his left arm, she took a step closer, and the movement caught his eye. He jerked in surprise and the drill slipped from his grip, but he caught it and swore. Then he met her gaze and smiled.

"You're here early."

"Didn't mean to sneak up on you like that." Even though she had.

"It's all right."

"What are you working on?"

"A portable office. My side job. Well, so far it's just a hobby, but I sold the first two I built for almost ten grand each."

"Impressive. So, this is how you spend your days off?"

"Most of them. And evenings when I have enough energy."

"Ranch work doesn't offer too many of those."

"No, but you won't hear me complain." He tilted his head, studying her with narrowed eyes, and she lowered her gaze. "Are you all right?"

She nodded, but at the reminder of what had driven her over hear, a lump formed in her throat, and she couldn't speak around it to tell him she was fine. It was a lie, anyhow.

"I don't mean to pry, but you look like you've been crying."

The concern in those hazel eyes—why hadn't she ever noticed how beautiful and kind his eyes were, as rich in color as tea with a sprig of mint brewing in the sun?—invited her to stop trying to be strong and independent and to lean on him and let him help her.

"I just got off the phone with Dustin… and it hurt worse talking to him again than it did to break up with him." Tears burned her eyes again, and she stubbornly fought them back. "And before you start thinking I regret breaking up with him, I don't. I'm more sure of it now than I was before. But he's a great guy, and for a while, I thought he might be the one. But when he pulled out that stupid ring box, I realized he wasn't. He wants the perfect little family, and that's just not me. And to call my parents' house hoping they'd help him convince me otherwise? What the hell?"

The words were coming too fast, so she snapped her mouth closed to stop them. At once, she wanted to find out if she would find comfort and understanding in Jeremiah's arms as she had on her birthday. And yet, she hesitated. She'd already kissed him twice, and rather passionately, so why did a hug seem so much more intimate?

She knew why. Physical desire was easy—a matter of giving free rein to her body's wants. Emotional need was something else entirely.

Hesitantly, she took a step toward him and waited to see if he would invite her to come closer. Relief sighed through her when he set his drill on the concrete floor of the shop and opened his arms. She slipped into them, hooked her arms around his waist, and let out a breath.

"I'm sorry," he whispered. "If you need more time…."

She shook her head. "I don't need time. I need *this*."

"In that case, why don't I call it a day and put my tools away so we can head up to the Ramshorn?"

"I don't want to interrupt your work."

"This is more important."

Lowering her head to rest it on his shoulder, she drew a ragged breath and let it out slowly. For the first time, she let herself feel the full pain of her breakup. With Jeremiah's arms around her, holding her together, she could do it. When he settled his chin on the top of her head, she closed her eyes, and a ghost of a smile curved her lips. This felt good. Better than kissing him. Better than anything she'd felt in quite a while. He was so steady and patient, and he seemed as content to hold her as she was to have him do it.

"Thank you," she murmured. "It's been a long time since I've been able to let go and let someone help me. A *really* long time."

"You're welcome."

She could stay right here for the rest of the day, but Murphy finally crawled out from under the trailer and greeted her with his tail stump wiggling enthusiastically.

"Oh, *now* you decide to greet me," she murmured fondly, reaching down to pet the dog without slipping out of Jeremiah's arms.

"Yeah… he has to make sure I'm okay with people before he greets them. At least until he knows them *well*. Then he makes an idiot of himself."

"Is that just his nature or a learned reaction?"

"Learned. Everything that could go wrong for him did. According to the Aussie rescue group I got him from, his first owner died of a heart attack, and he was sent to the man's granddaughter, who's boyfriend was a real piece of work. The prick beat him or kicked him hard enough to crack a couple ribs and then dumped him off at the local pound. He was only ten months old or so when I adopted him and still healing."

"I get it—his name," she said. "Murphy's Law."

"Yep."

With some reluctance, she slipped out of Jeremiah's embrace and knelt on the floor. Murphy wiggled into her lap, and she scratched under his collar and up and down his back. "Poor guy. But you finally got lucky, huh? Found yourself a good forever home with Jeremiah."

"He's not much of a cow or sheep dog, but he's the best companion. Goes everywhere with me."

"So I've noticed. Was it love at first sight?"

"Pretty much. I took a cue from Aaron and Brodie Dunn and met with several dogs until I found him, and we both knew immediately."

Heather frowned as she stroked her hand over Murphy's head, but it didn't last long. The happiness in the dog's blue eyes was irresistible. "Sometimes I really hate people."

She gave the dog a few more loves and pushed to her

feet. "If you're sure you don't mind quitting early, I'd love to hit the hot springs. But first… can I have a tour of your project?"

"Yeah. Of course."

He finished screwing the sheet of metal siding in place—the last one to go up, she noted—and then walked with her around the trailer. The galvanized siding covered the bottom half of the walls, and basic T1-11 siding painted a subtle medium gray-green covered the top half. He'd used the same corrugated metal for the roof, and it made for an aesthetically pleasing contrast with the paint color he'd chosen. The custom-made door was a dark purple just a little too blue to be eggplant. He opened it and stepped back to let her enter.

Inside, it was still bare studs with a wafer-wood floor, but the electrical was in, and when she noticed a battery and converter, she asked if he was planning to use solar power for it.

"Yep. And I have a tiny wood stove ordered, so it'll be off grid."

"Nice."

The door was in the rear driver-side corner, leaving plenty of room in the passenger-side corner for the tiny wood stove. The three windows on the other walls were small—two feet square—but they were plenty adequate for the seven-foot-by-nine-foot space. She listened as he described how he was going to finish out the interior with a creamy yellow paint, a blue-pine log desk that would wrap around from the front wall to halfway down the side walls, and a light, speckled carpet that wouldn't show the dirt as much as a solid-colored carpet would.

"I want one," she said, able to picture it in stunning detail. "Seriously. This is going to be an amazing office."

"Thanks. If or when that day comes, let me know, and I'll build you one. Shall we go swim?"

"If you're ready, yes."

"I am. Wasn't much in the mood to work today, to be honest."

"Oh? Why not?"

"Zach's officially a free man with a house and a job. Aaron talked to his PO this morning."

"I'm sorry, Jeremiah."

He shrugged. "Nothing I can do about it but hope his freedom is more important to him than revenge."

"You think he'd come after you for ratting on him?"

"Yeah, I do."

She slipped her arms around his waist again and touched her lips to his, hoping she could distract him as well as he'd soothed her. "In that case, we'd better get out of here and quick. A soak will do us both some good."

She lavished his dog with attention while he returned his tools to their homes, watching him all the while, marveling at how effortlessly she'd opened up to him about Dustin. It couldn't have been a comfortable thing for him to hear, especially not with his cousin's release weighing on his mind, but he hadn't said a word of complaint, nor had he asked for details, and damn, it had been nice to get it all off her chest without having to delve any deeper into it.

She was so used to people listening to reply rather than to understand that she was all the more aware of how soothing his quiet support was. How had she been so blind to the kind and generous soul behind that boyishly charming face? That question was followed immediately by another that she had no hope of answering right now.

What had she been missing out on all these years?

"Are we taking separate trucks?" he asked as he shut off the lights and ushered her out the door.

"Nah. I'll ride with you, if you don't mind swinging by my place so I can pick up my swimming gear."

Jeremiah opened his door and snapped his fingers. "Load up, Murph."

The Aussie bounded into the truck and plopped his butt in the middle of the bench. Heather laughed as she climbed in next to him. "How'd I know you were a spoiled boy? No riding in the bed of the truck for you, huh."

He eyed her as if to ask if she had a problem with that, so she ruffled his ears and was rewarded with a dopey smile and happy eyes.

Luke and his wife Ryan were in the pool house when Heather and Jeremiah arrived, and Heather was surprised to see them—school wasn't out for summer yet—until she glanced at the clock and realized it was already after five. Had she and Jeremiah really been in the shop that long?

She watched as her date chatted with the Conners, inquiring after their beautiful baby girl Ashleigh and remarking on how relieved they must be that the school year was almost done. When more customers arrived, he quickly paid for their swimming before she recovered her wits enough to even think about pulling her wallet out of her back pocket.

"You two enjoy yourselves," Ryan said with a smile that said a whole lot more than her words. She glanced between Heather and Jeremiah.

"Thanks," Heather replied. "We will."

She headed right into the women's changing room, oddly gratified by the other woman's apparent approval of her new relationship. She didn't know Ryan well, but that small glimmer of support was a welcome change from her family's disapproval. She changed into her bikini in a hurry, bolstered by hope. Luke at least, and probably Ryan, too, knew Jeremiah far better than her family did. The Conners and Hammonds had been good friends longer than her family had been in Northstar; if she recalled correctly, Luke's mother June and his honorary aunt Aelissm O'Neil had gone to college with all three of the Hammond brothers. All evidence pointed to that friendship extending to Jeremiah.

Despite her haste, Jeremiah beat her out of the pool house, and he was waiting in the larger pool for her... wearing a T-shirt. The surge of disappointment surprised her.

He wasn't ripped, but he had great muscle tone, and the wet cotton clung to him, leaving pretty much nothing to the imagination.

"What's with the shirt? You can't possibly be shy," she remarked as she angled her body over the edge of the boardwalk and lowered herself into the water beside him. "And if you are, I hope you realize that shirt isn't hiding anything right now."

"It's not that. Not exactly."

The quiet way he'd said it instantly piqued her curiosity. He met her gaze for a fleeting moment before looking away, but it was plenty long enough for her to catch a glimpse of the shadows in his eyes.

"Jeremiah?" She glided around him so that she was facing him, and when she did, she ran her hand up his arm, sliding her thumb under his sleeve and over the mark she'd spotted earlier. "Is this a burn scar?"

He nodded.

"Are there more?"

After a moment of indecision, he pulled his shirt over his head and turned his back to her. The left side of his body from his shoulder blade to his lower ribs was also marred by burn scars. The sight of them shocked her, and hesitantly, she reached out to skim her fingertips lightly over them.

"What happened?"

"House fire."

She wanted to ask him for details, but the hardness in his voice gave her pause. If he was willing to talk about it, he wouldn't have given her such a curt answer.

"I'm sorry. You've had some shit hands dealt to you, haven't you? More than your fair share, I'd say." She slid her arms around him and rested her head on his shoulder with her hands folded against his chest. "It's my turn to ask if *you* are all right."

"About that? It happened a long time ago."

"I figured. I meant about your cousin being a free man now."

He shrugged and swiveled in her arms, so she re-hooked them around his neck and pressed her body against his. She kissed him slowly, grinning when she snagged his bottom lip between her teeth and tugged on it as she pulled back.

"How about now?" she asked huskily.

"What were we talking about?"

Laughing softly, she dragged one hand down his chest, took his hand and placed it on her hip, holding his gaze the entire time. Hunger surged as his pupils dilated. He wanted her—that much was obvious even before she nudged her leg between his and he made a sound that was half groan, half plea for more. She kissed him again, harder, and curled her hand around a fistful of his hair. He shivered.

Good God, she felt *powerful*.

"Heather?"

"Hmm?"

"You realize we're in a public pool, right?"

"So?"

"You keep doing that, and this is going to get awkward in a hurry."

She growled, annoyed because he was right. Sighing, she loosened her grip on his hair and put a little distance between them… but not much because she couldn't bring herself to let go of him. His brows drew together and the muscle in his jaw twitched. She might've thought he was fighting to regain control of his desire were it not for the flash of pain she'd seen before he'd pinched his eyes closed.

"Tell me this isn't a dream," he whispered. "Tell me this is more than a rebound to you… because as incredible as that was, it felt like there was a fair amount of anger behind it."

He opened his eyes again, and the vulnerability in them shocked her to her core.

She started to argue that she wasn't angry at all and that she'd been caught up in the moment, but she snapped her mouth closed.

He was right.

The way he'd reacted to her bold kisses and demanding touches had given her such a rush of power, and she'd seized it, latching on to the control.

"I'm sorry," she murmured. "You're right. I *am* angry. But not at you. I'm angry that the people who should know me better than anyone don't seem to care how much it hurts that they don't."

His shoulders drooped with disappointment, and he looked away. She tightened her arms around his neck, but he wouldn't look at her. Finally, she laid her hand against his cheek and drew his face back to her. She didn't like the doubt in his eyes, and she wished she could allay it, but what if he was right about that, too? What if she *was* only using him as a rebound? She hated the idea of doing that to him, of hurting him when he'd been nothing but understanding and sympathetic.

"Maybe you need more time, even if you don't think so," he said quietly. "I've waited this long. I'll wait a little longer."

"I don't need more time," she assured him. "But maybe I do need to slow down. Give myself a chance to let go of the anger and, more importantly, get to know you better."

"That might be a good idea." He let out a breath, and a faint smile erased the doubt from his face. "We're going to be swamped the next couple weeks getting the herds ready to move them up to the summer allotments. And Henry thinks he might've found a buyer for that office I'm working on, so I'll need to spend some time working on that."

"I could help, if that'd be all right." She grinned. "It might be a little more difficult to get frisky if we're covered in insulation."

"That'd be… great. I'd like that." He gave her an adorable lopsided smile. "You still haven't told me this isn't a dream."

Laughing, she clasped his face and kissed his lips lightly. "This isn't a dream."

Five

"YOU'RE SURE THIS IS WHAT you want to do with your day off?" Jeremiah asked as he closed the door on the horse trailer. "More of the same you do for your job?"

"Says the man who spends his days off building portable offices," she retorted. "Besides, I haven't seen nearly enough of you in the last two weeks."

That was probably for the best, though he didn't say it out loud. She needed time to put emotional distance between her and her relationship with Dustin even if she didn't want to admit it to herself.

"And it's a gorgeous day," she added.

"That it is."

The late spring sun burned off the morning's chill, so checking the Lazy H herds up here in the allotments would be a downright pleasant task. Certainly a better one than driving them up in a fine rain a week ago had been.

He stroked his hand over her horse's golden shoulder. Good lord, the beast was tall—over sixteen hands—with the long, clean lines of his breed. "So this is your famous racehorse."

"Yep, this is my Jinx."

"Jinx, huh?"

"Well, his registered name is Sunfire Gentry, but he has a story a bit like Murphy's. I bought him my senior year of college from a classmate who thought he'd be better for dressage or pleasure riding than he was at racing and tried to beat the new skills into him, so… after almost getting into a fistfight with the jackass in the middle of class, I offered to buy Jinx. Cleaned out what was left of my savings after paying for college to do it."

"Ouch."

"He's worth it even without taking into account his lineage. His grandfather was a Kentucky Derby winner, so really, I got him cheap."

"Why do I feel like the old fart chaperoning a couple of moony-eyed kids?" Austin asked, joining them. He slipped his rifle into the boot of his saddle.

"Maybe because you are?" Jeremiah replied teasingly. "Let's get this done, shall we? Come on, Murph."

He held his arms out and the dog obediently jumped into them so he could be lifted onto the chestnut gelding's back. Jeremiah swung into his saddle, and Murph settled onto his thighs.

"He really does go everywhere with you," Heather remarked. "Spoiled boy."

"Maybe just a little."

They'd parked the trailer in front of the tiny log cabin that came with these allotments. It sat at the tree line across the narrow dirt road from a broad, sloping meadow that gleamed emerald beneath the brilliant morning sun. The first wildflowers of the season were beginning to pop their heads above the lush grass, and above it all, the towering granite dome of Comet Mountain rose into the crystal sky.

Many of the Hammonds' cows and calves were grazing at the southern edge of the meadow, on the opposite side from the cabin.

"Should we start with them?" Jeremiah asked, pointing.

"Might as well," Austin replied. He climbed into his saddle.

With Murph holding tight to his legs, Jeremiah nudged his gelding down the dirt road toward the scenic byway and the gate at their intersection. The rope loop holding it closed was high enough that he could lean down and slip it off the post and nudge the gate open with his boot. Heather followed behind him with Austin bringing up the rear. After the ranch hand closed the gate, they headed across the meadow at a brisk walk, content to enjoy the stunning morning.

The cows and their calves barely noted their passing, and Jeremiah called out ear tag numbers for Austin to note on the check sheet. Nearly half this herd was in the meadow. They found another quarter in the narrow strip of meadow behind the island of pines and the rest scattered in the trees. The steers were in the allotment to the south of the meadow, and it took a bit more work to find them through the forest. When they were all accounted for, Jeremiah,

Heather, and Austin broke for lunch on the small porch of the cabin.

"Have either of you stayed up here with the herds?" Heather asked.

"Just a couple times," Jeremiah replied. "The last time was a few years ago, when we had some trouble with a big tom mountain lion—the same one that got a few of the Robinsons' sheep."

"That was the summer Luke and Ryan got together," Austin said. "We ran into a pretty little mama with a couple of cubs on the fall color trail ride up to Hall and Hopkins."

"I remember hearing about that." Heather glanced thoughtfully at their surroundings. "I'd like staying up here. It's so quiet."

"As if Northstar is noisy," Jeremiah teased.

She laughed and took another bite of her sandwich.

Jeremiah studied her. On any given day, she was beautiful, but with the sun on her face and the peace of their home in her eyes, she was exquisite.

Austin leaned in close and whispered, "You gonna eat or what? You can stare at her after the work's done."

With his face heating, Jeremiah returned his attention to his food.

His companion nudged him. "It's good to see you so smitten with her. I was beginning to think you'd end up a lonely old grump like me."

"Weren't you married once, Austin?" Heather asked.

"To Shane's mother, yes. Until she walked out on us."

"Burned by love, and yet you're still a romantic."

"I've watched plenty of love stories play out. Just

because I haven't found my happy ending doesn't mean I don't believe in them." Austin draped his arm over Jeremiah's shoulders. "And this kid here deserves one more than most."

Jeremiah hazarded a glance at Heather and didn't know what to make of her contemplative expression that wasn't quite a smile but definitely wasn't a frown. Suddenly, he wondered what her family thought of them dating. She hadn't said much about it, but from what she'd said about her family riding her about her decision to break up with Dustin, he suspected he wasn't their idea of a good match for her. With his past, and the mistakes he'd made….

In a community as small and tight-knit as Northstar, it was difficult to reconcile how little he knew her family. Politely aloof, he would describe them. He'd met them a few times, but they'd never had much to say to him.

He jerked his gaze from her and reached to give his dog some love.

He didn't think Heather would care what her family thought of him, but even so, it certainly couldn't be pleasant to have her choices questioned by them, and he didn't like the idea of causing her that kind of frustration.

Shaking his head, he finished his sandwich after tossing a bite to Murph and picked up the remnants of their meal while he waited for Heather and Austin to finish eating. He stowed their trash in the pickup, and by the time he was finished with that, they were ready to go.

He stubbornly kept the thoughts of Heather's family from his mind as they headed east to check on the bred heifers, starting at the eastern edge of the meadow. It was a routine and pleasant check of the herd until they turned back west toward the cabin.

They found the dead heifer less than two hundred yards east of the cabin. She hadn't been dead too long but long enough for rigor mortis to set in. Jeremiah's heart sank.

"Son of a bitch," Austin muttered, riding closer to investigate.

Jeremiah followed his companion, and the cause of death was immediately evident—a single bullet to the head between the eye and ear. It was possible she was the victim of a stray bullet, perhaps from someone doing a little recreational target practice, but that wasn't the thought that came first to his mind.

Zach.

He fought the suspicion. Aaron had talked to his cousin's PO just this morning, and so far, Zach had been a model parolee—doing well at his job, which he'd been at yesterday evening when the cow had likely been shot. And yet, Jeremiah couldn't ignore the coincidence of a cow dead from a gunshot and his cousin's release from prison. Zach hadn't built his drug running business into the empire it had been by getting his own hands dirty.

"I know what you're thinking, boy," Austin said. "And it can't be him."

"Can't it? He gets out of prison, and a couple weeks later, a cow turns up shot."

"His PO verified that he was at work when this girl died."

"Doesn't mean he didn't get someone else to do it for him."

"Why shoot a cow? Most likely she got hit by a stray bullet from some drunk jackass up here doing some target practice."

Jeremiah shook his head. "I don't know."

"You're just jumpy, kid. And probably with good reason. Your cousin's a right piece of shit, and I'm sure he'd love to make you pay for taking him down. But this ain't gonna get the job done, now, is it."

"No, other than it hurts the Hammonds, and you can be sure Zach knows I work for them." *And probably that they're as close as family to me.* He kept that thought to himself.

"They can afford to lose one cow. Come on. Let's take a look around and see what we can find."

As they scouted the surrounding forest, Heather rode close beside him. She didn't say anything, but he sensed the questions churning in her mind. Surely he sounded paranoid to her. Hell, he sounded paranoid to himself.

"It's stupid, I know," he said. "I'm just jumpy. Like Austin says."

"You know your cousin better than any of us," she replied gently. "And from what I've heard, he's a touch crazy."

"Not crazy. Smart. Irresistibly charming. Devious. Possibly psychotic in that he seems to lack empathy and has no regard whatsoever for the law."

"Sounds like a real winner. How did you get mixed up with him?"

"Desperation. It was just Joe and me by then, and we were barely scraping by. Hey, Austin, take a look at that."

He pointed to a homemade target made of scrap two-by-fours and wafer wood just on the other side of the allotment's northern fence. It had been shot to pieces; there wasn't anything left of its center. They checked the area for any sign of where the shooter had shot from, crossing out of the allotment through a gate to the east of the target. They fanned out, scanning the forest floor for shell casings or anything else that might provide information.

"Here we go," Jeremiah said, nudging his gelding toward the glint of brass in a shaft of sunlight.

As they converged on the spot, he spotted about a half a dozen casings. Not nearly as many as he would've expected given the state of the target, and they were widely scattered as if the shooter had tried to pick up the brass but had missed a few. That in itself wasn't inherently suspicious—there were plenty of people around here that reloaded ammunition—and if the shooter had wanted to hide his activities, he would've taken the target with him.

The angles were totally wrong. The target was straight behind him, and the dead heifer was almost directly to his left.

"Well," Austin said, yanking his cowboy hat off and scrubbing his hand through his silvering blond hair. "Doesn't look much like an accident anymore. Let's check on the rest of the herd, then get to the Royal R, call John and Tracie, and see if Jim or Jessie or any of their hands saw or heard anything."

It was a quick task to complete the check, and Jeremiah and Heather stayed at the cabin while Austin drove over to the Royal R to talk to the Robinsons and call the Hammonds. Jeremiah perched on the porch of the cabin where they'd eaten lunch and ran his hand through his hair. Without invitation, Murphy sat beside him with half his body draped over Jeremiah's legs.

A cow shot intentionally….

Why wouldn't his brain let go of the idea that Zach was somehow behind it?

There was no rhyme or reason to it. If his cousin was planning something, killing one of the Hammonds' cows would bring unwanted attention. The logical explanation was that some jackass, likely drunk, had been up here target shooting and decided his target wasn't challenging enough. Frowning, he stroked Murph's head, and the dog squirmed the rest of the way onto his legs, leaning against him.

"You're not still thinking your cousin is behind this, are you?" Heather asked quietly.

"It doesn't make any sense," he admitted. "And I'm probably just being paranoid. But, Christ. For eleven years, I've wondered what he would do to me when he got out. Eleven years of building a solid life for myself and putting distance between me and the mistakes I made. And him being out of prison…. Everything's just a little too close to the surface again."

She slipped her arm around his waist and rested her head on his shoulder. She didn't say a word, but her silent companionship was all he needed.

They were still sitting like that when the cavalry arrived. Jim Robinson along with his foreman, Andy Epperson, and Shane had followed Austin back, and they all showed up the same time as John, Nick, and Aaron. While the others investigated the dead cow, Jeremiah and Heather unsaddled their horses and loaded them into the trailer. Then, because the others weren't back yet, they stepped into the cabin.

It wasn't much—a single room with a built-in wooden bunk without a mattress in the back left corner, a woodstove in the back right, a small counter with a cabinet below and above in the right front corner that served as the kitchen, and a scarred wooden table with two old chairs between that and the door. Two windows with old, wavy glass flanked the door on the south-facing wall. There was an old-school hand pump around the side that provided the only water, and an outhouse a few yards away in the woods.

"I've never been in here before," Heather remarked. "It isn't much, but it's more than I was expecting."

"It's kinda fun camping out up here."

Jeremiah poked around the cabin. There were no obvious signs that someone had stayed in here recently, but there was no dust on the bunk while there was a thin layer on everything else, and when he opened the wood stove, there were a few pieces of charred wood inside. The stove had been completely cleaned out when they'd moved the cows up to the allotments.

"Someone's been here in the last week," he said quietly.

"Probably our shooter."

Nodding, he stepped out of the cabin. Voices to his left drew his attention, and he spotted the Robinsons, Hammonds, and McGuires returning. He waited for them on the porch with Heather standing beside him and Murph leaning against his leg. While the others chatted more about the dead cow, Aaron joined Jeremiah and Heather on the porch.

"What's the consensus?" Jeremiah asked.

"I don't see how it could've been an accident. That hill behind the target was all soft dirt—nothing for a bullet to ricochet off. And we didn't find any other casings anywhere else that might've made me think the shooter took a few shots from the north."

Jeremiah nodded. "I think I ought to stay up here for a while. As a precaution."

"I don't think that's necessary, Jere. This was likely an isolated incident."

"Maybe. Maybe not. Someone's slept in the cabin since we moved the herds up."

"That doesn't mean anything."

"No, but if I'm up here, it might deter whoever did it."

"You have an office to finish. How are you going to do that if you're up here with the cattle?"

"It can wait. I don't have a buyer for it."

"Actually, you do. Henry ran into a guy in town this morning who saw your ad for the last one in the Devynite Daily. He'll be out this evening to take a look at it, but it sounded like he was already sold on it."

Jeremiah scrubbed his hands through his hair. "Fine. I'll finish it this week, and then I'll come up here, if that's all right with your dad and Nick."

Aaron studied him with narrowed eyes for the better part of a minute. Finally, he said, "You aren't thinking Zach is behind this."

"The thought crossed my mind," he replied. "But even I have to admit it seems implausible."

"Good, because you realize that not one of us would allow you to stay up here if we thought for even a second that your dickhead cousin had anything to do with this." Aaron wrapped his hand around the back of Jeremiah's neck and pulled him close. "Because no cow is worth putting you at risk."

Jeremiah pressed his mouth into a flat line and nodded. "So you think it's a good idea?"

"I don't know that I'd call it a *good* idea, but I'll talk to my dad and Nick about it." Suddenly, Aaron laughed, glancing sideways at Heather. "If I didn't know any better, I might think you were looking for a little privacy."

"That thought hadn't even crossed my mind, Aaron."

"Uh-huh. Sure."

"It crossed mine," Heather remarked, grinning.

Jeremiah swore under his breath and stepped off the porch. Murph followed him, bouncing around his legs like this was some fun new game, so he indulged the dog for a few moments while the itch of embarrassment slowly receded. When he finally looked at his companions again, they regarded him with matching smiles of amusement.

"Has he always been this shy?" Heather asked Aaron.

"Yep. He seems to be laboring under the misconception that he's not worthy of a woman like you."

"I beg to differ."

"So do I."

Chuckling, Aaron trotted down the steps and sauntered over to his father and brother. Jeremiah stuffed his hands in his pockets and watched them. They were too far away for him to hear what they were saying, but when Nick, John, and Austin glanced his way, he was certain they were discussing the pros and cons of having him stay up here with the cows. At last, Nick approached him with a nod from his father.

"Dad wants to wait," the eldest Hammond brother said. "He says—and we all agree—that you need to finish that office."

"Fine. Shouldn't take me more than a week."

"I can help, too," Heather said. "After work in the evenings. It'll be fun."

"Good," Nick said. "When it's done, we'll reassess the situation. Hopefully there'll be no need for you to stay up here."

Nick glanced between them with a knowing gleam in his eyes but didn't comment. "We'll stay here and take care of the cow if you two wouldn't mind taking the horses back to the ranch. Would you let Mom know we're going to be late for dinner?"

Nodding, Jeremiah opened the driver-side door of the pickup and told Murphy to load up. With Heather belted in to the passenger seat, he drove the trailer to the turnaround at the end of the road. The space wasn't big enough to simply drive around, but he'd been hauling trailers long enough now that he had no trouble backing this one and getting the rig turned back down the road toward the main road.

Heather laughed.

"What?" he asked.

"You can even back a trailer better than Brock."

He lifted a brow at her, not sure he wanted to be compared to her brother.

"He made a smart remark at the big family meeting a couple weeks back. I might've told him that you were a better rancher than he is… and you keep proving me right."

"I appreciate the compliment," he said slowly, "but I'm not sure using me as ammunition against your brother is the best idea."

"Probably not. But he pisses me off so much."

"I'm sorry to hear that. Joe and I were close, so I can't imagine fighting with him like that."

"Then you were lucky."

"It's not just me and Joe, though. Nick and Aaron and Henry have their disagreements from time to time, but they don't fight."

"No, they don't," Heather murmured. She turned her gaze out the side window.

Jeremiah took the hint and let the topic drop.

As he drove down the winding pass into the Northstar Valley toward the Lazy H, he let her draw him into conversation about the portable office he now had just a week to finish. Why hadn't he given himself more time? The only thing he'd had time to do in the last two weeks was the insulation, which left him with the paneling, painting, trim, carpet, desk, cabinets, and shelves to complete. He could get it done, but it was going to take some late nights to make it happen. It was a nice distraction—laying out everything he needed to finish and what order he needed to do things in to make the best use of his time—but even that couldn't get the dead cow off his mind.

It made no sense, but his gut wouldn't let go of the idea that Zach was behind it somehow.

* * *

Heather laughed as a big drip of cream-colored paint splattered the toe of her old tennis shoes.

"You're having way too much fun with that," Jeremiah remarked as he hopped up into the portable office to check her progress.

"I really am."

"Thanks again for helping me with all this. Not sure I could've gotten all this done without you."

"It has been my pleasure, Mr. Mackey." She used the relatively paint-free back of her hand to brush a strand of hair from her face, wiggling her lips and nose to assuage the lingering tickle. "Seriously. I'm having a blast. It's been a great change of pace."

She didn't say it out loud, but working with him every evening for the last five days had also saved her from two dinners with her family. They weren't pleased that she'd blown them off to help Jeremiah finish his project, but when she was with him, she couldn't bring herself to care.

She rolled the last section of wall while he watched, and when she was finished, she turned to him with a broad smile. "Second coat's all done, boss. How'd I do?"

"Fantastic. It looks great."

She glanced around the space. The color he'd chosen was bright and cheerful without being too yellow. It seemed to change color with the light, sometimes more yellow, sometimes with more of a pink tint. For the small area, it was perfect, and it also brought out the golden tones in the blue pine desk, cabinets, shelves, and trim he'd spent the last hour coating with the third and final layer of spar urethane. The plan was to install all that and the carpet tomorrow, and after that, the office would be done and two days ahead of schedule.

The sense of accomplishment was incredible.

"This thing is going to be gorgeous when it's all finished."

"Not to be arrogant, but yeah, I think it will be. I

learned a lot from the first one to this one, and it shows."

"I'm not sure you know *how* to be arrogant."

He met her gaze for a moment, then looked quickly away, and she couldn't help but grin. There wasn't an arrogant bone in him. If there was, he'd at least know how to take a compliment without blushing.

Of course, she was glad he didn't. She liked his humility. It was endearing and set him apart from many of the men she'd dated. More than that, she liked the effect it had on her. When she was around him, she was calmer somehow, and she knew it was because he didn't judge her. He was happy to be with her, exactly as she was.

Abruptly, she turned toward the door and dropped out of the trailer onto the concrete floor of the shop to inspect the blue pine pieces that would complete the office. There was something incredibly beautiful about the wood—all locally sourced, he'd informed her—even if that blue-gray staining was the result of the fungus carried by the destructive mountain pine beetle that had decimated forests across the Rockies. It added a unique infusion of contrasting color to the pale gold wood.

Jeremiah had left the uneven bark edge—sanded down to remove the bark and reveal the worm tracks beneath—on the desktop, the front edge of the shelves, the outside edges of the trim pieces for the windows and door, and the inside edges of the cabinet doors. The desk would have log legs on the front side with the back mounted to the walls, and along with the bark edges, they would make the whole thing eye-pleasingly rustic and one-of-a-kind.

He was one hell of a craftsman.

"Where did you learn to do all this?" she asked.

"My grandparents owned a construction company in Devyn, remember?"

"Yeah, that explains the office itself… but what about this?"

"Dad and Grandpa were also pretty gifted at building furniture. I didn't think I'd picked up much of that before they died, but I guess I did. At least enough that I was able to fill in the gaps."

"How'd they die?" she asked, latching on to the comment. He talked about his family so rarely that her curiosity was morphing into a ravenous thing.

"Grandpa? Heart attack."

"I'm so sorry."

"It was hard. He was a good man."

"If he was anything like you, I believe it."

He glanced sharply at her, then—as usual—ducked his gaze.

"You don't believe that?" she asked.

"That I'm a good man?"

"Yeah."

"Good men don't do the dumb things I did."

"Even the best men make mistakes."

He nodded, but she could tell he didn't agree with her. How long would it be before he stopped letting his past mistakes be one of his defining characteristics?

"You up for dinner at the Bedspread?" she asked. She peeled off some of the paint that had dried on her hands and rubbed off some more that was still tacky, but it was going to take some hot water and a scrub brush to get the rest off. Dropping her hands, she turned her gaze on Jeremiah. "I'll buy. Or the Ramshorn, if you'd prefer. I wouldn't mind taking another swim. We worked our butts off today, and we can't do anything else until the paint and the urethane is dry, anyhow."

He frowned and didn't immediately answer. Finally, after half a minute, he replied, "Uh, yeah. That'd be great."

"If you don't want to go… we don't have to. I'm a terrible cook, but I can whip up something easy."

"It's not that." He chuckled. "Sometimes I get into a gotta-get-it-done mindset and it takes me a while to stop looking for what I need to do next."

"Understandable. Do you want to get cleaned up before we go out?" She glanced at the clock on the shop wall. "Holy crap. It's already almost eight. I didn't realize it was that late. I don't think Pat and Aeli would mind if we showed up covered in paint, but maybe we oughta skip the Ramshorn tonight because getting this junk off us will eat up most of the time we have left before the pools close."

Shaking his head, he laughed a little louder.

"What?" she asked.

"You're cute. The Bedspread is fine, and no, I don't think Pat and Aeli will mind. This won't be the first time I've walked in to their restaurant covered in paint or sawdust or dirt."

"And I'm sure you aren't the only one to do it. This *is* a ranching community, after all."

She helped Jeremiah put tools away and clean up their rollers and brushes, and by the time they'd finished that, it was a quarter after eight.

"Come on, Murph," he called to his dog. "Time to go home."

The dog crawled out from under the trailer and

pranced over, stopping briefly beside his master for some pets before continuing on to Heather for more.

"He's warming up to you faster than he warms up to most people," Jeremiah remarked. He turned off the lights in the shop and followed Heather and his dog outside into a golden June evening. "Take that as a compliment."

"I do," she replied. "Is he coming or staying home with Austin?"

"I think he'll stay home this time."

Murphy put his ears back and lowered his head at the word *stay*.

"Say it isn't so, Dad," Heather whimpered, giving voice to the dog's dismay.

"Oh, he'll enjoy it. Austin spoils him rotten."

Heather opened the door of Jeremiah's truck. "Load up, Murph."

The dog obeyed without question. He *was* warming up to her. When she'd tried to let him into the truck on Tuesday, he'd glanced at his master and waited for Jeremiah to echo the command. Heather ruffled his ears fondly.

"Yeah, we're getting to be good friends now, aren't we, sweet boy?"

Murphy wiggled his tails stump in agreement.

Austin was sitting outside on the porch of the bunkhouse when they pulled up, and he tipped his imaginary hat to her in greeting, none too discreet when he glanced between her and Jeremiah with a twinkle in his eyes. She couldn't help but smile.

It was nice to be around people who approved of her relationship with Jeremiah.

Plus, she valued Austin's opinion. She'd gotten to

know him well back in high school when she'd gone out with Shane, and the fact that he felt as he did about Jeremiah—like the man was his second son—made it even easier than it already was to trust him.

Why couldn't her family see it?

"Nope," she muttered. "Not going to think like that tonight."

Because she didn't want to be alone in the truck with her thoughts for even the few minutes it would take Jeremiah to get his dog in the house and fed, she followed him into the bunkhouse.

"You two look like you got a fair amount of work done on the office this evening," Austin remarked, eyeing her paint-spattered clothes.

"We did," she replied. "Should be done tomorrow. I know it's ridiculous because I am exhausted enough to sleep for a week, but I've really had fun helping Jeremiah."

"He's good company. Easy to be around."

"Yes, he is. I was just thinking that myself a little while ago."

"Gossiping about me again, Austin?" Jeremiah asked when he'd finished dishing Murphy's kibble.

"Only good things," Heather said. "We ready?"

"Yep. Stay, Murph, and be good."

The dog gave him a pitiful look, but it lasted all of two seconds before he was distracted by his food bowl. Chuckling, Jeremiah opened the door for Heather and promised Austin he wouldn't be out too late.

"What the hell do I care when you come home?" the older man asked. "You're a grown man. Have some fun."

"I don't think I have the energy left for any more

fun," Jeremiah replied before closing the door behind them.

Heather climbed in his truck, amused that they seemed to take it more places together than her newer Silverado. The old Ford was a reliable vehicle, and there was something classic and timeless about riding shotgun in it.

Was it the truck… or her date?

Both, but mostly her date. He was always so laid back with her and never tried to show off or prove his masculine prowess, and the stubborn independence that would usually have her demanding she drive was silent. She was content to surf her hand on the wind and watch the familiar landscape roll past as the balmy early June air wafted through the cab.

"Are you going to keep going on the restoration of this old girl?" she asked.

"That's the plan. If I can sell a couple more offices, I'll finish the bodywork and have it painted. That and the trim is all I have left. The mechanics are all done."

"What color would you paint it?"

"A nice, rich metallic root beer—a nod to that brown and cream color scheme she was originally."

"That'd look great on her."

How much fun would it be to take a road trip with Jeremiah in this old girl all freshly painted? Just him and her and Murphy cruising down some two-lane highway with the windows down and the music blasting…. Her lips curved at the thought.

"That was a smile I've never seen," Jeremiah remarked as he turned into the Bedspread Inn's U-shaped driveway. "Whatcha thinkin' about?"

"A road trip," she replied. "Don't know when we'll

ever be able to take one, though. Ty keeps me pretty busy, and I know there's always work to be done on the Lazy H, and if you make a go of it with your portable offices…. And you should, by the way. They're adorable."

"I don't think there's enough of a market for it to be anything more than a hobby."

"Pssh. You've already sold a couple, right? And this one already has a buyer. Plus, didn't Henry say he talked to a guy who might be interested in one?"

His lips quirked upward. "Yeah, I guess so. But that doesn't mean it'll last. Devyn isn't exactly a deep market."

"No," she agreed. "But by the time you run out of buyers here, you could have the means to expand your radius."

She liked the way he let out a huff of laughter as if he didn't believe her but wanted to. Grinning, she turned her gaze out the windshield and barely held back the groan when she spotted Curtis's truck parked by the steps up to the deck of the Bedspread's restaurant. By the time Jeremiah parked his old Ford a couple cars over from it, her brother and his wife and their two young children were walking out the door.

"Let's just hang out here for a minute," she said quietly as if her brother might hear her.

"Why?" Following her gaze, Jeremiah asked, "Isn't that your brother and his family?"

"Yes, it is, and I'm having a great evening. I'd rather not ruin it by talking to him."

"Why would talking to him ruin it?"

Instead of answering, she glared in her brother's direction with her lips pressed into a flat line.

"I'm going to go out on a limb and guess your family doesn't approve of you dating me."

"That's a nice way of putting it," she muttered.

"Come on."

Before she could beg him to stop, he'd shut the engine down and jumped out of his truck. This time, she let the groan out and followed him outside. They passed her brother and his family on the steps, and to his credit, Jeremiah smiled brightly and commented on what a lovely evening it was. Curtis looked him up and down, glanced between him and Heather, and then forced a smile.

"Yes, it is."

"Christina, right?" Jeremiah inquired, turning to Curtis's wife with his hand extended. "I don't believe I've ever had the pleasure."

Christina glanced uncertainly between her husband and Heather but shook Jeremiah's hand. "Jerry Mackey, right?"

"Jeremiah. And who are these two cuties?"

"Our son Sebastian and our daughter Rosalie."

Heather now found herself holding back a laugh as Jeremiah made goofy faces at nearly-two-year-old Rosalie until she was giggling uncontrollably and then flipped a switch and greeted four-year-old Sebastian as if he were a man of great importance. As entertaining as her boyfriend was, his antics were not nearly as hilarious as her brother's discomfort. Curtis had a constipated look on his face—the expression of someone desperately wanting to escape an unpleasant situation but unable to do so without being incredibly rude.

"Well, gorgeous," Jeremiah said, turning to Heather

as he straightened and conspicuously took her hand, "we'd better get inside."

"Excellent idea. I'm starving."

"You four have a wonderful evening."

Without waiting for Curtis or Christina to respond, Jeremiah gave Heather's hand a tug and they left her brother and his family standing on the stairs with matching frowns of confusion and consternation. The doors had barely closed behind them before Heather lost the war against her laughter. It spilled out of her, and her tired body soon slackened with it. She hung on Jeremiah's arm as he guided her toward a booth on the left side of the dining room.

"That… was… *incredible!*" she said breathlessly with laughter still tumbling out of her. "The look on his face was priceless."

"I'm surprised he didn't try to give me the big-brother threat. 'Stay away from my sister, scumbag.' Or something like that."

"Nah. That's not Curtis's MO. Brock's maybe. But they'd have to care enough about my wellbeing to bother threatening you, so don't worry."

He tilted his head and studied her with his brows furrowed. "You think they don't care about your wellbeing?"

She squirmed in her seat. This was *not* what she wanted to talk about tonight. She'd had fun with Jeremiah this evening, and she wanted to hold on to that and savor it. "I wish I could say they do, but most of the time, it sure doesn't feel like it. Let's not talk about this tonight, okay? It's depressing, and I want to have fun with you. Austin *did* say he didn't expect you home too soon…."

He didn't complain when she sidled around the table and slid into the booth beside him, nor did he stop her when she slipped her arms around his neck and kissed him. There weren't any other diners in the restaurant, or she was certain he would've put the brakes on. As it was, she suspected he didn't because he sensed she needed the distraction. The concern in his eyes after she touched her lips to his again before pulling away confirmed it. He wasn't going to forget this conversation, and desperately, she hoped they'd get to a place that she felt comfortable enough to answer his questions about her relationship with her family.

The potential was there.

Just being with him soothed her jittery heart, and the way he'd boldly headed off what could've been a very awkward encounter with her brother gave her a sense of security she hadn't never realized she needed. Without her asking him to, he'd protected her from her own brother, and he'd done so despite the fact that he was the target of Curtis's scorn.

No one had ever done that for her before.

Pinching her eyes closed, she curled her hands around his arm and rested her head on his shoulder. When he draped an arm around her, she let out a breath and let herself be vulnerable for once in her life.

"Thank you," she whispered.

She thought she'd said it too quietly for him to hear, but he whispered back, "You're welcome."

Six

"STILL THINK IT'S UNNECESSARY for me to stay up here?" Jeremiah asked, gesturing to the dead calf.

Aaron leaned over his saddle horn to peer at the unfortunate animal, frowning. The calf hadn't been dead more than a day or two—Austin had marked the number on the ear tag as accounted for on his check the day before yesterday—but a bear or mountain lion or wolves or coyotes or who knew what else had chewed it up pretty good.

"There's no way I can see to tell what killed it," Aaron said at last.

"Dead's dead. And that makes two Lazy H cows in two weeks. We need someone up here to keep an eye on the herd. I should've come up here right after the first."

"We were all hoping it would turn out you wouldn't

need to come up at all. Two weeks without a single problem... and now this. Even if it was an animal that killed it, we can't ignore two dead cows."

Jeremiah felt no sense of triumph in hearing Aaron admit he was right. He would much prefer being wrong. As much as he'd enjoyed his previous summers in the cabin, he wasn't particularly looking forward to it. It would mean seeing less of Heather, and though he hadn't seen as much of her over the past week since they'd finished his portable office, they'd still managed to steal at least an hour a day to spend with each other.

Aaron chuckled. "Having second thoughts about volunteering to stay up here?"

"Maybe a few."

"Let me guess. Heather's the big one."

Jeremiah rubbed his hand over the back of his neck as he fought the smile that threatened. He lost the battle, and the grin spread even wider in triumph.

"You want to ask Austin if he'll trade you places?"

"No. He hates staying up here. I'll just have to suck it up."

Aaron laughed. "Guess that answers the question about how you two are doing. You were all geared up to stay up here two weeks ago, but it sounds like Heather's given you quite a reason to want to stay closer to home."

He nodded.

"So things are going good with her."

"I think so. She seems to be past the rebound stage, at least, and she's definitely not shy about... anything."

"Sounds like there's a 'but' in there somewhere."

Jeremiah frowned and straightened in his saddle,

eliciting a grunt from Murph, who had to readjust his position so he didn't fall off his master's lap or the horse. Jeremiah stared out at the bright meadow without seeing it. How could he explain his worry that this thing with Heather wouldn't last? It *was* going great, and with any other woman, he'd have no cause to worry. But she'd had relationships in the past that had seemed to be going great, too, until she ended them with the decisiveness of a slammed door. She'd been with Dustin for two years before she'd called it quits with him. He was thirty-three now, and in a few months, he would turn thirty-four, and it was beginning to feel like whatever chance he had at settling down with a woman was slipping away. Until recently, he hadn't given much thought to whether or not he wanted that, but the more time he spent with Heather, the more he wanted that kind of companionship. Austin was great company and all, but it wasn't the same.

"I don't want to put everything I have into a relationship with her, pin my hopes on it, and have it crumble."

"Ah."

Jeremiah looked to his companion. "I don't want to think like that, but…."

"She does have a troubling trend with men. But you aren't like the others. Maybe you have something she needs that they didn't."

"Like what? You've known Ty his whole life. The guy has it all, but she dumped him anyhow. What could I possibly have that they don't?"

"For one, Ty's heart already belonged to Shannon, and Heather was smart enough to know it. I honestly can't say what she's looking for, Jere. I don't know her well, but I *do* know that she knows her own mind better than almost anyone I've ever met. If she's with you at all, there's a reason. So, instead of worrying about what might happen down the road, enjoy what you have for however long it lasts. And who knows? Maybe it'll last forever. You'll never find out if you let fear get in the way."

Jeremiah sighed. Aaron was right, of course, but agreeing with that advice was far easier than following it. Still, everything with Heather had been a breeze so far. After years of waiting to catch her attention and expecting a constant battle to keep it once he did, it was a surprise that his relationship with her was as easy as it was.

"Give me a hand getting this calf loaded in my truck so I can take it in to town and have the guys at the FWP take a look at it, see if they can figure out how it died," Aaron said, swinging out of his saddle. "Then I'll help you get everything together for cleaning and stocking the cabin."

Jeremiah joined him on the ground, leaving Murph in the saddle. When the dog angled his body like he was considering jumping down to investigate the tantalizing and mercifully faint scent, Jeremiah commanded, "Leave it."

With a disappointed sniff and shake of his head, Murph put his head on his paws but watched intently from his perch.

Wrapping the remains of the calf in a tarp and tying it securely was a grisly chore. It didn't matter how many cows and big game animals he'd seen butchered, he would never get used to it. Even Aaron, who'd held his first wife in his arms as she'd died from a gunshot wound and helped clean up gnarly wrecks on the highways, grimaced.

"Death never gets easier," he remarked.

Jeremiah shook his head, agreeing.

They loaded the horses in the trailer and the dog in the truck, and Aaron drove down to the ranch. While he made his phone calls to Fish, Wildlife and Parks about the calf, Tracie and Beth helped Jeremiah gather the cleaning supplies he'd need to make the allotment cabin livable. In the middle of it all, Heather showed up. Murph bounded over to greet her, and she lavished him with pets until, beside himself with pleasure, he flopped on the ground and rolled onto his back, demanding belly rubs. Jeremiah grinned. There weren't too many people his dog trusted enough to bare his belly to.

"I thought you had to work today," he remarked, settling the broom, mop, and bucket in the bed of his Ford.

"Just the daily chores," she replied still petting his dog. "Ty had to head out of town for an auction in Billings, so I get the rest of the day off. I could work a few of the horses if I wanted to, but we're ahead of schedule as it is, and I figured the horses could use a day of rest, too. What's all this for?"

"I'm heading up to the allotment cabin."

"I thought the Hammonds hadn't decided on that yet."

"Aaron and I found a dead calf this morning."

"Was it shot, too?"

"Can't tell. There's not much of it left."

"Want a hand?"

He regarded her with a brow lifted. "What is it with you and working on your days off?"

"That's the pot calling the kettle black. How many times are we going to have this conversation? Let's just admit we're both workaholics and leave it at that."

"Yes, ma'am," Jeremiah replied, chuckling. "Of course I'd love your company, even if you just want to kick back and relax."

"I'll help," she said huskily as she slipped her arms around his neck, "and maybe tonight after all the work is done…"

"Heather…."

"…we'll have a picnic dinner at the cabin and play a card game or two." Mischief danced in her eyes, and with her hands knitted against the back of his neck, she leaned back in his arms and laughed as Murph bounced around them, wanting some of the attention. "No need to be shy with me, Jeremiah."

"Not shy, just… still can't quite believe this is real and trying to savor everything because—" He snapped his mouth closed and shook his head. He couldn't give voice to that thought, afraid that doing so would make it true. He'd already given it too much power admitting it to Aaron this morning.

"Because what?" she pressed.

Because I'm afraid it will end. Again, he refused to say it out loud, so he smiled in response. "Because it's better than I imagined and too good not to enjoy every second of it."

"I never knew you were such an eloquent romantic."

He grinned at that, pleased to have surprised her and even more pleased that she seemed to like that he had. After he climbed into the bed of his truck to secure the rest of the cleaning supplies for the ride up to the cabin, he braced one hand on the tailgate and swung his legs over it, landing lightly on his feet beside her.

"Show off," she muttered fondly.

"Not trying to be. Just in a good mood."

"Looking forward to some quiet time up at the cabin, huh?"

"Not so much."

"Then why are you in a good mood?"

He kissed her on the cheek and let that be his answer.

She grinned, but there was an edge to it. "Nice to know I can put *someone* in a good mood."

"Uh-oh. That doesn't sound good. What's up?"

"Nothing more than usual. Brock's pissed at me again because he doesn't like the price I quoted him to train the green-broke colt he bought yesterday. Seems he thought I was joking when I said I wasn't going to train any more of my family's horses without payment."

Jeremiah's brows rose. Her family expected her to do the work for free? Horse training was no quick, easy job, and any work she did for them without pay took time away from her paying jobs. He slipped his hand around hers as they started to the house and gave it a reassuring squeeze. "That's rather selfish of them."

She shrugged. "I made the mistake of training Brock's old mare for free when I first started working for Ty right after college. I didn't trust my skills back then, and I figured I could use the practice."

"I get that, but how many horses have you trained for them without pay?"

"All of them."

"That's ridiculous. Do your brothers and your

brother-in-law get paid for helping on the ranch?"

"Of course."

He shook his head, frowning. "That'd be like John expecting Aaron or Henry to work the ranch for free. You help bring in the money, you ought to get a cut of it."

"Well, that blow up over Rain the day of that first lesson with Jessie finally pushed me over the edge. Not my fault Brock thought I was joking."

"No, it isn't. Your brother sounds like a dick."

"He is. We've never gotten along. Got along better with Curtis, but even he's been *off* lately."

"I'm sorry."

She turned abruptly to him. "What the hell do you have to be sorry for? It's not your fault my family is a bunch of uptight, self-centered pricks."

"I'm not apologizing." He opened the front door and stood back to let her enter first. "I'm expressing sympathy. I wish they weren't a bunch of uptight, self-centered pricks. It's good of you to tolerate them despite that."

She tilted her head and regarded him with a quizzical frown.

"What did I say?" he asked slowly.

"You aren't going to tell me I should suck it up and deal with it because they're my family?"

"Why would I? Them being your blood doesn't give them the right to take advantage of you."

"You're the first to say that."

Abruptly, she slipped past him into the main house. He stared after her a moment before following, reaching the kitchen just in time to see her wrapped in a warm hug by Henry's wife. With a deliberate cheerfulness, Heather scooped Henry and Lindsay's little boy up in her arms, and Jeremiah frowned. This thing with her and her family…. It bugged him. Maybe he'd been spoiled by the Hammonds, who were among the most caring people he'd ever met, but it didn't seem right that her family should be a source of anxiety for her. And clearly they were.

"When did you come in, Linds?" he asked the redheaded woman.

"Just a minute ago. Hey, I know you need to get the allotment cabin set up, but you're still coming to Noah's birthday party after, right? And you're going to bring this pretty lady, too, I hope."

"Crap. That's tonight? What day is it?"

"Friday, honey. Tracie, I think we need to get him one of those watches with the day and date."

"Wouldn't do any good," the Hammond matriarch remarked. "He'll just break it out working."

"Hey," Jeremiah retorted, "at least I remembered to wish him a happy birthday *on* his birthday. And I called him before any of the rest of you did, I'd like to add."

"Yes, you did," Tracie laughed. Then she shook her head. "Nineteen already. I can't believe it."

"Uncle Jere?" Archer asked.

"Yes, Bubba Louie?"

"Can I stay in the cabin with you?"

"Maybe one night, if it's all right with your mom and dad."

"Fine by us," Lindsay replied. "It's been a while since Henry and I have had a night to ourselves. Might just go out dancing. How upset is Will going to be that he won't be the one to stay with the herd?"

"He'll have to deal with it," Tracie replied. "We didn't let Nick, Aaron, or Henry stay up there until they were eighteen, and we're not going to change the rules for Will. We promised he can do it next year, whether or not we actually need anyone to stay up there with them."

From the corner of his vision, he caught Heather watching him with an odd expression, but when he turned fully toward her, it was gone, replaced by a relaxed smile. He glanced between her and their companions.

"Well?" he asked. "Would you mind postponing our picnic dinner to join me for Noah's birthday dinner?"

"I'd love to," she replied. She turned to Lindsay and added, "If you're sure me coming along wouldn't be an intrusion."

"I'm positive."

"In that case, we'd better get to work. Tracie, where are the linens? I can take those up in my truck so Jere doesn't have to make two trips."

Jeremiah tilted his head. That was the first time she'd called him by the shortened name the Hammonds had started using after he'd told them he didn't like being called Jerry. It made him smile—the familiarity and comfortableness of it. He embraced Lindsay and followed Tracie and Heather into the laundry room under the stairs and let them load his arms with the sheets, blankets, and hand towels he'd be taking to the cabin.

"I'll call the boys in and have them bring down the mattress," Tracie said. "While you're up at the cabin, I'll get the cooler together for you so you can take it up with you after dinner. Any special requests?"

"You know what I like," he replied. "And even if you

didn't, whatever you give me will be great."

"We've trained you well, young one," Lindsay teased.

Heather opened the doors for him, and in short order, he had the linens stuffed into the back seat of her truck. Will and Noah arrived with the twin mattress just as she closed the doors, and he told them to toss it in the back of his truck.

"Can't believe it took both of you to carry a twin," he teased. He gave Noah a welcome-home hug. "How was your drive back from Washington, birthday boy?"

"Uneventful," Noah replied. "But man am I glad to be back."

They chatted for a few minutes about Noah's boring visit with his father and stepmother and about Will's mild disappointment that he wasn't allowed to stay up at the allotment cabin yet. Jeremiah reached up to ruffle his blond hair, and the kid took it good-naturedly—he was every bit Nick's son, just as laidback. As they strode away, Jeremiah turned to Heather and again caught that odd look he's glimpsed in the kitchen. This time, she didn't hide it.

"What?" he asked.

"You're not a Mackey anymore. You're a Hammond."

Not sure exactly what she was getting at or why it was so important to her, he waited for her to elaborate.

"They're great people—the kind who treat everyone like family," she said slowly as if trying to find the right words to explain her thoughts. "But they don't just *treat* you like part of the family. You *are* family."

"They sure make me feel like that," he replied. Sensing what she was getting at, he said, "Family is more than blood, you know. It's the people who care about you and love you and want the best for you."

"I know that."

"Do you?"

She glanced sharply at him.

He'd hit a nerve, and unable to tolerate the naked pain in her beautifully expressive eyes, he opened his arms, offering support. But he didn't take a step toward her, letting her decide if she needed or wanted to accept his invitation. She stepped into his arms after a moment's hesitation and tucked her arms around his waist.

What the hell was wrong with her family that they'd done this to her?

"I'm sorry if that was out of line," he murmured. "You don't talk much about your family, and what you *do* say doesn't exactly give me the best impression of them."

She didn't offer any explanation—she didn't say anything at all—but she let him hold her. That in itself was incredible. Heather was one of the most strong-willed and self-sufficient women he knew, more than capable of handling her own soothing. And yet she seemed to find comfort in his arms.

After more than a minute, she straightened, slipping slowly from his embrace as if she was reluctant to leave it.

"Daylight's burning," she said quietly. "And we have a cabin to clean and set up before we get to party with Noah tonight."

Nodding, he obeyed her unspoken request to end the conversation about her family. He kissed her cheek and walked around to the driver side of his truck. Realizing his dog was nowhere around, he let out a single, high whistle.

Murph rocketed around the side of the house from the backyard, and half a second later, Archer's disappointed cry explained why the Aussie had been back there.

"Load up," he told his dog.

After jogging around the house to apologize to Archer for stealing his dog back, he climbed in behind the wheel, patting the dash of his truck as it started up like the finely tuned machine it was. "Atta girl."

As he drove up the valley and pass to the allotment cabin, he hoped Heather would someday trust him enough to tell him about her family and why she didn't feel like they cared about her.

By the time they arrived at the cabin, Heather had shed her vulnerability like a winter coat and was again her bold, vibrant self.

"We're gonna have to make use of all this privacy," she remarked, turning to him and pushing him against the doorframe.

The way she kissed him—brazenly without a hint of restraint—left him breathless, but he was beginning to recognize that this was her way of subverting her troublesome thoughts… and that it was dangerous.

"You're doing it again," he whispered against her lips.

"Doing what?"

"Trying to burn away your dark thoughts with physical distraction."

He expected her to jerk back, but she didn't. She only smiled and kissed him again.

"I'm serious, Heather."

"You mean to tell me you don't like this?"

She pressed her body against his, and he inhaled

sharply.

"I'd like it a lot better if you were doing it because you wanted *me* and not because you need an outlet."

At last, she stepped back and regarded him with narrowed eyes.

"You're fire." He took a deep breath, hoping the words that came to mind were the right ones. "I already have burn scars on my body. I'd rather not end up with some on my heart, too."

Her eyes rounded. "Jeremiah, I'm sorry. I…."

"It's okay." A strand of hair had pulled loose from her ponytail, and he tucked it behind her ear. "Just… try not to scorch me, all right?"

She laughed softly at that and twined her arms around his neck. Crazy as it might sound, it was just as nice to be hugged by her as it was to be kissed by her. Better, even. In her embrace, there was only affection, and he buried his face against the curve of her neck.

She smelled good—like a mountain summer. The natural fragrances of their home clung to her like the sweetest perfume, and beneath it and the faint hint of the rosemary-mint-scented shampoo she preferred, she was all warm woman. He inhaled deeply and let his eyes slide closed as desire shot through his veins.

He wanted what she'd offered on several occasions now, but not until there was nothing in her touches and kisses but passion and desire for him. He didn't want to share her with her anger over her breakup or her anxiety about her family. And if he wanted that to happen, he'd better put the brakes on again, right now, before the scent of her drove everything but the pounding hunger from his mind.

The insistent grunt-growling of his dog, demanding to be included in the love fest, made it easier to put an end to their moment of passion. Letting go of Heather, he leaned down to give his dog some loves. When he started to straighten again, a glint of silver on the floor beneath the bunk, peeking from behind its leg, caught his attention.

"Would you grab me the broom out of my truck while I move the furniture?" he murmured, staring at it.

Oblivious to his distraction, she pressed her lips to his cheek and slipped out the door.

Bracing his hand on the bare bunk, he leaned under it and snagged the necklace. Absently, he stroked Murph's head as he studied the pendant on the silver chain.

What remained of the haze of carnal desire vanished as quickly as if someone had dumped a bucket of ice water over him. There was nothing special about the necklace. It was a plain, sterling silver cross, as common as could be except for the diagonal grooves that made an X across the joint of the bars.

But Zach had worn a cross just like this.

Had it been dropped here… or planted?

The chain wasn't closed, but when he hooked the clasp to the eye, it appeared to function properly, suggesting the necklace hadn't fallen here by accident.

"This isn't his," he told himself as if saying it out loud would make it easier to believe.

Hearing Heather coming up the porch steps, he tucked the necklace in his pocket and inhaled deeply. After a count of five, he let it out slowly, but it didn't clear the jolt of unease from his mind. So he tried to reason it away. He was just spooked by his and Aaron's find this morning.

And yet… he couldn't shake the deep-seated premonition that the necklace and the two dead Lazy H cows were more than coincidences.

When Zach had first invited Jeremiah to join him in his money-making scheme—long before Jeremiah had any clue how his cousin made the money he enviably seemed to have no shortage of—the first thing he'd done to scare Jeremiah into compliance was show him what happened to the people who crossed him. One of Zach's lackeys had screwed up and gotten busted that same week. Zach hadn't been content to simply cut him loose. He left little clues everywhere—small, personal things like this cross necklace that the man would recognize—to remind the man of Zach and let him know that he was being watched, that Zach could get to him any time he chose.

After a year of it, the man had killed himself.

Was that happening again? Was this Zach pulling strings, reminding him of his reach and power?

Jeremiah shuddered.

* * *

Noah's birthday party was a simple affair—dinner and swimming at the Ramshorn—and Heather was glad to have been invited. It was fun to watch Jeremiah goofing around with the Hammonds, confirming what she'd realized this morning. Nick's, Aaron's, and Henry's kids all called him Uncle Jere. Noah, Will, and Jessie were all old enough to remember the Hammond family before Jeremiah had been part of it, but to their younger siblings—Nick and Beth's twins Caleb and Cade, Aaron and Skye's son Eric, and little Archer—Jeremiah had always been a part of their family, and they made no distinction between him and their blood uncles. And the way the whole family poked fun at one another only to reaffirm their love for each other immediately after with a hug or a touch.….

Her family didn't do that. Not *like* that, with such uninhibited affection for one another.

She squirmed as she remembered how succinctly Jeremiah had called her out this morning.

Family is more than blood.

I know that.

Do you?

Apparently she didn't. She had some idea that there were two kinds of family and she'd heard the Conners and O'Neils note plenty of times that sometimes the best family is the one you choose. But God, with the exception of Ainsley and Christina and Ty, no matter who she was with, she always felt like an outsider. And of late, Christina had made her feel like an outsider, too.

She let out a growl. That line of thought wasn't appropriate for a gorgeous evening like this, so she tipped her head back and stared at the indigo sky dusted with thin streamers of cirrus clouds. It was a warm evening—almost too warm to be soaking in the hot springs, but after cleaning the allotment cabin, the hot water felt good.

The current of the water shifted, announcing Jeremiah's approach. She turned her gaze on him and smiled. At some point, he'd shed the T-shirt, and though the sight of his scars still shocked her, she appreciated the reminder of his words at the cabin. The way he was looking at her with that adorable twinkle in his eyes and looking damned sexy with water droplets glittering on his skin, she'd need all the help she could get to keep a lid on her physical urges. And she needed to because he was right. Her anger was still too hot.

The last thing she wanted to do was hurt him.

"I just realized," she said. "It's officially summer now."

"Ah, that's right. Today's the solstice. Sorry I've been ignoring you."

"I don't mind. I'm quite enjoying just watching you interact with your surrogate family."

It was cute and endearing, the way he ducked his head with that shy smile.

"But… it *is* getting late," she sighed and glanced at the wisps of clouds over head that now blazed like molten gold. "And if we want to watch the stars come out at the allotment cabin, we should probably head up there."

"I suppose we should."

The way he said it wasn't quite a sigh, but she got the same impression; he wasn't ready to leave yet. The faint frown drawing his brows together as he watched the Hammonds engaging in a boisterous game of Marco Polo confirmed it.

"We don't have to go," she said, unable to fully keep the disappointment from her voice. "We can stargaze some other time."

His gaze snapped to her, and his frown deepened. She had to give him credit for that—he was incredibly sensitive to her moods.

"I still want to stargaze with you." He flashed her a smile. "It's just been such a fun evening. It's not often we get a chance to get *everyone* together without it involving work. You're having a good time, aren't you?"

"I'm having a fantastic time," she replied. "The Hammonds are as inviting as the Conners and O'Neils and Carlyles and Evanses and Dunns… and pretty much every other family in Northstar but mine. I couldn't have a bad time with them if I wanted to."

He lifted a brow, and for a terrifying moment, she thought he would press her about her family. But he only shook his head and kept whatever questions he had to himself. Why did she keep bringing her family up to him? She was usually much better at pushing them out of her head. Maybe it was the fact that they were so vocally opposed to her dating him; their voices were always at the edges of her thoughts when she was with him.

That was part of it, but it wasn't all of it.

"All right, if we're going, let's go," she said, pushing off the floor of the larger pool and swimming for the stairs.

"You aren't leaving all ready, are you?" Lindsay asked as she made her way back to the pool with a bottle of water from the pool house.

"We still need to get Jeremiah's cooler for the cabin before we head up," Heather replied. "And he said something about wanting to pick out some books to take up with him."

"Understandable." The redheaded woman smiled. "I'm glad you came, Heather."

"I am, too. Have a good night."

Lindsay nodded and jumped into the pool, drenching her husband and sons with her tidal wave. Their laughter followed Heather all the way around the boardwalk and into the pool house. Smiling, she waved at June and Ben Conner as she passed. She couldn't begin to explain why Lindsay's comment—and the genuine way she'd delivered it—made her chest tighten.

Despite taking time to say his goodbyes to the Hammonds, Jeremiah beat her out of the dressing rooms. He didn't say a word about her hasty departure, and as she drove to the main house with him sitting quietly in the passenger seat of her truck gazing out the window with a faint smile gracing his boyish features, the spark of anxiety eased.

Glancing over him, she laughed softly to herself. He was in his thirties, but he could still easily pass for nineteen or twenty.

"What are you laughing about over there?" he asked, turning his eyes on her.

The merriment of Noah's party still twinkled in those eyes, and her smile widened.

"Just thinking that you don't look much older than Noah. How old are you, anyhow?"

"Old enough to start appreciating it when people say that."

"Smart ass. I'm serious. What are you, thirty-two?"

"Thirty-three."

"And your birthday's in September?"

"On the first—same day as Celeste Dunn, but I'm a few hours older. We keep meaning to have a double party, but it hasn't happened yet. Maybe next year, for thirty-five."

"That'd be fun. So, what do you want for your birthday?"

He narrowed his eyes, studying her for a moment before he turned his gaze back out the window. "It's still a ways off."

She frowned. *That was an evasive answer.*

They'd arrived at the bunkhouse, and Austin, who hadn't felt up to partying it up with the rest of the Hammond clan, was sitting out on the porch with Murphy at his feet, so she didn't get a chance to probe Jeremiah's odd response.

"Feeling better?" Jeremiah asked as he climbed out of her truck.

As soon as he reached the bottom step up to the porch, the Australian shepherd took a flying leap into his arms. Judging by the ease with which Jeremiah caught him, Heather guessed this was a well-rehearsed ritual between them. Silly dog.

"A bit better, but still not great," Austin replied. "It's hell to get old, kid. I don't recommend it."

"Heather was just pointing out that I don't have much choice."

"Har har," she retorted. "That's not what I said."

He grinned at her, then turned back to Austin. "At least it's a nice evening to sit out and recuperate."

"It is indeed."

Jeremiah looked at Heather and tilted his head toward the door. Taking the hint, she bounded up the steps and opened the screen door for him so he didn't have to set Murphy down. She followed him into his small bedroom, curious to get a glimpse of the one space in the world that was entirely his.

It was… surprising.

While it was tidy enough, every bit of shelf space was lined with books—hard covers, worn paperbacks that looked like they'd been read a dozen times, and crisp, brand new books he hadn't yet gotten around to reading. What wasn't taken up by books was littered with crystals, unusual rocks, and other odds and ends he'd picked up over the years. The space was definitely lived in with one glaring exception. He had very few photos. Just three, in fact. The first and newest was of him and the entire Hammond clan taken in front of the Christmas tree, and as she glanced from one face to the next, she was amazed they'd managed to fit everyone in. The next was older. In it, Jeremiah was young, maybe twelve or thirteen. Beside him was a young man who looked similar enough in appearance that she guessed he was Jeremiah's brother, Joe. An older couple stood next to the brothers. They must be his grandparents. In the third photo, he was even younger, eight or nine. It was a family photo like the one of him and the Hammonds, but far less crowded. She spotted his brother, his grandparents, a man and woman who must be his parents, and another woman who she guessed might be an aunt.

What had happened to them?

Suddenly feeling like she was prying, she turned away from the photos.

Jeremiah was currently skimming the books stacked on his nightstand while Murph watched from the middle of the bed with a bored expression. She noted the titles of the nearest books and was shocked by the variety. He had a little bit of everything. She spotted the *Hunger Games* trilogy in the stack of books on his night stand, a well-worn, single-volume edition of *The Lord of the Rings* on his dresser, and George R. R. Martin's *A Song of Ice and Fire* books on top of the bookshelf by the window. He also had several nonfiction books, memoirs, a romance or two, some mysteries and thrillers, literary fiction titles, sci-fi, and a rather large collection of Westerns. Hell, he even had *Macbeth* and *Romeo and Juliet*.

"I had no idea you were such a bookworm," she remarked, watching as he piled half a dozen books on his bed.

"Had to make up for not graduating from high school somehow."

"You never graduated?"

"Nope. Got my GED after I got out of prison, though, thanks to Tracie and Aaron."

He reached under his bed, pulled out a suitcase, and carefully settled his selected books inside.

"I know what I'm going to get you for your birthday. An e-reader."

His lips twitched. "Thanks for the offer, but save your money. Tracie bought me one a couple years ago, and I never use it. There's just something special about a physical book…."

He was so adorably serious when he said that that she couldn't help but laugh. "Nerd."

"Yeah, I guess I am."

"Nothing wrong with that. Just one more thing that makes you so damned cute."

Once his books were in the truck, he returned to his room to pack a couple changes of clothes. He'd be down to the ranch every other day at least, so there was no point in packing for the whole summer. Besides, the allotment cabin was only fifteen miles or so from the ranch, so if he needed anything, it would be a short hop and a skip to get it.

Thinking of that and the number of books he'd packed, she chuckled.

Lastly, he grabbed Murphy's bowls and the kibble and treats he'd already measured out earlier and loaded everything in his truck. They bid Austin good night and headed down to the main house to pick up the cooler Tracie and Beth had packed. The women had also put together a tub of non-perishable foods for him, and their thoughtfulness struck Heather. It was something her mother would've done, too, but it would have lacked the love and affection that radiated from Tracie and Beth's care package—they'd included his favorite treats. Her mother would've tossed in whatever.

Nope. Not gonna think like that.

She helped Jeremiah carry the cooler and tub out to his truck. When he went back in, she followed him. What had they missed?

Nothing.

He plucked a pen and a notepad out of the junk drawer to leave a note for Tracie and Beth and another for Aaron.

While he wrote his notes, she glanced around the house. She and Jeremiah hadn't turned on any lights. The last rays of the sun, peeking over Carol Hill to the west, bathed the yard outside in rich golden sunlight, and enough reflected into the house to give them plenty of light. She hadn't been in here many times, but the place was always so full of life that the cool shadows away from the windows and the quiet that had settled over it with the whole family up at the Ramshorn was jarring.

"You ready?" Jeremiah asked.

"Yep."

Because she wouldn't be staying the night—tempting as the idea was—she followed him in her truck. By the time they arrived, only the very tip of the big granite dome that was Comet Mountain still glowed with the ruddy light of the dying day. They'd timed it perfectly. They had just enough time to get everything settled in the cabin and light the lanterns before the light failed completely. And then it would be stargazing time.

Jeremiah dug out the powdered lemonade mix Tracie had tossed into the tub and freed two bottles of water from the case they'd brought up earlier when they'd cleaned the cabin. She stood in the open door and watched him shake the bottles to mix the lemonade, beaming and trying hard not to laugh when he did a goofy little dance for her amusement.

It was amazing how the cabin had gone from a bare, rustic shell to something that almost resembled a home since just this morning.

"It's actually pretty comfortable in here now, isn't it," she observed.

"It is," he agreed, handing her one of the bottles.

She set it aside and slipped her arms around his neck. With a perfect summer night falling outside and no one else here but him and his dog, she was filled with a curious sense of contentment. She didn't kiss him right away, taking her time to enjoy the feel of his body against hers, and after a few moments, when he realized she wasn't going to jump him, he tucked his arms around her waist and eased deeper into her embrace. Finally, she touched her lips to his in a feather-light kiss and then laid her head on his shoulder, sighing happily.

Maybe she *would* stay the night.

And not because she was overcome by any ravenous need for sex. That was the furthest thing from her mind right now, and its absence was strangely refreshing. No, she wanted to stay because she needed the serenity he exuded. She wanted to wrap it around herself for a few hours and feel what it was like to let go of the constant hum of energy and anxiety.

"This is delightful," he murmured.

"Mmm-hmm." Idly, she trailed her fingers across his chest. "I can't remember the last time I had a moment like this, so peaceful and just… nice. That sounds like such a boring way to describe it, but I need this."

"Well, if peace is what you want, how about we take this out to the porch, pull our chairs together and snuggle while we watch the stars come out?"

"That sounds like heaven."

She grabbed her lemonade and followed him out to the porch. They set their camp chairs side by side so the arm of hers overlapped his and sat sipping lemonade as the cool mountain night settled over the meadow. It was silent but for the soft breeze wafting down from the peak and sighing in the pines and the faint gurgling of the small creek that meandered through the meadow. Only a few times did the cattle disrupt the quiet; apparently they were enjoying the evening as much as she was, content to graze quietly on the tender alpine grasses.

She twitched with the prick of a tiny needle and instinctively slapped her upper left arm. When she lifted her hand away, there was a smashed mosquito stuck to it.

"Great. The first skeeter of summer. You have bug juice up here, I hope."

"I do. I'll go grab it."

In the time it took him to dig out the insect repellant, two more of the tiny bloodsuckers buzzed her, but she was able to chase them off with a wave of her hand. There didn't seem to be too many out tonight, but even so, they coated themselves with a light spray.

As she settled back into her chair, lifting her head from his shoulder occasionally to take another sip of her lemonade, she laughed.

"Nothing like a little bug juice perfume to really bring out the romance."

Jeremiah chuckled. "It's better than getting eaten alive."

Nodding, she pointed out the first glittering star. Even with the bug juice, which couldn't fully mask the more desirable fragrance of the mountain air, it was still an exquisite night. And in fact, that humorous note added rather than detracted from it; it made this all feel real.

Jeremiah Mackey, the man she'd barely given two thoughts to before she'd pulled over to see if he needed help on her birthday, was turning out to be a wonderful surprise.

Seven

AFTER ALMOST TWO WEEKS mostly alone in the allotment cabin, the Fourth of July potluck and barbecue hosted by the Bedspread Inn was a welcome change of pace. Jeremiah sat on the bench of one of the two dozen picnic tables with his back to the table's top and watched the festivities. Almost everyone who called Northstar home was here along with several dozen other people from Devyn and other nearby ranching towns. Now that the heat of the day had broken at last as the sun slipped closer to the western hills, people were beginning to congregate around the small stage that had been set up for the live band. Beside him, Heather sipped her Jack and Coke with a faint smile of contentment dancing about her features.

She'd spent a lot more time with him up at the cabin than he'd expected; she'd been up almost every evening for several hours, from the time she got off work around six until the sun went down. He suspected she would've tried to convince him to let her spend the night if the bunk wasn't a twin and if she hadn't needed to get up for work in the morning. On the two days she'd had off in the last two weeks, they'd sat out on the porch until after midnight, doused in mosquito repellant or inside at the table with windows open playing cards until the wee hours of the morning.

It was heaven.

"You wanna dance?" she asked after she drained the last of her drink.

"Love to."

She bounced to her feet and held out her hands to him. He took them and let her help him to his feet, amused when she wrapped his arm around her, broadcasting loud and clear to anyone who cared to notice that they were together. If there were any trace of that fiery vindictiveness, he might've been concerned, but tonight, she emanated bliss.

Catching sight of her family, he wondered how long it would last. They sat apart from the Northstar crowd at a pair of picnic tables with a few people who'd come up from Devyn, and they watched him escort her toward the band with disapproving frowns.

He shrugged it off. What they thought of him and of Heather dating him wasn't his problem unless she said it was. And so far, she didn't seem to care what they thought.

Determined to push them from his mind, he tucked Heather into his arms and led her through a slow dance. They were surrounded by their friends and neighbors, and

Jeremiah couldn't imagine a better way to spend the Fourth of July.

As they danced, he couldn't help but notice how warm everyone was to Heather. She was every bit as much a part of this community as any of them, and he knew she'd worked hard to earn her place among them. Her family, on the other hand…. It was hard to ignore how little they cared to interact with everyone else. He wanted to ask her about that, but he wasn't willing to interrupt her enjoyment of the evening.

He was going to need to find out before too much longer, however, because he was beginning to suspect they were a big reason why she had burned through one man after another. If her bond with her family was as toxic as it seemed, how could she recognize a healthy relationship?

Maybe that was where he needed to start to keep her from walking away from him, too.

They danced without break until the sun dipped behind the hills and plunged the Northstar Valley into shadow. Jeremiah was thoroughly enjoying himself, but it was getting late, and he needed to get back up to the cabin.

"You're not going to stick around for the fireworks?" Heather asked.

"I never do."

"How come?"

"I don't like fireworks."

There must've been something off in his voice because she narrowed her eyes and tilted her head.

"Then I'll go up with you."

"You don't have to do that. Stay here and enjoy the show."

"I've seen plenty of fireworks displays. Missing this one won't break my heart."

"If you're sure… I'd love the company."

"Just let me say goodnight to my family. I'm sure they expect me to watch with them since I've ignored them all day."

He nodded and located the Hammonds while she talked to her parents and siblings. It took him a while to bid them all goodnight as they were scattered around the yard chatting with their valley neighbors, and Heather should've been ready to go long before he was. She wasn't, and as he made his way back to her, he caught the unmistakable tones of anger.

"Hey, what's going on?" he asked her, resting his hand lightly against her back.

Her body was rigid.

"Stay out of it, Mackey," her brother Brock snapped. "This isn't any of your business."

"She's my girlfriend, and if she's upset, that *makes* it my business."

Brock lunged to his feet. "You want to start something? Bring it, little man."

Little man? Jeremiah snorted. Brock was barely two inches taller than him and ten, *maybe* twenty pounds heavier. "I'm not bringing anything. Heather, are you ready to go?"

"Yeah."

They started to walk away, but Brock grabbed his shoulder and wrenched him around. Before he had a chance to react, Heather shoved her brother hard enough to make him stumble over his own feet. When he took a step toward them again, she drew her fist back.

"Don't," she said in a low, warning voice.

Jeremiah glanced at her family. Her mother, sister, and sisters-in-law all sat quietly with their faces down-turned, embarrassed perhaps. Her father and older brother were more concerned with sneering at him than they were about the brewing fight. Jeremiah held their gazes with a sneer of his own, and finally, they looked away.

Wow.

"So that's it?" her father asked. "You're going to ditch your family again… for *him*?"

"I didn't realize that needed clarification," Heather remarked.

"Fuck you, Heather," Brock retorted.

"Bend over."

Brock lunged toward her, but Aaron—who had been chatting nearby with the Conners—jumped in front of him.

"Hey, now," the sheriff said with equal measures of placating gentleness and commanding sternness. "None of that."

"She started it."

"I don't give two shits who started it. It stops *now*."

With a growl of disgust, Heather stalked away. As she turned away, Jeremiah saw her expression shift from fury to despair. He clenched his fist at his side as he stared after her. With deliberate movements, he turned back to her family.

"I know you don't like me, and that's fine. But don't take that out on her."

"Shut your mouth," Brock growled, taking a menacing step toward Jeremiah with the rest of his family looking on like they would love to see them fight. "I told you once already. This isn't any of your business."

Jeremiah shook his head sadly. "You're hurting her. Do you know that?"

"Better we hurt her than you."

His jaw dropped. *What the hell?* Disgusted, he retorted, "Better *no one* hurts her."

"Jere," Aaron interrupted, "I thought you two were heading up to the cabin."

"We were," he replied.

Gratitude diluted his irritation, not only for the out Aaron provided but for his inclusion of Heather in his statement. It drew a line for the Browns, let them know that her relationship with Jeremiah was acknowledged and accepted by others. "She just wanted to say goodnight to her family before we left. That's all. And instead of accepting her choice to be with me, they derided her for it."

"Fancy word for a little man who never graduated high school," Brock sneered.

Jeremiah sighed. "Fancy words, empathy—it's amazing what you can pick up from reading. You oughta try it sometime. Good night, all. Enjoy the rest of the party."

Even with Aaron remaining behind to talk to the Browns, Brock's continuing taunts trailed after Jeremiah as he walked away. He wasn't remotely tempted to acknowledge them. Rather than goad him into a fight, as Heather's brother no doubt intended, they just made him tired. He was beginning to get an idea of exactly what Heather's trouble with her family was.

"I don't give a damn what you think about him. I say he's not good enough for my sister," he heard Brock say.

"Seems to me that's Heather's choice," Aaron replied. "Regardless of how you feel about him, you need to put yourself in check. I suggest you start by making that beer your last. Good evening, all. I hope I won't need to speak to any of you again tonight."

Brock was lucky Aaron wasn't like his predecessor. Rogers wouldn't have hesitated to throw his weight as an officer of the law around and dragged him from the party in cuffs. Of course, he probably would've put Jeremiah in cuffs, too, for daring to respond at all.

Halfway to the table where Heather was sitting with Henry, Lindsay, Noah, and Archer—interesting that she'd gone to them instead of Ty and his family or Ainsley and hers since they were her best friends—Aaron caught up to him.

"That was big of you back there," the sheriff remarked. "You'd've been well within your rights to hit him. What kind of brother says 'better we hurt her than you'?"

"A shitty one."

Aaron snorted. "Yeah. You got that right. But, that aside, I'm proud of you for the way you handled yourself."

"Thanks." Jeremiah grinned. "I'm glad Henry taught me how to properly defend myself, but I sincerely hope my brawling days—as short and pathetic as they were—are long over. I don't want to be that person ever again."

"I don't think you were ever him to begin with."

Since they'd reached Heather and Henry and family, Jeremiah acknowledged Aaron's praise with only a nod.

"I gotta say," Henry remarked, rising from the table to briefly embrace Jeremiah with a slap on the back, "you going out with this beautiful lady has certainly answered the question of why her family hasn't ever tried to be a part of the Northstar community. They're a bunch of judgmental dicks."

"I coulda told you that," Heather muttered.

She sat close to Lindsay with the older woman's arm around her shoulders and glared in her family's direction. She seemed to have calmed down some but not enough for Jeremiah's liking; the now familiar instinct to lash out at whomever and however she could was back in place. Now that he'd seen what she was like without it, he wanted to find a way to bring her back to the place she'd been his first night in the allotment cabin… and fast.

"Well, you know what the Conners and O'Neils say about the family you choose being more important than the one you're born to, right?" Henry asked.

"Yeah, I do. Thanks, Hen."

"Aw, she's even calling me Hen already."

Playfully, she punched the younger Hammond twin in the arm.

"See, this is how big brothers are *supposed* to treat their little sisters," he continued, unfazed. "Tease them a little and then let them beat on you for it."

"How would you know?" his wife asked. "You don't have any sisters."

"True, but that's common knowledge."

"I wish I had brothers like you," Heather muttered so quietly Jeremiah didn't think she meant it to be heard.

Henry caught Jeremiah by the back of the neck and dragged him close, grinning as he glanced between him and Heather. "Well, you know, there is a way to make that happen. You see, one of my brothers is still unmarr—"

"Okay!" Jeremiah said quickly, ducking out of Henry's grip. "I see Pat bringing out the fireworks, so it's time for us to go. I've already caused one scene, so I'd rather not cause another."

His companions nodded in understanding, but he didn't think for a second Henry would let the matter drop. Not that he was going to complain. He was glad for the reason for the teasing and even more glad to have someone who loved him enough to tease him.

Heather drove up to the cabin ahead of him while he stopped down at the bunkhouse to retrieve his dog. When he arrived at the cabin, she was sitting out on the porch, staring blindly across the darkening meadow. As soon as he let his dog out of the truck, Murph raced right to her, and as a testament to her mood and the Aussie's ingrained need to improve it, even the rattle of kibble in his bowl couldn't lure him away from her.

"I've been wanting to ask you what your deal is with your family," he said as he sank into the chair beside her, "but I think I have a pretty good idea now. Do they always treat you like that, or is it just me they don't like?"

"It isn't just you," she replied quietly. "But them not liking you or me going out with you is definitely making the problem worse. I'm sorry, Jeremiah. I never wanted to drag you into the middle of my family's dysfunction, and I certainly didn't want them to make you the scapegoat for it."

"It's okay. It doesn't have any impact on how I feel about you."

She finally turned her gaze on him and managed a faint smile. He leaned over and hugged her, laughing when Murph tried to wiggle into the embrace, too. He didn't like the sadness in her eyes—it was worse than the fire—so he patted his leg, and she didn't hesitate to leave her chair and settle in his lap. A sigh escaped her as he wrapped her tightly in his arms, and he pinched his eyes closed for a moment.

"I was wrong," he murmured. "It *does* change how I feel about you. It makes me want to hold you until none of it matters. To find a way to make it go away."

She was quiet for a long time, content to let him hold her. At least he could do that for her. She rested her head on his chest, which was a bit awkward in the camp chair since she wasn't that much smaller than him, and idly, he skimmed his hand up and down her arm while he watched the afterglow of the cloudless sunset fade into a lavender twilight. They'd be lighting off the fireworks soon, and with his helpless anger over his encounter with Heather's family, he was glad he was too far away to see any flashes or hear any of the booms.

As if she sensed the shift in his thoughts, she asked, "Why don't you like fireworks?"

He didn't immediately respond. Habit stopped him from talking about his phobia—to most people, it probably seemed silly—but being the Fourth of July, those thoughts and memories were already front and center in his mind, so what would it hurt to tell her about them?

"Does it have anything to do with your scars?"

"It has everything to do with them. It's how my parents and aunt died."

Twenty-two years removed, he had no trouble recalling that horrific night, but at least the edges of the memory and the pain of that loss had dulled.

"It was the Fourth of July. I was eleven, and we lived on a cul-de-sac in the suburbs of Huntington Beach. We'd spent the day out in the boat—water-skiing, inner-tubing, knee-boarding, swimming—and as much as I wanted to stay up to watch our neighbors set off their fireworks, I was wiped. We all went to bed early with music playing in the house to help drown out the noise. The boat was in the driveway, up close to the garage door, and I guess the spare gas can had a leak. A misfired firework landed in the boat, and it ignited the gasoline. Then the house caught fire."

He swallowed. The memories and pain might have been diminished by time, but they hadn't faded nearly enough and he doubted they ever would. He shifted his gaze from the failing twilight to Heather's face; she'd sat up and was watching him as he spoke, and her expression was one of unveiled sympathy.

"I remember waking up to the screams of the neighbors and someone pounding on the door. And I smelled the smoke. My room was downstairs, but my parents and my Aunt Ruth were upstairs. I tried to get up to them to wake them up, but by then the fire was too intense, and I couldn't get through it. And the smoke…."

He could still feel the burn in his nose and throat and lungs and the stinging in his eyes as if it had happened yesterday, and he shuddered.

"I passed out on the stairs," he continued. "Our next-door neighbor broke down the door, dragged me out, and turned the hose on me, which probably kept my burns and their scars from being worse than they might've been otherwise. I don't remember any of that—I woke up in the ambulance, screaming for my parents and my aunt. They didn't make it out."

"Oh my God, Jeremiah. I had no idea."

He shrugged. "It's not something I talk about much."

"I totally get why. Christ. I can't even imagine."

"Some days it's so real I can still feel the heat, but others… it seems like a dream or something that happened to someone else and I've somehow tapped into their memories. Anyhow, Grandma and Grandpa and Joe flew down, and after the funerals, I moved to Devyn to live with them."

"Do you have any other family?"

"Just Zach and my paternal grandparents, but I've never met them, and Zach…. Well, I'm sure you can guess what that relationship is like."

"Is he your aunt's son?"

He nodded.

"Where was he when she died?"

"With his dirtbag father." He snorted. "I remember Mom saying once that Aunt Ruth had a knack for picking losers. Mom was the younger of the two, but you'd never know it; she was the responsible one, always trying to look out for Aunt Ruth. Of course, she couldn't stop Aunt Ruth from getting pregnant with Zach by the biggest loser of all. She was eight months pregnant when they got married, and it lasted all of four years. Zach was a few months older than Joe, and they got along great when they were little kids, but as he got older, Zach started spending more and more time with his dad. Joe's relationship with him crumbled, and I never really had one with him."

"How the hell did you ever get mixed up with him, then?"

"His dad was shot and killed when a drug deal went south, and he moved up here to escape. Grandma and

Grandpa were dead by then, and it was just Joe and me, and we were in rough shape, barely scraping by."

"Wait. When did your grandparents die?"

"Grandma of cancer a year after the fire, and Grandpa had a heart attack on a job site a year after that."

She swore under her breath and slipped her arms around his ribs, folding her hands behind his back and giving him a squeeze. "I don't know what to say other than life has been seriously shitty and unfair to you."

"It's gotten a lot better. This right here is pretty great."

She tilted her head up and smiled. "It is, huh?"

"Yep."

"I think I know how to make it even better."

"Yeah? How?"

Tenderly, she pressed her lips to his. Then she shifted in his lap and hooked her arms around his neck, deepening the kiss. God, she could kiss. He'd had a few girlfriends—not many compared to some—but at the moment, he couldn't recall any of them.

"This is a good start," he whispered when she released his mouth.

"A start? You mean you're going to let me do more tonight?"

"Maybe."

"Don't tease me, Jeremiah."

Suddenly, the playfulness left her eyes, and she brushed one hand back through his hair while the other rested against his neck with her thumb against his jaw. Beneath her probing gaze, he felt naked and vulnerable, but rather than make him uncomfortable, it emboldened him.

"Are you going to let me stay the night?" she asked gently.

His voice refused to cooperate. Right now, he wanted nothing more than to spend the night with her tucked snuggly in his arms, to let the warmth of her body keep the memories from haunting his dreams. More than that, he wanted to keep *her* bad thoughts at bay, and since being with him soothed her as much as she soothed him, he nodded. He still wanted to take their relationship slow, but since he doubted either of them were going to be up for more than a few kisses, he figured they were safe enough.

"I am," he replied, finding his voice at last. "I think we both need it."

"Mmm. I think we do, too." She let out a sniff of laughter. "Is it silly that you being up here by yourself bothers me?"

"How so?"

"I don't know. What if something happened to you?"

"The Royal R is only a couple miles away if I need help in a hurry."

"I know. It's just…. What if you're right about your cousin?"

Jeremiah shrugged. That thought had crossed his mind more times than he could count, but so far, Zach had been on his best behavior, and even if he *did* show up, Jeremiah wasn't the same scared and impressionable kid he'd been the last time they'd met. When he said as much to Heather, she nodded.

"I like that you worry, though," he murmured. "It's nice."

Murph jumped to his feet and leapt off the porch

with a warning bark.

"They must be starting the fireworks down in the valley," Heather remarked.

"It's about that time."

He held his breath, listening for anything that would confirm that but heard only the quiet sounds of the creek and the wind in the trees. Straining his eyes in the dark, he looked for his dog. Murph stood in the middle of the dirt road, growling, hearing something Jeremiah couldn't.

"It's all right, Murphy," Heather called to the dog. "Just the fireworks."

But Murph's attention wasn't focused toward the valley; he was staring in the opposite direction.

Echoes, Jeremiah told himself. *The sound is echoing off the trees. That's all.*

"You up for a game or two of cards before bed?" he asked Heather abruptly.

"I thought we could just snuggle tonight instead, if that's all right with you."

"You bet. Come on, Murph."

The dog gave one last growl before bounding up the stairs and racing into the cabin ahead of them. Heather wasted no time in stripping out of her clothes, and Jeremiah had to avert his eyes. She had an incredible body. So sleek and strong. He wanted to run his hands over her, to savor every line and curve and revel in the softness of her skin.

"Do you have a spare T-shirt I can borrow to sleep in?" she asked.

"Um, yeah. Here." He dragged his duffel bag from under the bunk and pulled out a clean black tank top. "Will this work?"

"Perfect."

He made the mistake of glancing at her when he handed her the tank top. She was naked but for her delicate black lace panties, and a groan of pure need escaped him. She was the most beautiful woman he'd ever seen.

Catching his look, she grinned with feminine pride, she slipped the tank top over her head, freed her dark, silken hair from its ponytail and shook it loose, then turned down the blankets and climbed onto the bunk. Realizing he was still fully dressed, he quickly stripped down to his boxers, clicked off the battery-powered lantern, and slid in beside her. When she draped her arm across his chest and her leg over his, he let out a breath.

Nightmares, sad memories, and dark thoughts wouldn't stand a chance tonight.

* * *

Heather opened her eyes to a cabin faintly illuminated by a dim predawn and smiled as sleep vanished like a dreamy summer breeze, leaving her fully rejuvenated and wondrously serene. Considering that dawn was just beginning to brighten the world and that she'd spent the night on a cramped twin bunk with Jeremiah, it was amazing she was so rested. It was even more amazing because it had taken hours to fall asleep. *He* had drifted off within minutes, but she'd lain awake reviewing his heartbreaking revelations.

He lay on his stomach beside her, right on the edge of the bed with his face turned toward her. With sleep slackening his features, he looked even younger than he usually did. Despite all the tragedies and traumas in his life, he had somehow managed to maintain a heartening optimism and even a glimmer of innocence. It wasn't too hard to imagine how a cunning, charismatic psychopath—everything she'd heard about Zach led her to believe he quite likely fit the clinical description of the term—had manipulated him.

Gently so as not to wake him, she sat up and let her gaze drift over the puckered scars on the left side of his back. It was only her unwillingness to risk disturbing him that kept her from skimming her fingertips over them. How horrible to not only lose his family like he had but to also bear the scars of that fire as a lifelong reminder.

As much as her family drove her nuts, to lose them like he'd lost his parents and aunt would break her. She loved them even though they probably didn't deserve it most days. At the thought of them and the horrible things they'd said about Jeremiah last night, the ghost of a sensation tickled her left wrist, reminding her that she'd taken her wrist band off after Jeremiah had fallen asleep last night. With the blissful serenity slipping away, she snatched it off the corner post of the bunk where she'd set it and slid it on to hide her scar beneath it again, letting her eyes take in Jeremiah's scars again as she adjusted the laces.

His scars, my scar…. We've both been damaged.

Suddenly, a need to be close to him overpowered her desire to let him sleep in peace. She slid back under the covers and wrapped herself carefully around him, and though a soft moan escaped him, he didn't wake. She pulled the blankets higher around them to ward off the chill in the cabin and tucked her arm around him. The firm warmth of his body was comforting.

He was comforting—his very presence.

She tightened her arm around him. In her two years

with Dustin, she'd never slept as peacefully or woken as rested as she had this first night with Jeremiah.

Why couldn't her family understand that he was good for her and that that was more important than the mistakes he'd made in the past and long since atoned for?

She would *not* cry. She'd given them that power—and more—over her before, and she would not let them have it ever again. Pinching her eyes closed, she inhaled deeply, held it for several seconds, and let it out slowly.

"G'morning," Jeremiah mumbled.

It took her a moment before she dared to look at him. She pulled her head back to focus on his face, and her lips curved when her eyes met his sleepy ones. "Good morning to you. How'd you sleep?"

"Great. You?"

"Same."

Her treacherous voice cracked, betraying her.

And Jeremiah, in his remarkable awareness of her, caught it. Concern erased the drowsiness from his kind eyes, and he lifted his head. "What's wrong?"

She sucked her lips between her teeth and shook her head, trying to show him he didn't need to worry, but he wasn't convinced. She sat up and drew her knees up to her chest, wrapping her arms around them. She tried to hold it back; he had more than enough traumas of his own to bear without adding hers to the pile. But the harder she tried to keep the despair and anger inside, the harder it railed against her efforts. Finally, she couldn't hold it in any longer, and the words came spilling out of her.

"I'm so sick of my family giving me shit about you. I'm sick of them judging you for something you did *years* ago. And I'm sick of them expecting me to marry some perfect man and settle down with him in a perfect house and have three perfect children. I'm not fucking perfect, and I never will be. I'm...."

The words vanished, and she gasped for air to fill the sudden void created by their absence. She buried her face against her knees.

"You're flawed?" Jeremiah finished for her. "Why? Because you don't fit into your family's idea of perfection?"

Unable to find her voice again, she nodded.

"Is that the reason for this?" he inquired, lifting her left wrist and drawing it to him.

She jerked her head up and snatched her hand back. He didn't move to take it again. There was a disarming tenderness in his gaze that put her at ease, and letting out a breath, she extended her hand to him. His fingers were gentle as he took it.

Instinctively, she knew she could trust him with this secret as she had trusted no one else but Ainsley.

With a light touch that sent pleasant tingles rippling over her skin, he loosened the laces and slipped the wrist band off. She closed her eyes as he brushed his thumb over the thick white scar on the inside of her wrist. The cut had needed stitches, but she'd done her best to bandage it without them.

When he hadn't said a word after at least a full minute, she opened her eyes and searched his face.

"You don't look surprised."

He shook his head. "I don't know if I'll ever be able to forgive them for this. You may be flawed, but everyone is. Some of us are just more aware of our flaws than others."

He lifted his gaze from her scar to her eyes, and it sent a shock of electricity straight to her core. She didn't know how, but he understood—*truly* understood—in a way no one ever had.

"When did this happen?"

"When I was seventeen. It was the winter after Mike Thompson and Carol Landers were killed."

"I only met Mike a few times—we didn't exactly run in the same circles—but he seemed like a nice kid. Did you know them?"

"Yeah. I went out with Mike after Carol broke up with him, and I wasn't friends with Carol, but I knew her and liked her well enough. I was having a particularly bad day—one of those days when grief just kinda hits you out of nowhere—and my sister was getting ready for the winter ball, going on and on about her stupid dress, and I don't know why, but it pissed me off so much. I said some not-so-nice things to her, and Brock jumped in to defend her like he always does. We started yelling at each other, and then Brianna started crying, like she always did… and he punched me. Right in the mouth."

"He *what?*"

"That's how I got this," she said, pointing to the tiny scar on her upper lip. Over the years, it had faded to the point of being mostly unnoticeable. She balled her right hand into a fist and showed him how the base knuckle on her middle finger was bigger than it should be. "And this. I hit him back—broke his nose… and cracked my knuckle in the process. I also cracked one of his ribs."

"Jesus."

"Brock likes to think he's a brawler, but he's a piss-poor fighter. Too much fire and not enough focus."

"And you know how to box. When did you start?"

"Middle school. Thought it might win my dad's favor, but I was wrong again. In his opinion, girls don't fight. I kept it up anyhow, just to piss him off. It's a bad habit of mine, doing things out of spite."

"Bad habit, good habit—that's a matter of opinion. Sounds like boxing has served you well."

She smiled at that. "Anyhow, Curtis came in and broke us apart, and instead of yelling at Brock for starting the fight, he yelled at me for breaking Brock's nose. I've never felt so betrayed in my life. Curtis was *my* brother like Brock's was Brianna's. Until that night. I ran out to the barn, and Mom and Dad sent him out to get me because they had to take Brock to the hospital—they couldn't get his nose to stop bleeding. Curtis didn't try very hard to get me to come back to the house, which felt like another betrayal. I found a knife stuck in a bale of hay, and I wondered… would my family even miss me if I was dead."

The breath she drew was ragged. Damn, that was hard to say.

"I, uh… I pressed the point to my wrist. Just to see, you know? I don't think I really meant to do it, but a barn cat knocked over a bucket and startled me, and I jerked the knife. It sliced deep, and damn…." She shook her head and rubbed her wrist as if she could massage away the memory. "It hurt. That shocked me, and suddenly, I realized what I was contemplating, and it scared the hell out of me. Then my horse Orion—he was my first—whinnied, and I went to his stall and cried on him for, God, an hour? That's when I knew that I was on my own and that horses would be my way to take care of myself."

"Have you ever told anyone?"

"Just Ainsley. I couldn't stand to be in my house that night, so I went over to hers. I thought I'd be able to lie to her about how I'd cut my wrist, even hid the bandage under a long-sleeved shirt, but she knew something was wrong." She combed a hand through her hair, shaking the knots loose. "To my knowledge, she's never told anyone, either. Not even Christina. We both agreed Chris might let it slip to Curtis, and the last thing I needed was my family knowing."

Jeremiah pulled her into his arms, and she let him, glad for his support and quiet understanding. Her eyes focused on the burn scar that curled over the curve of his neck, and tentatively, she reached for it. When he didn't seem to mind, she skimmed her fingers over it. Her brows drew together.

"As horrible as my family is sometimes, at least they're still alive."

"Don't do that. Don't think your heartbreak is less than mine. It isn't."

"Isn't it? I still have a family, even if they *are* assholes to me."

"Yeah, maybe the only blood family I have left is a cousin who didn't try to hide the fact that he wants me dead, but I knew my family loved me. I never doubted for even a second that they cared about my wellbeing. And now I have a new family who remind me on a regular basis that I matter. I have three brothers there to help with anything from working on my truck to finding the courage to ask you on a date. Can you turn to your family when you need help? Or do you avoid them because they'll only make things worse?"

A tear slipped down her cheek. Then another.

"I'm so sorry," he whispered. "I'm sorry they have no idea how incredible you are. And I'm sorry they've tried so hard to crush everything that *makes* you incredible."

More tears came, silent but healing. She didn't know how long she cried, but Jeremiah didn't say a word as he held her. Right now, he was exactly what she needed. He was probably what she'd needed all along. For the first time in her life, she had someone who could truly empathize, and the release that came with that realization was breathtaking.

After a while, the tears stopped, and as they did, the serenity she'd woken up with returned.

"How did you know?" she asked.

"I've been there. When my brother killed Erica and then turned the gun on himself, I lost the only thing I had left in the world."

"Did you… attempt it?"

"No. Thankfully, I was in prison and I was never given the opportunity. But I wanted to, and I spent a fair amount of time trying to figure out how to do it before the guards could stop me."

"Thankfully," she echoed. "I get it now."

"Get what?"

"How you can be so grateful that Aaron arrested you."

She tilted her head up to look at him just in time to see his lips twitch with the hint of a smile. He brushed the tears from her cheeks and bent his head to kiss her.

"You're pretty incredible yourself," she murmured. "I'm sorry I didn't see it sooner. And I'm sorry for what my brother said to you last night. That was low, even for him."

He shook his head and kissed her again. "Don't apologize for him or for any of them. I don't care what they think of me. I know who I am and what I've done and how hard I've worked to be better. All I care about is what *you* think."

She couldn't find the words to adequately express what she thought. All she knew was that he made her feel like she was perfect just as she was. And that was everything.

Eight

JEREMIAH STEPPED INSIDE to pull his fleece on while the sausage cooked on the Coleman stove out on the porch. In a sharp contrast to last night's blissful warmth, it was downright chilly this morning, and a fine rain drifted from the sullen gray sky, dampening the world and dimming the vibrant colors of summer. It was cold enough that he could see his breath. Heather lingered in bed, staring blankly out the window. The far-off look in her eyes made his chest tighten.

"You all right?" he asked.

She nodded but didn't look at him.

Sighing, he turned to the wood stove to stoke the fire—good thing he'd cleaned the flue pipe when he'd moved in—and left the cozy warmth of the cabin to turn the sausage and scramble eggs on the second burner.

He couldn't wrap his head around it.

Not that she'd contemplated suicide. That part he understood even if it broke his heart.

He didn't understand how her family could see her strength and independence as a fault. How could they not appreciate how hard she'd worked to get where she was, to build a successful career for herself from something she loved? That was an incredible feat few people managed.

When breakfast was ready, he set the table while Heather slipped into her jeans. She sat hunched over the table in the old spindle-legged chair across from him with her hands folded in her lap. Because she didn't seem too inclined to dish herself breakfast, he did it for her, and when he returned to his chair, he reached for her, resting his hand on the worn table top with his palm up in invitation. She didn't seem to notice, so he withdrew his hand, uncertain.

"Are you okay?" he asked more firmly this time.

Finally, she met his eyes, and he flinched at the exhaustion in them.

"Looks like you have one hell of an emotional hangover right now," he murmured.

She nodded, and her lips twitched with the faintest hint of a smile. "That's a good way to put it. I've never talked about it like that before. Not even with Ainsley."

"Did it help at all… or just make it worse?"

"It helped. But, like you said, I have an emotional hangover."

"Do you still want to come with me to check on the cows, or would you rather stay here in the toasty warm cabin?"

"I'll go. I could use the fresh air."

They ate in silence, and after they'd finished, Jeremiah checked the pot of water he'd set on the wood stove to heat for dishes, but it wasn't hot enough yet. Heather wandered over to the bed and sat on the edge of it, staring out the window again. Concerned, he sat beside her and rubbed his hand across her back. After about two seconds of that, she leaned against him with her head on his shoulder.

She let him rub her back for some time, and he was happy to do it, more so as she slowly came back to life again. About the time he figured the water was hot enough, she tilted her face up and kissed him, tugging on his bottom lip as she stood. She pushed him back onto the bed and straddled his waist, kissing him with increasing demand. When she slid her hands under his fleece, pressing the heels of her hands hard against his bare skin as she worked them up his body, he shuddered.

There was no trace of that dangerous fire in her, no warning going off in his head telling him to stop or risk getting burned. Only pure, delicious need. So he gave in.

"You're not going to stop me," she said huskily. It was more a statement than a question, but she searched his eyes, seeking clarification.

"Do you want me to?"

She shook her head. "No. I don't."

Without warning, she claimed his mouth again, and just when he caught up to her, she shifted her attention to his jaw, nipping at it before raking her teeth over his neck. He swore under his breath, and she laughed with a feline smugness. She grabbed the front of his fleece and pulled him upright just so she could remove it slowly and torturously, trailing kisses from his stomach to his collar bone as she lifted it over his head.

He wasn't exactly inexperienced, but he'd never been with a woman as bold and confident as Heather, and beneath her demanding touches, he felt like an unseasoned boy. He tried to tell her to slow down, that he wanted to savor every moment and every exquisite touch, but the words wouldn't cooperate.

When her fingers slid over his scars, exploring the puckered texture, he winced.

"Sorry," she murmured, nipping at his jaw with her teeth again.

Damn, he liked it when she did that. "'S okay," he mumbled. "I'm a little self-conscious about them. It'll pass. Oh, God."

His eyes rolled back into his head when she sat deep into his lap and slid her hands under the elastic waistband of his flannel pajama pants to grip his buttocks. He couldn't explain how she did it, but she used her arms and shoulders to push his upper body back while she worked his pajamas down his hips. He could do nothing but obey, so he laid back and lifted his pelvis off the bed so she could slide them and his boxers—both at once—the rest of the way off.

Then she dragged her hands down his body all the way from his jaw and wrapped a hand around him. He groaned.

She let go long enough to shimmy out of her jeans. She left the black lace panties on for now but she pulled his T-shirt off slowly, teasing him. As if he wasn't already achingly aroused. Suddenly impatient, he grabbed her around the waist and yanked her onto the bed. He skimmed his hands up her legs and drew her panties down them.

Laughing breathlessly, she whispered, "Atta boy."

Ignoring the sensation of surreality, he ran his hands over her sleek body with hunger pounding through him, reveling in the feel of silken skin beneath his palms. He kneaded one breast and latched onto the other with his mouth, and she arched into him. A soft moan escaped her, demanding more. He obliged, rocking his hips against hers. Encouraged by the way she dug her fingers into his back, he slid his hands between her legs to massage her until she begged him to take her.

She was already there.

"You're sure you want this?" he asked hoarsely.

She clasped his face and kissed him. "I'm sure. I need this. I need *you*."

Catching her bottom lip between his teeth, he plunged into her, gratified by her gasp of pleasure.

There was no take-it-slow-and-savor-it; impatience and ravenous desire ruled them both, and as he thrust deep, Heather clawed at his back and gripped his hips with her thighs. She was exquisite, and as they reached the peak together and crashed over it, he knew there would never be any woman who could ever compare. There never had been.

She hooked her arms under his with her fingers curled over his shoulders and her nails biting into his skin, clutching him to her as her body clenched around him. Panting and trembling, he didn't know how much longer he was going to be able to hold himself above her before his arms gave out.

"Heather, I—"

"Shh."

When she finally released him, he sank onto the bed beside her and rolled onto his back with his head turned toward her. He watched the rise and fall of her chest slow as she caught her breath, and when she had, a smug, feline grin curved her lips. He couldn't help but grin in response. He might've felt totally inexperienced there for a while, but he'd still managed to satisfy her.

She rolled onto her stomach and pillowed her head on her arms, smiling at him. "You are full of surprises, Jere."

"How do you mean?"

"You usually wait for me to make the moves—both physically and emotionally—and I love that. But I didn't expect you to take command like that. That was… incredible." She pushed against his shoulder. "And don't look so smug about it."

"Smug? No. For a while in there, you made me feel like a green-broke boy."

She laughed huskily and stretched her neck to kiss him. "Coulda fooled me."

They lay there for a while, naked and sated atop the blankets while he trailed his fingers lightly over her back. Finally, the sound of boiling water drew his attention.

"Crap. I forgot about the dishes."

"We could always go for round two while we wait for the water to cool."

"Tempting." He chuckled. "So damned tempting. But I still have cattle to check on."

"Bummer."

"We'll probably need some warming up after, though."

She answered him with a grin.

He kissed her as he rolled off the bed. Yanking on his boxers, pajama pants, and fleece, he grabbed the water bucket and headed around to the water pump.

The task of washing their dishes took far longer than it should; Heather flirted and played, sliding her hands over his arms and shoulder and chest and back and nipped at his neck in a most distracting way as he worked, trying to draw him back into bed.

"*You* may have the day off," he said huskily as he fended off another advance, "but I have to work."

Finally, with his chore out of the way, he dressed quickly while Heather went out to use the outhouse. When she returned, she stuck her bottom lip out in the most adorable pout but changed into her clothes.

"Murph, you coming?" he asked his dog.

The Australian shepherd perked his ears but didn't lift his head or otherwise move a muscle to get off the bed.

"Spoiled dog," Jeremiah muttered.

"Can you blame him?" Heather asked. "The weather sucks."

"You wanna stay here with him?"

"Tempting," she replied, slipping into her wind breaker. "But nope. Let's get this over with."

Jeremiah grabbed the rifle leaning against the wall beside the door. He didn't usually take it with him on his rounds, but the patter of rain and the growing wind would make it more difficult to hear any disturbance amongst the cows, and he didn't want to be caught off guard and unprotected by a bear or mountain lion. Not that he'd seen signs of either in the two weeks he'd been up here. He tried not to think it, but it wasn't a predator of the four-legged variety he was most concerned about; the autopsy on the dead calf had revealed that the cause of death was a bullet to the head just like the heifer.

Despite the cold drizzle, their ride around the allotment to check on the cows and inspect the fence line was pleasant. Heather let him ride Jinx, who she'd been keeping up here at the allotments with his chestnut gelding, Flame—what *was* it with him and fire?—and he marveled at the thoroughbred's smooth gates. He definitely wasn't a cow horse, and while he eyed the cattle with curiosity, he was too well-trained and trusted his rider's promise that the bovines were safe for him to ride through.

Jeremiah had thought himself spoiled by Flame, who'd been trained by Ty Evans and responded to his rider's lightest commands, but with Jinx's easy gaits combined with that same, remarkable sensitivity, he was in awe… not only of the horse but of his owner. Heather had trained her ex-racer entirely herself, and Jeremiah knew she was incredibly talented, but to enjoy her handiwork himself was something else entirely.

"You are a magnificent animal, Jinx," he murmured, patting the palomino's damp neck.

They headed west from the cabin and looped south, east, and finally north, talking rarely, happy to enjoy each other's company. Heather was much more her usual self, but some of her intoxicating vivaciousness was missing, replaced by a quiet contemplativeness. He might be tempted to think she was still struggling with her emotional hangover, but it was too natural. It seemed more that this was a side of her few people were ever lucky enough to see—her soft and fragile core that she protected with her bold and blunt mannerisms.

The worry that she would walk away from him as she'd walked away from so many other men had been subdued, but it lingered, a tiny voice deep in his mind reminding him that he had made the choices that had earned her family's scorn. Maybe he wasn't that man anymore, but he had been once upon a time. And it didn't help that he hadn't yet figured out what her previous boyfriends had lacked that she needed. Still… the fact that he was only the second person she'd told about contemplating suicide when she was seventeen—and the first she had discussed it with in such detail—had to mean something. At the very least, she trusted him with that immensely private and deep-rooted secret.

To lose her after that would break him.

He loved her blunt way of speaking, her vibrant spirit, her dedication to her career, her incredible body…

He just loved her.

Maybe he was a fool bound to have his heart burned to ashes, but he couldn't help how he felt. He'd known from the first time he'd met her that she was exactly the kind of woman he wanted. Their time together and now their deeply revealing chats only solidified that.

She had changed the relationship by telling him about the teenaged fight with her brother and her suicidal thoughts after. His selfish desire to have her in his life had shifted to a powerful need to make sure she had someone who appreciated everything she was, exactly as she was with all her facets and flaws. Ainsley certainly did, but she had a family of her own now, and Jeremiah suspected that left

Heather feeling a bit like a third wheel with no one left who had the time or inclination to hold her together those times when she needed to fall to pieces.

He started to ask if that was why her other relationships hadn't worked out and what those seemingly perfect men had been lacking, but the out-of-place, dim reflection of gray sky on glass caught his attention. He tipped his head toward it. "See that?"

She nodded. "Looks like a vehicle."

They rode closer to investigate, and as they neared, the vehicle took the shape of a black Ford Bronco sitting abandoned on the road just beyond the northern fence line a couple hundred yards east of the cabin not far from where they'd found the shot-up target the day they'd discovered the dead heifer.

When they reached it, Jeremiah swung out of his saddle, landing lightly on his feet, and handed his reins to Heather. The Bronco hadn't been here yesterday afternoon when he'd done his herd check before the Bedspread's barbecue, and upon closer inspection, he spotted footprints by the driver-side door. He was no expert tracker, but he didn't have to be to know the tracks were fresh. If he had to guess, he'd say they belonged to a big man; next to his size nine ropers, the tracks were huge—long, wide, and deep with mud pushed up into squishy ridges around them. Peering through the windows, he noted a couple dozen empty beer cans. He tried the handle, and the door popped open, and his lip curled at the unmistakable stink of stale alcohol. Half a dozen shell casings spilled out into the mud, glinting faintly in the gloom.

He'd spent enough time around Aaron that he picked

them up with a stick and slipped them into his saddle bag without touching them. Most likely, the vehicle's owner had nothing to do with the deaths of the two cows… but maybe he did. The roads around here got a fair amount of traffic—mostly adventurers enjoying the mountain trails on four wheelers or dirt bikes—but it was too coincidental that the Bronco should be this close to the Hammonds' allotments after two cows had turned up dead by gunshot to the head.

He returned his attention to the tracks, following as they led away from the Bronco. Realizing the direction they were going, he lifted his gaze to Heather. "These head to the cabin."

"Good thing you grabbed the rifle this time."

Jeremiah didn't comment, but neither did he ignore the prickle of unease. The sharp fragrance of wood smoke drifted to him on the chilly breeze, and he hoped the man was nothing more than a drunk who'd gotten stuck out in the mountains and caught that same sent and gone looking in search of warmth. It wasn't freezing, but it was cold enough that a night spent in a broke-down vehicle would be uncomfortable.

When they reached the cabin, a giant of a man stood on the porch, talking gently to the dog snarling with hackles raised like porcupine quills. Murph glanced only briefly at them, too intent on barring the man from entering the cabin to give them much of his attention.

"I just wanna get warm, dog," the man said.

Jeremiah slipped the rifle out of its boot on his saddle and laid it unthreateningly across his thighs. "Can I help you?" he called.

The man jumped, and when he glanced over his

shoulder at Jeremiah, Murph barked and snapped, startling him. He nearly fell down the stairs. He was still a little drunk, it seemed. He swore as he regained his balance.

"Easy, Murph," Jeremiah called.

His dog sat in the doorway and stopped snarling, but he didn't take his eyes off the stranger.

"Sorry to bother you folks," the man said, turning only halfway to Jeremiah and Heather so he could keep an eye on the dog. "I've been in that damned Bronco all night, freezing my ass—" He glanced at Heather. "My butt off— sorry, ma'am. I smelled your fire and followed it here. Thought I might be able to get warm and find someone who could point me to the nearest phone so I can call for a tow."

"What were you doing up here?" Heather asked.

"Just wanted to take a drive in the mountains. Borrowed the Bronco from a friend, and he said I'd have no trouble with it but the damned—darned—thing just up and died on me."

"What's your name?" Jeremiah asked.

"Oh, sorry." The man cautiously made his way down the steps, wincing when Murphy let out a growl.

A jolt of recognition sizzled through Jeremiah when the stranger turned his face fully toward him. Then it faded, leaving him with a vague inkling that he'd seen the man before.

The man lifted his hand in greeting. "Greg Jones."

The name didn't elicit the same spark of recognition, which put Jeremiah even more on edge. Shaking the offered hand, he said, "I'm Jeremiah and this is Heather."

"You're the ones staying in this cabin?"

"Yes, sir."

"Would you, uh, mind…?" He gestured to the open door and shivered. "I'm freezing my balls off. Sorry, ma'am."

Heather shrugged.

How much of what he said was true, Jeremiah had no idea, but he wasn't faking the part about being cold. His teeth were beginning to chatter. "Yeah. Come on in and get warmed up. Then I'll give you a tow over to the Royal R. You can call for a tow into town from there."

"Thanks, Jerry. I really appreciate it."

Heather glanced sharply at Jeremiah, and he nodded. He caught the nickname, too. Greg wouldn't be the first person to screw up his name, but it was one more thing that stretched his willingness to believe Greg was here by coincidence toward the breaking point. Heather volunteered to unsaddle the horses while Jeremiah headed into the cabin with their uninvited guest.

He stoked the fire and put the coffee percolator on the wood stove, watching Greg as he worked. Murphy clung to Jeremiah's legs, nearly tripping him, with his eyes trained on the stranger. Jeremiah couldn't blame the dog for his wariness. His own instincts were on high alert, though he couldn't begin to explain why. There was nothing threatening about the man other than his size—he had to be as tall as Pat O'Neil and Luke Conner and half again wider.

"Good dog you got there," Greg observed.

"One of the best."

Heather came in right about the time the coffee was ready. He handed her a cup first, with milk and sugar like she preferred.

"You learn quick," she remarked quietly with a grin. "You're going to spoil me."

"You deserve to be spoiled. You've busted your ass on your own long enough."

Greg didn't say anything else while he drank his coffee, but Jeremiah sensed the man's eyes on them. He couldn't shake the feeling that he'd met the man before. He'd love to see his reaction to the mention of Zach's name but couldn't think of a way to bring his cousin up without being totally obvious. Maybe Aaron could run the plates on the Bronco, see if that turned up anything.

"You ready for this?" Jeremiah asked, taking the empty cup from Greg. "Heather, do you want to stay here?"

"I'll come. We can take my truck—more room."

There was nothing obvious about her demeanor, but he sensed an undercurrent of intensity in her, and the way she held his gaze just a moment too long didn't sit well with him. Then he caught the slightest movement at her side— she'd formed her hand into the shape of a gun. That's right. She kept a .38 in the center console of her truck.

"Good idea," he replied. "That way Murph won't have to stay here. Not sure he'd forgive me for leaving him behind again."

He reached down to ruffle his dog's ears. Still the Australian shepherd would not be distracted from his death stare. At any other time, it might've been comical.

Jeremiah ushered everyone out the door and closed it behind himself. "Let me just grab the tow strap out of mine."

Heather let him drive.

It didn't take long for them to hook the strap to

Greg's Bronco, and with him behind the wheel steering it, Heather and Jeremiah were free to talk. They didn't immediately say anything; instead, she grabbed a scrap of paper and a pen out of the center console and jotted down the license plate number of the Bronco along with the name the man had given them.

"Murph sure doesn't like him," she remarked.

"He doesn't like most people at first, especially men," he said. "But he seemed to take a special disliking to this guy. Maybe it's just that Greg spooked him… but maybe not."

"You think his name is really Greg?"

"No. And I know him from somewhere. I just can't put my finger on it." He let out a growl. "I hate this. For all we know, he might have nothing to do with Zach or the dead cows."

He glanced at her in between checking his rearview mirror to keep an eye on Greg and the Bronco and watching the road in front of him.

"Everything he said makes sense—it's logical."

"But there are too many coincidences."

He nodded. "Am I losing my mind?"

"I couldn't say. Everything you've told me about your cousin makes him sound like a pretty ruthless guy. And…."

She didn't immediately continue, and for the time being, he was too focused on the task of towing the Bronco and making sure Greg didn't rear end Heather's beautiful, dent-free truck to press her. Once they were on the scenic byway, it was easier, and he glanced at her. Her brows were knitted in a frown of deep thought or old memories—he wasn't sure which.

"And what?" he asked.

"And the shot cows, the signs of someone staying in the cabin before you moved into it, and now this guy just happening to break down so close to where we found the target…. I don't know. It kinda reminds me of the summer JP killed Mike and Carol—when he was fucking with Luke's head. I mean, this is nothing as bad as that, but come on. There are just too many coincidences."

"Screwing with heads is right up Zach's alley."

"I think you ought to call Aaron when we get to the Royal R and let him know what's going on."

"I was planning to."

"Good."

He flexed his fingers on the steering wheel and glanced in the rearview mirror again as he mulled over Heather's words. It was bad enough that he was thinking like he was, questioning that this was Zach messing with him and thinking that it was indeed exactly what he feared. That this situation reminded her of JP's manipulations did nothing to alleviate those fears.

This is nothing as bad as that.

He pressed his mouth into a flat line.

Yet.

* * *

Jeremiah looked up from his book with a trickle of adrenaline heightening his senses. He listened for a minute, but when whatever he heard didn't come again, he let out a breath and sank back into his camp chair, returning his attention to his book.

This was getting ridiculous. In the three days since he

and Heather had discovered the broken-down Bronco and returned to the cabin to find its driver trying to get past Murph, he'd spent far too much time thinking about that encounter. He could've used some company to keep his mind off it, even if it came in the form of Aaron or Nick or John or Henry telling him he was being paranoid. Heather's company would've been a far better distraction, but she'd been up only for a couple hours the day after—she'd been swamped at work and with getting ready for her family's trip to watch Curtis's final boxing match. So, he'd finally decided it was time to lose himself in a book. But as much as he loved *The Hunger Games,* the book wasn't working. Every time he heard a vehicle going by a couple hundred yards away on the scenic byway or caught the distant buzz of four-wheelers out on the numerous trails through these mountains, he was jerked out of his book with a shock of adrenaline just like now.

Aaron had run the Bronco's plate numbers, and the vehicle was clean—registered to a Randall Cochran in Missoula. Under the pretense of checking up on suspicious activities near where the vehicle had been found, he'd even called the man to verify that "Greg Jones" had borrowed the vehicle. That should've eased Jeremiah's suspicions. After all, Greg had said he was a friend of the owner, so that part checked out.

If anything, he was more suspicious now.

He knew the name Randall Cochran; recognized it with that same sense of vague familiarity he'd felt upon seeing the man. He still couldn't figure out where he'd encountered the man, but he knew with a gut certainty that the name Randall Cochran and the man who called himself

Greg Jones were one and the same.

Slipping his makeshift bookmark—a corner he'd torn off an old herd check sheet—between the pages, he set the hardcover on his chair and wandered into the cabin. He slipped the silver cross from under his mattress and stared at it for a long while.

Zach was behind this.

He had no idea how it was possible, since his cousin had been checking in with his PO on a regular basis and hadn't missed a single day of work or shown up even fifteen minutes late. Maybe Aaron would find some connection between Zach and this "Greg Jones" and Randall Cochran.

Murph, who'd remained in his spot beside the camp chair, gave a happy yip, so Jeremiah returned the cross to its hiding place and joined his dog on the porch. He couldn't see the truck yet, but it sounded like Heather's.

The prospect of seeing her again was a warm summer breeze that drove away the clouds of dark musings. He reached down to give Murph a good behind-the-ears scratch and watched her blue-gray Silverado materialize through the trees.

"This is a welcome surprise," he called as she parked beside his truck. "I thought you had dinner with your family tonight."

"I did. But I missed you, so I ditched them again."

"I bet they're not too happy about that."

She shrugged. "They ought to be used to it by now."

"How have they been since the Fourth?"

"Same as ever. Maybe a little less insulting to you, but that's only because I walk away any time one of them so much as mentions you."

He winced. He did *not* like being a source of friction between her and her family.

"Don't give me that look, Jere. It isn't your fault they are the way they are."

"I know, but…."

She didn't let him finish that thought, wrapping her arms around his neck as she crested the steps. She kissed him, and he was too glad to have her back in his arms to let thoughts of her family distract him. When she raked her hands back through his hair, his eyes slid closed. That felt good.

"It's getting long again," she murmured.

"Yeah, I know. I need to ask Tracie if she can cut it for me sometime this week."

"Mmm. I don't know. It kinda suits you."

He opened his eyes and grinned. "Are you just saying that to get me into bed?"

She tipped her head back and laughed. "Maybe. But we'll save that for later. We probably ought to get dinner started, though, if we want to eat before midnight."

"Dinner?"

"Yeah. You didn't think I came all this way up here just to say hi, kiss you, and be on my merry way, did you?"

"No." He chuckled. "Henry brought me up a couple good looking T-bones this morning. Steak all right?"

"Sure. And what to go with it?"

"How about some of Tracie's famous potatoes and a salad?"

"You got it."

She released and followed him into the cabin. He filled one of the plastic wash basins with enough water to scrub the three potatoes and then handed her a knife and a cutting board and asked her to slice them into thick French fries. While she was doing that, he sliced the onion into rings, halved them, and laid them on a sheet of aluminum foil. Heather scattered the potatoes on top, and he added several pats of butter and some salt and pepper and folded it all into a nice little pouch.

"That's all she puts in them?" Heather asked.

"Yep. Simple, huh?"

"Yeah, but damn they're good."

"They're my favorites. She says the trick is to use a sweet onion, especially a Walla Walla. If you grow them yourself, even better."

"Mom's tried to replicate these, but I don't think she ever tried sweet onions. I know she tried adding brown sugar once. That was… interesting." She snorted. "Mom likes to think she's a gourmet chef, and she's a good cook and an even better baker, but coming up with her own recipes or figuring someone else's without directions is *not* her strong suit."

Jeremiah fired up the little camp barbecue and set the potatoes on to cook while he seasoned the steaks.

"Those *are* good looking T-bones. Lazy H beef?"

"Naturally."

"Who do you guys have do your butchering?"

"Top of the Hill, right here in Northstar."

She made a sound that was half disgust and half annoyance. "I keep telling my dad to try them, but he won't listen."

He wanted to ask if her father had any idea that she was the child who should inherit his ranch, but he already knew the answer. If Brian Brown had refused to teach his daughter to box even though it was obvious she had a natural talent for it purely because she'd been born female, he wasn't the type to think she could handle running the ranch by herself. And yet he had no problem letting her do it when it suited him… like this next week so he could go watch his eldest son fight.

"I know that look," Heather said, prodding him in the chest. "It's the same one I get whenever I think about how backwards my family's stance on gender roles is."

He laughed at that, not because it was funny—it wasn't—but because of the way she delivered it with that adorably exaggerated eye roll and because it was better to laugh than to dwell on everything she'd told him the morning after the Fourth of July barbecue. It was bad enough to know that she suffered because of her family's expectations for her, but knowing there wasn't a damned thing he could do to stop them was excruciating.

And that was an entirely new feeling. He'd never been in a position like this before, to have someone trust him with such an incredible secret and to want to help but be unable to do so. He had always been the one needing help.

"Now that look…. I don't know that one."

"Just thinking I wish I knew how to make them see *you* and not what they want you to be."

"Yeah. Good luck with that. I've been trying for thirty years, and nothing has worked. Not the barrel-racing trophies, not the couple of junior boxing fights I won, not the successful horse-training business… even if it's a partnership with Ty for the time being."

"Maybe you just need to draw a line in the sand for them. Make it clear that they either meet you on your terms or you'll cut them out of your life."

"I can't do that. Cut them out of my life. They're my family."

"Just because they're your blood, that doesn't give them the right to treat you like they do. I know, I know. My blood family's all dead except for the one cousin I wish wasn't a blood relation, so I don't really understand the whole 'you must love your family' bullshit. It's abuse, what they do to you, and you don't owe them a damned thing."

"Hey, easy," she cooed, folding her arms around him like he was the one being wronged. "I get what you're saying. And you're right. I don't owe them anything. But they *are* my family, and…. I don't know. I love them despite everything."

"You can love them and still set boundaries with them."

"Like not agreeing to watch the ranch for them while they're away? I've been regretting that since I said I'd do it."

"That'd be a start."

"I don't think I've ever heard you swear like that." She sighed and brushed her hand back through his hair again. "I'm beginning to wish I'd paid a lot more attention to you long before now. You're a pretty amazing guy, Jere."

"Thanks. I, uh, hate to interrupt this little heart-to-heart, but I need to get the steaks on the grill."

Reluctantly, she released him and wandered over to the camp chair he'd vacated just before she'd arrived. He watched her from the corner of his eye when he wasn't shooing his dog away from the barbecue. She picked up his book and opened it to the first page.

"*The Hunger Games*, huh?" she asked. "I've seen the movie, but I haven't read the book."

"The book is better," he replied.

"They always are." She shook her head with a faint, poignant smile gracing her features. "You keep surprising me."

"Oh?"

"Yeah. You're nothing like I expected."

"What did you expect?"

"Not much." She glanced sharply up from the book. "I didn't mean that how it sounded. I just meant that you're so quiet and reserved around most people that I didn't expect a bookworm cowboy with a spoiled dog who talks to his truck. There's a lot more to you that whan you let people see."

"What's that saying? Something like the quietest people have the loudest minds."

"That's definitely you. More so than me. I'm pretty loud."

"That doesn't mean you have a quiet mind. Far from it. You just hide what's really in your head behind the blunt talk."

"That's probably the most complimentary way I've ever heard it described."

"Maybe I just know you better than most."

"Maybe you do. Hey, is that Aaron?"

Jeremiah turned around to follow her point. Sure enough, Aaron's truck cruised down the low rise south of the allotment, slowing to turn onto the dirt road to the cabin. The sight of his truck triggered a now-familiar tingle of nerves. He wasn't expecting Aaron tonight, which meant he had news of some kind, and Jeremiah suspected it wouldn't in any way connect Zach to any of the incidents up here.

A minute or two later, Aaron was climbing the steps to the porch.

"Something smells great," he greeted. "Those the steaks Hen brought up?"

"Yep," Jeremiah replied.

"Heather, sweetheart, how are you?"

"Good. And you?"

"Can't complain."

Jeremiah tried to ignore his aggravation, but it came spilling out despite his efforts. "Why are you here, Aaron?"

His surrogate brother regarded him with concern. "I'm sorry this is so hard on you, Jere. I am. I wish I had more answers for you, but I *do* have some good news. Those shell casings you found?"

"Yes?"

"They're the same caliber and manufacturer as the bullets that killed the cow and the calf."

The rush of relief—of validation—was incredible. "And?"

"That was enough to get a search warrant for the Bronco, Randall Cochran's home and Greg Jones's home. Only… I'm having trouble tracking down Mr. Jones."

"That's because Greg Jones *is* Randall Cochran."

"It's beginning to look that way."

"Still no ties between him and Zach?"

"No, but I'll keep looking."

Jeremiah sighed and stepped away to turn the steaks.

His gut said there was a connection, that Zach was somehow orchestrating all this despite all the evidence to the contrary. The very fact that there *was* so much evidence and none of it pointing to Zach made him even more certain of it. Since Heather had made the connection to the way JP had toyed with Luke and the Conners, he hadn't managed to get it out of his head. It was just too Zach. He was too good at manipulating situations and people for his reformed sinner act to be real—it was too obvious.

"Aaron, you are great at anticipating small-time criminals, and thank God that's really all you have to deal with in this county. But Zach isn't like them. He's *smart*. He is a master manipulator. He didn't build the biggest drug-running empire in this county by being stupid and leaving easy-to-follow trails. I'm telling you, he's pulling strings again."

"I believe you, Jere, but I have to operate within the law, and the law requires evidence. We have none. My gut says the same thing yours does even if my brain can't figure out how it's possible. I'm doing everything I can."

Jeremiah let out a growl, and Heather came to stand beside him with her arms around him. That helped. "I'm sorry, Aaron. I'm just frustrated. And this is making me a little crazy."

"Which, if this really is Zach, is probably exactly what he wants."

He nodded. Of course, refusing to let this get to him was impossible. He'd spent too many years fearing the day Zach was released from prison, certain his cousin would make good on his unspoken threat at the earliest opportunity.

"Anyhow," Aaron sighed, "I just wanted to let you know what I found. Keep that rifle close, just in case. I'll leave you two to enjoy your evening. Heather, it's always a pleasure."

"Likewise," she replied.

By the time Aaron pulled out onto the scenic byway, the steaks and potatoes were done, and putting the salad together kept Jeremiah's mind occupied for a time. Heather's praise of his potatoes kept him occupied a little longer.

"I'm not kidding. These are *just* like Tracie's."

"You should make them for your mom."

She smirked conspiratorially. "I should… and pretend I don't know why they're better than hers. Speaking of cooking, I want to have you down for dinner sometime this week while my family's out of town. Just you, me, and Christina. I want to give her a chance to get to know you without her husband whispering in her ear."

"Dinner at your place? Sure."

"No, at the main house. I'm staying there while everyone's gone."

He eyed her over his plate. "Do you really think that's a good idea?"

"Yep. I won't get to see you much this week, and if my family doesn't like having you in the house, they can suck it."

"I just don't want to create any more drama for you."

"How many times am I going to have to say this? *You* aren't the one creating the drama."

"No, but I'm the reason for it."

"If it weren't you, it'd be something else. Like me

breaking up with Dustin. So you'll come? I already talked to Christina about it, and she's willing to give you a chance to prove you're not some degenerate out to drag me down into the criminal underworld."

It was meant to be funny, so he gave a half-hearted chuckle, but it just made him sad. Would he ever bury his past, or would his mistakes precede him every time he met people who knew him only by his reputation?

"I'm sorry," she said. "That was a bit much."

"It's not what you said. But it would be nice if people looked at me and saw *me* and not what I did as a stupid, desperate kid."

She reached across the table, offering her hand in a show of silent support, and as he took it, he met her gaze. What he saw in her eyes was breathtaking.

It was the soul-deep connection of someone who understood exactly the pain of being misunderstood. And that, he realized, was what made their relationship so beautiful and rare.

Was *his* ability to empathize with *her* also what he had that none of those other men did? If it was, he had a shot… a real shot at capturing her heart like no one else had.

A real shot at forever with her.

Nine

"SO, WHEN'S JERRY supposed to get here?" Christina asked, leaning against the counter in the main house's kitchen. When Heather glanced sharply at her, she winced. "Sorry. When is *Jeremiah* supposed to get here?"

"Thank you. He was going to get a haircut from Tracie and go home to shower before he came over. He should be here shortly."

Christina nodded. "Have you heard from Ainsley lately?"

"She called yesterday to say she and Rowan and Gavin and Moira were having a blast in Hawaii. We didn't talk long because they had a luau to get to, but she said enough to make me jealous."

"I bet. I've always wanted to go to Hawaii."

"So why don't you go?"

Her friend snorted. "With three kids under five and a husband who leaves all the kid wrangling to me? No thanks."

Heather's brows rose. Uh-oh. If that didn't sound like trouble in paradise, she didn't know what would. "Everything all right?"

"Fine."

The pinched look on Christina's face said everything was most certainly *not* fine, but it had been so long since they'd been able to have a real heart-to-heart talk that Heather didn't know where to begin. She'd suspected for a while now that something was off in Christina's life, but other than Curtis's surliness over the end of his boxing career, she had no real idea what.

"When a woman says everything is 'fine', that usually means the opposite, you know," she remarked.

"I'm okay, Heather. Just not feeling so great today. I'm ready to have this kid out of me."

"Ah."

That was *definitely* something she couldn't help with. Despite watching her sister, two sisters-in-law, and Ainsley go through a combined eight pregnancies now, she'd never cared to pay attention to their complaints.

Deciding it would be better to change the topic, she asked, "Speaking of kids, how are you enjoying your alone time without Sebastian and Rosalie?"

The smile that washed across her friend's face was one of immeasurable relief. "Don't get me wrong. I adore my children, but I am loving having the chance to focus on me. Of course, it would be even better if I wasn't a week away from my due date."

Christina's expression soured so quickly, that Heather jerked her head back and froze. When tears welled in her friend's eyes, she set the knife down. Instinctively, she wanted to hug Christina, but she didn't know if that was the correct gesture.

"What's wrong, Chris?" she finally asked.

Christina sucked her lips between her teeth, fighting a losing battle against the tears. A joke about hormonal and emotional moms-to-be popped into Heather's head, but she didn't have to be a mom to realize how deeply inappropriate giving voice to it would be. So she acted on her instinct and embraced her friend. As soon as her arms were around the woman, Christina burst in to full-fledged, gulping sobs. All Heather could do was be the friend she suddenly realized she hadn't been for the duration of Christina's marriage to Curtis and provide a shoulder to cry on while she kept an eye on the spaghetti sauce simmering on the stove.

"Hey," she murmured, "are you okay?"

"No," Christina cried. "I never wanted this."

"Wanted what, honey?"

"Three kids. I never wanted more than two, and I wanted a career, not to be stuck at home because my husband wants me to stay home with the kids. I thought I could do it—I did—but I miss having a purpose outside my family. I miss going to work and having adult conversations. I feel like I'm going insane, Heather. And I hate myself for it because I love my kids and I want to be there for them."

As Christina descended into incoherent blubbering, Heather gaped, glad her friend couldn't see her shock. So when she'd questioned Christina's happy marriage that day they'd had lunch with Ainsley, she'd been on the mark.

"I'm so sorry, honey," she whispered.

"And seeing Ainsley so happy with Rowan…. I am thrilled for her, but it just makes me feel worse, you know? Like, what am I doing wrong? Why can't I just be happy with what I have? I love my family. I do, but—"

"You're exhausted, Christina. You give so much of yourself to your family that you have nothing left for yourself. You have every right to be upset but, as far as I can see, no reason at all for feeling guilty. Curtis needs to get over himself, step up, and be a goddamned father and husband."

That triggered a fresh round of tears, and Heather let out a sigh. She could punch Curtis for this.

"After this baby's born and you have a chance to heal up, I will sic your kids on my brother and our parents and pay for a night away for you and me and Ainsley, too. We'll go someplace like Missoula or Bozeman and go shopping and go to a spa to get pampered."

Christina sniffed. "That sounds wonderful. I would love that."

After a couple more minutes, Christina pulled herself together enough to slip away from Heather. As she stirred the sauce and slid the noodles into the pot of boiling water, Heather watched her friend's expression smooth into a composed mask, and if she hadn't held her for almost ten minutes while she cried and if her eyes weren't red and her cheeks weren't blotchy and tear-streaked, she might not believe the woman had been sobbing on her shoulder. Even as Christina's ability to put on a happy face awed her, it broke her heart to know her friend had needed to master that trick.

"I've always admired you," Christina said after a moment. "The way you know exactly what you do and don't want out of life and the way you refuse to let anyone bully you into something you know is wrong for you. I wish I was more like you."

For the second time in fifteen minutes, Heather's mouth fell open. The way their friendship had been going the last few years, that was the *last* thing she would've expected.

"But I'm not like you. I'm a doormat, doing what's expected of me even when I don't want to. And look where it's gotten me. Fat and pregnant, married to a man who cares more about the dismal end of his lackluster boxing career than he does about making sure his wife has what she needs to be happy."

"You are *not* fat. Don't ever say that to me again. You are also not a doormat. My family is… overbearing. You either give them what they want or they grind you down to dust." She set the spoon aside and untied the laces of her wrist band. With only a flicker of hesitation, she slipped it off and held her bared wrist out to Christina. Unsurprisingly, her friend gasped. "I did this when I was seventeen. And I've kept it to myself all this time… until I told Jeremiah about it the morning after the Fourth of July barbecue. After my brother tried to goad him into a fucking fist fight right there with the whole valley watching. Ainsley knows, but I didn't even tell *her* the details."

Christina was shivering, so Heather hugged her again.

"You aren't the problem, honey. Curtis is. Our whole damned family is. Don't let him do this to you. I don't care if you have to file for divorce. If that's what it takes, I'll help you. But don't let this destroy you like it almost destroyed me."

How long they stood there, clinging to each other like they hadn't seen each other in years, Heather had no idea, but it was healing, and she began to see that she had seriously misjudged Christina.

"I owe you an apology," she murmured. "I have been unfair to you lately. For a long time, really. I've assumed you were turning into everything I hate about my family, and I never realized what you were going through. Never bothered to find out."

"It's not your fault."

"That much is. I'm strong enough and humble enough to own it. I've been a poor friend to you, and I am so, so sorry."

Christina nodded. "I haven't exactly been the best friend, either. I don't know your man other than what I've heard about him and what you've told me, but he seems to make you happy. And stronger. I'm sure there's a reason you never told me about this." She brushed her thumb over Heather's scar. "Probably the fact that I was already going out with your brother by then. But it sounds like Jeremiah has given you the courage to talk about it. And if he can do that for you... well, he must be something special."

Heather nodded, agreeing wholeheartedly. She couldn't say exactly what quality he had that set him apart, but like she'd thought about Luke and Shane that day she's had lunch with her two best friends, Jeremiah knew what it was to break and to heal. He understood her. "He makes me feel safe," she said slowly, testing the idea. It fit. "On a level I've never felt safe before."

"That's wonderful, Heather. It truly is. Maybe he's the one."

She snorted. "You know I don't believe in all that 'the one' crap. But I get what you're saying."

"I wasn't talking about all that 'the one' crap," Christina replied in a playfully mocking tone. When she let go of Heather and leaned back against the counter, she grinned. "I was talking about him being the one you can finally fall in love with."

"I've fallen in love before."

"Let me finish, dammit, woman. He may be the one you can finally fall in love with… and *stay* in love with. The one who brings out the best in you and makes you the strongest version of yourself."

A knock on the kitchen door announced Jeremiah's arrival and the merciful end to a conversation that was sure to turn embarrassing momentarily.

"Saved by the knock," Christina teased as she stepped around Heather and went to answer the door.

She greeted him graciously with an enthusiastic hug, but Heather didn't think it was contrived. Her smile was genuine when she stepped back to let Jeremiah in, and he glanced at Heather over her head with a questioning look. Heather shrugged.

"I owe you an apology, Jeremiah," Christina said. "To echo Heather's words to me just a few moments ago, I have been unfair to you. I've judged you based on your past and my husband's less than objective opinions, and Heather has pointed out rather bluntly—as is her way—that I have been wrong to do so."

"Fancy way of apologizing for judging a book based

on the opinion of someone who's never read it," he replied lightly. "But I appreciate it."

For one heart-stopping moment, Heather stared at him, stunned by the flippant, out-of-character response that treaded the line between being rude and standing up for himself. But then she glanced at Christina and let out a breath. Her friend was grinning. Somehow he'd known exactly what to say to put her at ease and win her over.

"I deserve that," she said.

"Well, that was quite an ice breaker," Heather said brightly. "So, I know you've met briefly before, but let me officially introduce you. Jeremiah, this is Christina, who is both my best friend and my sister-in-law. Christina, this handsome devil is Jeremiah, my boyfriend. I haven't mentioned it yet, but he is a bookworm like you, so you two should have *loads* to talk about."

"It's a pleasure," Christina said, extending her hand.

Jeremiah shook it. "It is indeed."

"So, while Heather is finishing dinner, shall we talk books?"

"As long as you two stop with the ridiculous formal talk," Heather muttered without heat, "have at it. He's re-reading *The Hunger Games* right now, if you want to start with that. I know it's one of your favorites, too."

"It is," Christina confirmed. "I've read the whole trilogy five times now."

"You've got me beat, then. I'm only starting it again for the fourth time."

Heather might've rolled her eyes, but they were too cute discussing the popular trilogy and their hopes for the next movie with animated expressions and gestures. At this rate, it wasn't going to take Jeremiah long at all to win Christina over. With a shake of her head and a smile, she pulled out the ingredients for the salad. Christina stepped over to help, but Jeremiah jumped in.

"Oh, no you don't," he said. "Sit back and relax."

Christina's eyes sprang wide, and as she perched on a stool across the island from them to watch, surprise gave way to relief. Heather again had to subdue the urge to punch her brother. It was a good thing he wasn't in the same state right now, but he was going to get a piece of her mind when he got home.

She kept an eye on her friend while she and Jeremiah chopped ingredients, concerned by the frown that occasionally darkened Christina's pretty face and the way she kept reaching to massage her back and shifting on the stool like she couldn't get comfortable. A week away from her due date, she probably *couldn't*, so with a snort, Heather tried harder to focus her attention on her task so she didn't chop her finger off. Jeremiah helped distract her, diving in to kiss her cheek or nuzzle her neck now and again.

Christina laughed at their antics. "You two make a cute couple."

"Thanks," Jeremiah replied, beaming.

With dinner ready, they opted to forgo the formality of eating in the dining room and instead set their plates around the island. Heather smirked inwardly. *That* would drive her mother nuts, and judging by the sly twinkle in Christina's eyes, she wasn't the only one feeling naughty… and proud of it.

Heather let out a breath. This was just like old times, and she was glad to have her friend back if only for this week while Curtis and the rest of her family were out of town. It was good to feel that connection again, and without focusing too much on it for fear of ruining the moment, she admitted just how much she'd missed it.

They lingered over their meal, eating slowly while Jeremiah and Christina tried to convince her to read their beloved books, and Heather finally relented. How could she not want to read something that both her best friend and her lover adored?

With everyone finished eating, Jeremiah shooed them out of the kitchen while he did the dishes. They sat together on the couch, talking in hushed voices like they'd done a million times in high school.

"I totally get what you see in him," Christina murmured, craning her neck to peer into the kitchen. "I can't believe I could've ever thought he was trouble."

"I can't, either. I also can't believe I let my family's opinions stop me from getting to know him better. I've always had this feeling he was a good guy. I mean, everyone else in Northstar loves him. The Hammonds, the Conners, the O'Neils, the Carlyles, the Strutherses…."

"So they do." Christina regarded her with a thoughtful expression. "I can't quite put my finger on it, but you're different with him. It's nothing obvious. That flirting over the salad—you would've done that with Dustin, too, so that's not it."

Heather glanced at her still-bare left wrist. She knew exactly how she was different with Jeremiah, but she wasn't going to make it easy on her friend. She wanted Christina to arrive at that conclusion on her own so it'd sink in deeper.

"You're more… *you*. Unreservedly so. I mean, you're

never shy about who you are, but there's always an edge to it, like you're always waiting to defend yourself for being who you are. And with him… I don't see that. I see you totally comfortable with yourself."

"That sums it up pretty well. Incredible, isn't it?"

"Yes, it—" Christina's hand shot to her belly, and her eyes sprang wide. "Oh!"

"Kick?" Heather asked, but there was something in her friend's eyes that concerned her—a shadow of panic.

After a few seconds, it subsided. "No, just a pretty strong Braxton-Hicks. I don't think I've had enough water today. They're stronger when I don't."

Heather waited, perched on the edge of the couch, for almost a minute more, but when Christina smiled reassuringly, she went into the kitchen to fetch a glass. She slid her hand along Jeremiah's back as she passed him on her way to the fridge, kissing him lightly when he turned his head to her.

She definitely felt free to be herself with him, and it was amazing.

When she returned to the living room, Christina wasn't there. Figuring she must've stepped into the bathroom, she set the glass of water on the coffee table and sank into the couch, resting her head on the back of it with a sigh of contentment.

Minutes ticked by and Christina didn't return. Finally, she heard the familiar creak of the loose floorboard in the hallway outside the bathroom.

"I was beginning to wonder if you'd fallen in," she remarked, turning her head toward the hallway.

She jerked upright. The lower skirt of Christina's

pretty turquoise sundress was wet, and the shadow of panic Heather had seen earlier had morphed into fully fledged hysteria.

"Oh God, what's wrong?" she asked, on her feet and rushing to her friend.

"My water broke."

"But you're not due for a week," Heather replied. She snapped her mouth closed. What a dumb thing to say. She had enough nieces and nephews to know that babies rarely debuted on their due date. But dammit, Curtis was hundreds of miles away and his fight wasn't until tomorrow! "Sorry, honey. Um... what do you need me to do?"

"I...." Christina glanced around, her eyes wild. And then she started crying again. "It isn't supposed to be like this! Curtis is supposed to be here."

"I know, honey." Heather embraced her friend, terrified and furious at once. Christina had already gone through this twice, so she shouldn't be scared and crying. She should be settling into that instinctual single-mindedness women in labor seemed to slip into. "I know. What do you need me to do? Do you have your OB's number? We should probably call her, right?"

Nodding, Christina seemed to come out of her panic a little. "Yes. I need to call her. And I need to head into town. We barely made it to the hospital in time with Rosalie after my water broke."

Oh, great.

Thankfully, that thought stayed locked in Heather's head. "All right. You call, I'll pull my truck over."

"Towels," Christina said distantly. "I don't want to wreck your seat."

"Towels, right."

Wreck my seat? Yeah, now I'm even less inclined to have kids.

Heather ducked into the kitchen. "We need to go. Christina's water just broke."

"Crap."

"Yeah. Pretty much my thought."

Jeremiah set the last pot in the drainer. "How can I help?"

"Um… can you grab some towels out of the bathroom while I pull my truck over?"

"Absolutely."

Heather slipped out the kitchen door and jogged across the driveway to her truck. She yanked her keys out of her pocket and cursed when she dropped them. Why the hell were *her* hands shaking? She wasn't the one about to give birth. She took several deep, measured breaths as she started her truck and swung it around to the front door of her parents' house, but they did nothing to calm the clawing panic.

Catching movement from the corner of her vision, she turned her gaze toward the door to see Jeremiah helping Christina outside with a couple towels tossed over his shoulder. In contrast to the Heather's rapid heartbeat and shallow breath's, his face was a mask of calm concern, and the sight of it soothed her.

There was no reason to panic. Everything would be fine.

She shifted her truck into neutral, set the parking break, and climbed out to open the passenger-side door for Christina just as another contraction seized her friend. Jeremiah didn't wait for it to pass; he picked her up, nodding his head to the towels on his shoulders. Heather folded them and set them on the seat, and he settled Christina gently in the truck.

"Your shirt's all wet now," Heather observed after he shut the door.

"Wouldn't be the first time I've had amniotic fluid on me."

Calving. Duh. No doubt he'd pulled his fair share of calves. "No, I guess not."

"You all right?" Jeremiah asked her quietly.

"I'm not the one about to have a baby."

"No, but your hands are shaking and you're paler than Christina is."

"She's done this before. I haven't."

"You want me to drive?"

"Um…." She pinched her lips between her teeth and closed her eyes. Nope, that didn't help, either. "Yeah. I think I do. If you don't mind."

Rather than slide into the back seat, she flipped the center console up and buckled herself into the rarely used center seat in front so her friend could lean on her. And Christina needed someone to lean on. She'd stopped crying, but tears still shimmered in her eyes, waiting to fall.

Damn you, Curtis.

On the heels of that thought came another, and she gave Jeremiah's leg a squeeze.

At least one man around here can be counted on. And ain't it funny it's the one they all say is unworthy.

* * *

Heather lifted her head and blinked the sleep from her eyes. The hospital room was dark except for the faint glow under the door and the dim blue of predawn peeking through the gap between the heavy curtains. Her body felt like it was made of lead. What a night. Christina hadn't delivered her baby until after midnight—unlike his big sister Rosalie, the little fella hadn't been in a rush to meet the world—and it had taken another hour or so to get mom and baby checked out and moved out of the delivery room. Which meant they'd all had less than four hours of sleep.

She sat up carefully so she wouldn't wake Jeremiah. How they'd managed to fall asleep at all, leaning against each other in the uncomfortable chairs, she had no idea.

Hunched over her legs, she dragged her hands over her face and rubbed her tired, gritty eyes, then turned her gaze over her shoulder to admire the sleeping man.

Thank God he'd come with them. She couldn't have handled Christina's labor and birth without him. He'd been the rock her friend needed—patient and steady even when Christina had gripped his hand so hard Heather was sure she'd break his fingers. He'd been the rock *she* had needed.

"What time is it?" he mumbled.

"Not quite five," she replied. "Sorry. Didn't mean to wake you."

"You didn't." He pushed himself straighter in the chair with a groan and opened his eyes. "The kink in my neck did."

He held out an arm, and she didn't hesitate to wrap it around herself and lean against him with the unforgiving arms of the chairs digging into her side. Despite her discomfort, she let out a huff of laughter.

"How the hell did we sleep at all?" she asked.

She sensed the smile that curved his lips even though

she couldn't see his face—his demeanor shifted somehow.

"Guess we were just *that* tired."

"Yeah, it was definitely a long night," Heather murmured. "That's the first time I've ever been in the room the whole time."

"Me, too. And I'm in no hurry to repeat the experience."

Her heart tripped a little. They'd never talked about whether or not he wanted kids, so she had no idea what he meant by that… and she was too scared to ask. Instead of commenting, she smoothed her hand across his chest and left it resting there, listening as his breathing slowed again as he dozed off. She closed her eyes, lulled into a blissful state of half-consciousness in which there were no worries about biological clocks and the societal pressures she'd bucked against her entire life. Jeremiah's arm warm around her and the steady beat of his heart beneath her palm—that was all she needed and wanted in this moment.

The insistent cries of a newborn jerked her from that wonderful netherworld, and if it was possible, she was even more exhausted than she'd been the first time she'd woken up. And this time, Jeremiah wasn't wrapped around her. Somehow, she'd managed to fall the rest of the way into a deep enough sleep that he hadn't woken her when he'd left his chair. She found him standing beside Christina's empty hospital bed looking adorably uncertain as he tried to soothe the crying baby in his arms. The tiny boy quieted after a moment, and Jeremiah smiled with a hint of *I-did-it* pride.

Something flickered in the deep, dark recesses of her being—an instinctual flutter at the confirmation her prospective mate could at least hold a baby without dropping him or running in the opposite direction. But that's all it was, a faint flicker. Heather didn't know if seeing him holding her new nephew *should* trigger some earth-shattering flood of maternal desire, but it didn't. Her mother was going to be *so* disappointed that the arrival of Christina's third child was having no more impact than the births of any of her other nieces of nephews. She was still every bit as certain as she'd always been that motherhood wasn't for her.

God, she's not even here *and she's in my head.*

With a disgusted growl, Heather lurched out of the chair, swaying faintly with a rush of dizziness from the lack of sleep. When her equilibrium righted itself after a second, she looked up to find Jeremiah watching her with his lips twisted in amusement.

"I'd offer to let you hold him, but I'm afraid he'll start crying again if I move him."

"Where's Christina?"

"Shower."

Now that he'd mentioned it, she realized she could indeed hear the shower running. "Ah."

"When she gets out, can I borrow your phone? I need to call Austin, see how Murph did last night and see if he can come get me."

"I'm sure Murphy is just fine. You know Austin spoils him rotten."

"I know, but he doesn't handle being away from me overnight very well. Separation anxiety, big time."

Heather's lips twitched. "Him or you?"

With a quiet chuckle, he said, "Both. Besides, I need

to get up to the allotment and check on the herd. Everyone's cutting hay today, so no one will have time to get up there."

"Why don't you just take my truck?"

He eyed her for a moment. "Won't you need it?"

"Nah. I won't be going anywhere for a while."

"If you're sure, that'd be great. Then I won't have to inconvenience Austin. If I head out as soon as Christina's done and ready to take this little guy back, I should be able to get back here in time for lunch."

"You *could* put him back in the basinet, you know."

"Yeah, but this is supposed to help them bond." He let out a soft laugh as he glanced down at the baby now sleeping comfortably again in his arms. "Or at least, that's what Lindsay said every time she wanted me to hold Archer for her. I think she may have been trying to trigger my paternal instincts."

Heather chewed on her lip, trying to stop herself from asking the question because she wasn't sure she wanted to know the answer. "Did it work?"

"Dunno. But at least I'm not terrified of dropping this little guy like I was the first time I held Archer."

That didn't tell her much, but at least he hadn't said all that time with Archer and now with Christina's son had convinced him he needed to have kids.

Christina's emergence from the bathroom looking much refreshed and not at all like she'd given birth only a few hours ago prevented her from dwelling on it too much. She watched her best friend take her newborn son from Jeremiah and noted the grateful smile she flashed him.

"I wasn't trying to eavesdrop," she said, "but I heard

you say you need to head back to Northstar."

"For a few hours," Jeremiah replied. "I should be back by noon. Is there anything you need me to pick up for you on the way back?"

"No, I don't think I need anything that can't wait until I go home. Thank you so much for all your help. I think Heather and I would've been a wreck without you. And… I'm more sorry than ever that I ever thought—"

He held his hand up. "You already apologized, Christina. No need to do it again."

Indecision flashed across her face, but then, as if driven by an irresistible impulse, she threw her free arm around his neck and dragged him into a hug. Heather might've laughed at the shock on his face if she weren't so surprised by the relief at her friend's about-face regarding him. By the time she released him, his shock had shifted into an expression Heather couldn't quite describe—there was a glimmer of the relief she felt but also something else. Gratitude, maybe? No, that wasn't quite it. Whatever it was, it touched something deep in her heart and made her want to wrap *her* arms around him… and never let go.

"All right, I'd better get out of here," he said. Turning to Heather, he kissed her and promised he'd be careful with her truck.

And then he was out the door, leaving her staring after him more than a little dumbstruck.

So many thoughts and conflicting worries and hopes spun through her head, and she sank into the chair she'd left only moments ago. She was vaguely aware of Christina settling next to her into Jeremiah's empty chair.

"You look… perturbed," her friend murmured.

"What's wrong?"

"I…." Heather snapped her mouth shut, not sure she could adequately explain her fear. "We've never talked about kids."

"So?"

"I don't want any."

"I know that."

"What if he does?"

Christina glanced down at her sleeping son, then offered her a sympathetic smile. "Would that be so bad?"

"Chris… I broke up with Dustin over it. He was going to propose, and he started off by saying how much he couldn't wait to start a family with me, and I knew… I knew I couldn't be the woman to give him that. It's just not me. And I knew everything would fall apart eventually when he finally realized that. So what was the point of staying together? He was looking for his forever woman, and I was never going to be her. I couldn't be."

Christina took her left hand turned it over, skimming her thumb over the thick white scar. Heather hadn't ever put her wrist band back on. "Before last night, I might've asked why you always say things like that as if you're the problem, but I get it now. You aren't broken, sweetie. You never have been. You just haven't found the right man for you… until now. I don't think you have to worry about Jeremiah trying to pressure you into having kids you don't want."

Heather's befuddled mind couldn't process anything after *until now*. Had Christina really just said she thought Jeremiah was the man she could spend the rest of her life with? Of course, there wasn't much more he could've done to prove his worth than stepping up in a crisis like he had last night. Finally, her brain caught on to the second statement.

"Why do you say that? Did he say something?"

"Not anything specific, but I get the feeling that he'd be happy with whatever you wanted. He sees you in a way I don't think any man ever has before. For one, he sees *you*—exactly as you are—and he seems to adore you for everything you are and everything you think you aren't."

Heather ran her hands through her sleep-mussed hair and then hunched over her thighs with her hands wrapped around her neck. Christina wasn't wrong, at least about Jeremiah knowing her better than any man she'd dated. Maybe that was because she'd told him more about her deepest insecurities than she'd ever told *anyone* else. Or maybe it was something else. Something deeper… a natural harmony of their spirits.

Recalling Jeremiah's comment about holding babies helping them bond, she sat up and turned toward her friend. "Can I hold him?"

Christina's brows rose. "Of course."

"Don't look so surprised. I may not want kids of my own, but I adore my nieces and nephews."

"I know you do. But you've never been too keen on holding newborns before."

She laughed softly as she remembered the rest of what Jeremiah had said along with that statement. "I've always been a little afraid of dropping them. They're just so tiny and delicate, and I'm used to dealing with big, strong animals."

"Yes, you are, but you also have a lighter hand with

them than anyone I've ever seen except Ty and his dad. Here."

Heather gingerly took the baby, but there was no need to fear him waking up; he was out cold, swaddled in a football-print blanket, all snug and warm. He truly was a beautiful little boy, and her heart swelled with pride and love.

"You think you're this big, awkward, unfeminine woman," her friend continued, "and I think your family has something to do with that belief. But they're wrong. You may be strong and stubborn, but you're also gentle and kind and as beautiful on the inside as you are on the outside."

"Thank you," Heather whispered. Sniffing and blinking her eyes to stave off the tears, she added, "Now stop it before you make me cry. I'd rather bond with your son without dripping tears all over him, thank you."

They were quiet for a while until the baby stirred and started crying. Heather gave him back to his mother and wandered over to the window while Christina nursed him.

"You remember when Sebastian was born, and I couldn't get him to latch after I took a shower?" Christina asked with maternal fondness thick in her voice.

"Yeah. You used some froo froo flowery body wash and he didn't recognize your smell. Looks like you learned your lesson."

"Oh boy. Ugh. I just wanted to be clean and feel human again. And you were the one who figured it out and told me to put my dirty old hospital gown back on."

"That's how Ty and I have gotten mares to take foals that aren't theirs—by making the foals smell like them."

"I just think it's ironic that you—who don't want

kids—are the one who figured it out. Not your mother, not your sister, not Brock's wife. Not even the nurses. And yet your parents give you hell about not wanting kids." Christina snorted. "You'd probably be the best parent of us all. And speaking of parents… this little boy's going to have a stronger bond with Jeremiah than with his own father. Just watch."

"That'll really piss Curtis off," Heather remarked. She left the window and sat with Christina on the bed, smoothing her hand over the baby's head with its dusting of super fine blond hair. Blond like his mommy instead of dark-haired like his daddy and his brother and sister were. She couldn't explain why that tickled her. "I think he's going to be *yours* more than Sebastian and Rosalie."

"I think you're right."

Heather laid back, across Christina's legs. "I've missed this."

"Missed what?"

"You and me. I could kill my brother for driving a wedge between us. I didn't realize until last night that he did. I just knew something was off."

"He did, didn't he. But now that we know it, we can fix it."

"Can't fix something when you don't know where or how it's broken," Heather agreed. She reached for her friend's hand and gripped it.

"I'm glad you finally gave Jeremiah a chance," Christina murmured. "I think he has a lot to do with us realizing that. Before you started going out with him, you just got impatient with me. You never asked what was wrong."

Heather pinched her eyes closed. As painful as it was to admit it, that was the truth. "I'm sorry, Chris."

"We're on the mend now, though, right? That's what matters."

"You bet. And we're definitely still on for that girls' night. Don't forget."

"I won't. Believe me." Christina laughed softly. "He's a good man, your Jeremiah."

Heather turned her head to her friend and smiled, and when Christina offered the fed and snoozing baby to her, she didn't hesitate to sit up and take him. Staring down at her adorable new nephew, she had an epiphany.

She was as certain as ever that she didn't want kids of her own, but if Jeremiah wanted one or if they found themselves facing an unplanned pregnancy… she could do it.

She tipped her head back, eyes closed, and let out a breath.

"You all right?" Christina asked.

"Um… yeah. I think so."

"You look like a woman who's just realized something earth-shattering."

Earth-shattering. Yeah, that summed it up pretty well. Had she really just admitted to herself that if Jeremiah wanted kids she'd do it?

What… the… fuck.

But she had. And it didn't matter how fervently she tried to deny it; now that thought had struck with the awesome brilliance of a bolt of lightning, she couldn't erase it. It was burned into her mind.

And the scariest part about it? She didn't know if she

should be terrified… or thrilled.

Ten

AS SOON AS JEREMIAH reached Northstar, the first thing he did was stop at the bunkhouse to get his dog, who maintained his aloof *I'm-mad-at-you* disdain for all of five seconds before launching into his arms. Then, with Murph happily settled in the passenger seat of Heather's truck, he drove down to the main house to check in with the Hammonds. He located Tracie in the house, cleaning up after breakfast.

The lingering aroma of bacon and syrup made his stomach growl, and with a laugh, the Hammond matriarch fixed him a plate of leftovers.

"You didn't eat before you left town, did you."

"Nope. Thanks, Mom."

She dipped her head in acknowledgement. "Did Christina have her baby?"

"Yeah. A little after midnight. He's a cutie."

"Everything went all right?"

"Define 'all right'. Because I have no idea, and that's not what I'd call *all right*. There weren't any complications, if that's what you mean."

"I take it you were there for the whole show."

"She wouldn't let me leave." Anger flared as he remembered the fear and anguish in Christina's eyes as she'd cried and cursed Curtis. At the one time when she needed her husband the most, he was hundreds of miles away. "What kind of jackass schedules a fight so close to his wife's due date?"

"I don't know. John wouldn't have dreamed of anything like that. Neither would any of my boys." She reached up to run her hand through his hair with an affectionate smile. "Including you."

"I don't think the thought would've ever crossed my mind, but it *definitely* won't now. Not after that."

"Well, you'd best hurry up and eat your breakfast and get up to the allotment. Sounds like Christina needs you more than we do today."

He scarfed his breakfast, and Tracie took the plate from him. Then he gave her a hug and zipped out the door. He stopped briefly by the lower hayfield to check in with John and Nick and took the good-natured ribbing from the rest of the hay crew for showing up in Heather's truck with a smile. He tried to apologize for not helping with the haying, but they didn't let him get it out. They had more than enough help, anyhow, so it wasn't a big deal, but Jeremiah didn't like slacking off... or feeling like he was even if he wasn't.

The contrast between the Hammonds—his family, he added; might as well get used to thinking of them like that on a regular basis because they were—and the Browns was even more striking this morning.

Every muscle in his body was sluggish and heavy with weariness and he wanted nothing more than to crawl into his bunk in the allotment cabin and sleep for a few hours, but he had work to do, so he drove up to the allotment with the windows down and the cool morning air swirling through the cab, hoping that would be enough to keep him awake. It was a gorgeous summer morning, but the forecast was calling for afternoon thundershowers. Too bad he'd be in town with Heather at the hospital. It would be nice to curl up with her in the cabin, cozy and dry while the storm raged outside.

He turned off the scenic byway onto the dirt road to the cabin and yawned so hard his eyes watered.

As the cabin came into view around the bend in the road, Murph let out a warning growl. With the wavering sheen of yawn tears still distorting his vision, Jeremiah couldn't see what his dog did, so he swiped at his eyes. He stopped the truck in the middle of the road in front of the cabin and stared up at it.

"What the hell is *that?*"

Shifting the truck into neutral and setting the parking brake, he stepped outside with a command to Murphy to stay, unable to take his eyes from the grisly scene.

Propped precariously on the railing where it joined with the post closest to the steps was the severed head of a whitetail buck with antlers in full velvet. There was a bloodless bullet hole between its glassy, lifeless eyes.

Heart racing and senses heightened, he froze, listening for any sound out of place, but he heard nothing other than the breeze and birds chirping and the calls of the Lazy H cattle. Cautiously with his eyes scanning the cabin and the trees behind it, he reached into the truck and felt around until he found the release for the center console and slipped Heather's .38 pistol out of it. The weapon was cold and heavy and alien in his hand, but he chambered a shell and released the safety. With slow, measured steps, he climbed the stairs to the porch, glancing at the deer head as he passed it. The door was still locked—after his surprise visit from the man who called himself Greg Jones, he'd gotten into the habit of locking it even when he was out checking on the herd. He slipped the key out of his pocket and opened the door. Everything inside was exactly how he'd left it. Locking it again, he picked up the deer head by an antler on his way down the steps. With the small pool of half-dried blood on the boards beneath it and a modicum of warmth still in the soft velvet, it was a fresh kill, and he wasn't about to leave evidence behind while he went over to the Royal R to call the Hammonds and the FWP.

As he descended the steps, he spotted something he'd missed before—a bloody boot print. It was only a partial, but more than enough to guess that it had been made by a big foot. Like Greg Jones's.

Settling the deer head in the bed of Heather's truck, he opened the driver-side door to climb in, but Murphy bolted out of the cab and made a beeline for the steps to sniff the crime scene.

"Get out of that," he told his dog, who sniffed the blood with one paw lifted and his entire body tense.

Murphy let out a growl that turned into a whimper and glanced sharply to the woods behind the cabin. His hackles rose.

"Has our uninvited visitor come back?" Jeremiah asked the dog. "Is he still here?"

With the gun gripped tightly in his hands, he crept around the eastern side of the cabin. Unlike that morning in the rain, there were no clear tracks in the dry dirt to follow; everything had been trampled over. Then he heard a car door slam in the direction of the road just beyond the northern edge of the allotments, and he headed toward it, placing his feet carefully to avoid stepping on anything that would make enough noise to give him away.

Sure enough, there was a gunmetal gray four-wheel-drive pickup—a late 90s Dodge Ram—parked off to the side of the road… and there was Greg-slash-Randall with a headless deer carcass on his tailgate, filling the animal's chest cavity with ice.

Jeremiah crouched behind a boulder and commanded Murph to lie down beside him.

What the hell was he supposed to do?

He wasn't stupid enough to confront the guy alone, but he also couldn't let a poacher escape. If he could just get the license plate number… but not from this angle.

For the first time in his life he wished he had one of those obnoxious smartphones. Then he could take a video of the prick.

Murph growled.

Jeremiah glared at his dog, but it was too late. Murphy growled again, louder this time as he rose to his feet in a single, fluid motion. Jeremiah grabbed him by the collar, but the cascading ice and the rustling of the tarp the man was wrapping the deer in ceased.

"Who's there? You might want to get your ass out where I can see you, or I'll start shooting."

Shit.

Jeremiah stood slowly, Heather's pistol aimed square at the man's chest as he straightened. "Hello again, Greg."

The man jerked toward him and blinked as if he hadn't actually expected anyone to answer him. He'd been staring toward the cabin, but Jeremiah was almost ninety degrees over.

"Or is it Randall?"

His eyes flashed—confirming Jeremiah's suspicion that he was in fact Randall Cochran, and that Greg Jones was a fake name, probably thought up in the heat of the moment.

The poacher's rifle was still resting in the bed of the pickup, leaning against the side, and he glanced toward it.

"You don't want to do that, Randall."

"Easy there, Jerry."

"My name's Jeremiah. The only person still alive who calls me Jerry is my cousin. Zach Neely. You know him?"

The spark of recognition—a flicker of angst—was so quick he almost missed it, but the confused frown that replaced it was too obvious, too rehearsed to be real.

"I don't know any Zach Neely. And my name ain't Randall. That's my friend."

"Bullshit. I know you. I know your name is Randall Cochran."

"Sure you know me. You gave me a tow to that ranch over yonder a couple weeks ago. Remember?"

"No, I know you from before that. And you know me. You recognized me that day. Barely, but you did."

"You're outa your head, kid. I never met you before that day. Put the gun down, would you? I don't want any trouble."

"You should've thought about that before you poached a deer… and I'm guessing two Lazy H cows—a heifer and a calf earlier this summer."

"Now you're *really* talking nonsense. My family's ranched for generations. I ain't gonna shoot another man's cows. Just put the gun down. Please."

"Not a chance."

"So we're just going to stand here like this until… what? Hell freezes over?"

"Or until Sheriff Hammond gets here."

"Yeah? And when will that be?"

"Any time." If Randall could lie, so could he. He'd said he would stop down at the ranch before he headed back into town, and if he didn't, one of the Hammonds would likely notice his absence—they were considerate, caring people like that—and come looking for him. That could take hours, but Randall didn't need to know the details. "He said he'd be up shortly with groceries for me."

Randall twitched toward his truck, and another flood of adrenaline shot through Jeremiah like a thousand icy needles. He watched the man's every move, his senses heightened to the point that everything seemed to happen in slow motion. Randall spun toward his truck, ducking as he grabbed his rifle and ran for the passenger-side door and yanked it open. He stayed low as he crawled awkwardly into the driver's seat and started the engine. The tires spun as

Randall gunned the truck, spraying dirt and forest debris behind him. The deer carcass and the cooler the ice had been in tumbled out of the back and crashed onto the road.

Jeremiah stared at the license plate, but he couldn't get a good look at it; between the dust kicked up, the shadow of the tailgate, and the fishtailing of the truck as Randall raced away, all he could make out was the four denoting Missoula County and the first letter and number after it. Hopefully that would be enough.

When the Dodge was out of sight down the road, Jeremiah sank to his knees, braced his hands on them, and hunched over as the adrenaline subsided. His entire body shook, and he carefully flipped the pistol's safety back on so he didn't accidentally shoot himself. Murphy, who he now realized had been superglued to his leg throughout the exchange, pushed his way under his arm. Jeremiah hugged his dog.

After a moment, he sat back on his heels with his head tipped back and took several deep breaths.

What now?

He had to get over to the Royal R and call the sheriff's department and the Hammonds and Fish, Wildlife and Parks to report the poaching. But did he dare leave the evidence here for Randall to come back and pick up as soon as Jeremiah left the area to make his calls? Would the buck's head be enough proof of the poaching? Surely it had to be…. And what were the chances he'd be a suspect in the poaching, since he'd handled the head and it had left a blood trail on the cabin where he'd been living all summer? What was there to connect Randall to the kill other than Jeremiah's word he'd seen the man prepping the carcass to take it out of the mountains?

No, he had an alibi, and Heather and Christina and at least half a dozen nurses could verify that he'd been at the hospital in Devyn until this morning. Tracie could vouch for his whereabouts until twenty minutes ago.

Abruptly, he straightened.

He was overthinking it like he had the night sixteen years ago when Aaron had arrested him.

"Thinking like I'm the guilty one," he muttered. "And I am *not*. Not this time."

He pushed to his feet. "Come on, Murph. Let's go make some phone calls. And figure out where the hell I know our friend Randall from."

* * *

By the time Heather dropped him off at the Lazy H's main house at seven that night, Jeremiah could barely keep his eyes open, but he had to stay awake a little longer. Heather had headed home to her cabin for a shower, but she'd promised to return by eight to deliver the two casserole dishes of lasagna and enchiladas Tracie had prepared for Christina. That would give her plenty to eat without needing to cook for the next couple days until the rest of the Brown family returned from Curtis's fight, which was due to start in a couple hours. Christina was at home already, figuring there was no reason for her to stay in the hospital any longer. She and the baby were doing great with zero complications, and this wasn't, as Heather had put it, her first rodeo. Besides, Heather and Jeremiah couldn't exactly stay another night in the hospital with her, and she didn't want to be alone. He could hardly blame her for that.

Heather had volunteered to stay with her the next

couple nights, and somehow Jeremiah had been roped into staying over, too, despite his reservations. Her husband already didn't like him, and he was pretty sure staying in the man's house would only make Curtis want to punch him more than he probably already did. That was the last thing he needed right now.

"I think she just needs to be reminded of the good in men," Tracie had remarked when he'd asked her opinion on the matter. She'd given his shoulder a squeeze and reminded him, "And you're about as good as they come."

Sitting at the dining room table with his half-eaten dinner in front of him, he rubbed his hands over his face. It wasn't that he wasn't hungry. He was. He was just too tired to go through the motions of binging fork from plate to mouth. His eyes drifted closed....

"Why don't you go sit on the couch to wait for Aaron, honey?" Tracie said, sliding her hand across his back. "Since you're apparently not going to eat."

"If I sit on the couch, I'll fall asleep," he mumbled.

"And that's a problem because...?"

He had a reason, but at the moment he couldn't remember what it might be. Oh. Right. He was waiting up for Aaron. He hadn't heard a word about what else the sheriff and the FWP warden had found or if Randall had been caught. An APB had gone out on the truck and the man immediately. They'd taken his statement, and he'd walked Aaron and the warden through everything, and then he'd completed his herd check while they scouted for additional clues. They'd found the gut pile quickly just a tenth of a mile up the road where Jeremiah had encountered Randall. But that was as much as Jeremiah knew. Aaron had sent him into town as soon as the herd check was complete.

There were two small bright spots in the whole situation. Because Randall had nearly finished wrapping the deer carcass, the ice had stayed mostly inside and prevented the meat from spoiling, so it could be professionally processed and donated. At least it wouldn't go to waste. The other was Aaron's praise for how Jeremiah had handled the situation.

"You're stressing about this poacher," Tracie guessed.

He nodded.

"You did well, my boy." She laughed softly. "Scared the hell out of me to hear what happened, but you did well. This'll be the end of it. We won't have any more trouble this summer."

Jeremiah wished he could agree with her optimism, but he couldn't.

When she folded her arms around his shoulders and rested her cheek against his, he sighed, forgetting the constant, dull hum of dread for a moment. "Have I ever thanked you for everything you do for me? For treating me like part of your family."

"Every day. And you aren't 'like' part of my family, Jeremiah. You *are* my family. And I love you as my own son… because you are now. You have been since you first stepped onto this ranch. Someday I hope you'll finally believe that."

Releasing him, she took his plate and shooed him into the living room. He glanced at the clock on his way to the couch—it was a quarter to eight. Aaron should be home any minute, and Heather should be on her way back down from her cabin. He could stay awake that long at least. But the couch embraced him, promising blissful comfort. Maybe he could close his eyes, just for a minute....

"It's not that I don't believe him, Heather. But I have *nothing* connecting Randall Cochran to Zach. As far as I can tell, they've never met, and they don't share any associates. No friends, no family, no coworkers, no former employers. The only thing on Randall's record is a single DUI, so I doubt they met in prison or through some mutual inmate friend."

"I know there's nothing, but come on, Aaron. This feels exactly like JP all over again. Maybe not so obvious, but what kind of poacher puts a bullet between a prize buck's eyes and leaves his trophy behind? I'm telling you, it was a *threat*."

Jeremiah struggled to free himself from the heavy blanket of sleep, but the fear mixed in with the anger in Heather's voice was a line he could use to pull himself out.

"We don't know that," Aaron replied.

"No, we don't *know* it, but we all feel it. Please, *please* don't let it get to the point that one of us finds a body. Because you know in your gut it's Zach doing this—I know you do—and that body will be Jere's. Or yours."

"I can't arrest a man on a hunch, Heather. I need *proof*. Like I've told Jeremiah at least a dozen times."

Dragging his body upright—when had he slumped against the arm rest?—Jeremiah opened his eyes, and even though it took a moment for them to focus, he had no trouble picking up on their tense postures. Aaron stood with his arms folded across his chest, and Heather made sharp gestures with her hands as she spoke.

"This is Zach," he mumbled. "When I said his name, Randall knew it."

"He's swearing up and down he's never heard of Zach Neely," Aaron replied. "Didn't mean to wake you, Jere."

"S'all right. Didn't mean to doze off."

"Can't blame you." Aaron flashed him a sympathetic smile. "You've had a hell of a twenty-four hours."

He stretched his hands out in front of him to loosen the knotted muscles in his back, then looked up at Aaron who was still standing near the front entryway with Heather. "You caught Randall?"

"We did. One of my deputies picked him up over in the Big Hole, heading toward the pass on his way home to Missoula. He's sitting in one of our fine jail cells as we speak."

"Good. Any word on whether or not he shot the cows?"

"He swears he didn't, but both the heifer and the calf were shot with the same caliber bullet as the buck—thirty-aught-six. Common, so it's not much to go on yet, but I'm betting on a ballistic match. Your statement coupled with the blood on the back of his truck makes a pretty tight case against him on the poaching, but I'd like to link him to the cattle, too."

Finally, Heather walked into the living room with her arms folded and a deep frown pinching her usually beautiful features. When she sat beside him, she tucked her arms around him and rested her head on his shoulder. He liked it when she did that. She was a strong and stubbornly independent woman, and he appreciated that she felt she could lean on him both to offer support and to receive it.

Aaron came over, too, perching in Tracie's recliner, leaning forward with his forearms braced on his knees and his hands folded lightly in front of him. Those blue Hammond eyes searched Jeremiah's, and once upon a time, that steady gaze would've made him shudder. Now they were a source of security and love. Fate was a funny thing.

"You think I'm crazy," he said quietly.

"I promise you I don't. But on the surface, it looks exactly like Randall acted alone."

"Of course it does. Zach isn't stupid." Jeremiah ran his hand back through his hair and met Aaron's gaze again. "You only caught him because I couldn't keep my shit together. No offense."

"Believe me. I know that."

"He didn't tell me hardly anything about his operation, so I always thought…. But he trusted me with the most damning piece of information—that it was all his—because I was his blood." Tipping his head back and sinking into the couch, Jeremiah snorted. "Family sticks together, no matter what. That's what he told me when he offered to bring me in to his operation. I never understood until just now that he actually believed that."

Aaron sighed. "I know you think this is Zach, and I want to believe you. Hell, my own gut says he is—yes, Heather, you're right—but I just don't see how it's possible. You gotta help me out here, Jere. How do *you* know Randall? Because that's all I've got right now."

Jeremiah's shoulders slumped. "I don't remember. But I *know* I've seen him somewhere."

"Well, when you figure it out, let me know. Until

then...."

"Life goes on as if I don't have a homicidal cousin breathing down my neck," Jeremiah muttered.

"Don't be like that."

"Sorry. It's been a long day after a long night, and I'm cranky."

Aaron let out a huff of laughter. "I guess you'd better get the man home to bed, Heather."

"I'm betting a hot shower would feel better first," she replied.

Jeremiah let out a groan at the thought of hot water pouring over him, washing away the day's toils.

"Yeah, I know." She bumped her shoulder against his. "Mine felt so good I might be tempted to join you. Come on, old man."

"I beg your pardon?"

"Well, you *are* closing on thirty-five."

"Thirty-four, youngster. I won't be thirty-five until *next* September, thank you very much."

Aaron chuckled a little louder this time. "Get a room, lovebirds. And while you're at it, Mom's got the casserole and enchiladas ready to go over to Christina. Give her our love will you, Heather?"

"Absolutely."

"And, Jere?"

"Hmm?" Jeremiah asked, rising slowly to his feet.

"I'm glad Christina asked you and Heather to stay over with her tonight. I may not be able to prove there's anything to worry about, but I think we ought to reassess you staying by yourself in the allotment cabin."

Jeremiah nodded in acknowledgement and turned to

help Heather to her feet but she was already standing beside him. Aaron embraced him, gripping his shoulder for a moment before he turned away and headed into the kitchen to fetch the dishes Tracie was sending over to Christina.

Think, Jeremiah, he snarled at himself. *Remember! How do you know Randall?*

* * *

"Dammit, Christina, would you go sit down? I am perfectly capable of getting linens for Jeremiah and me. Eat some of Tracie's enchiladas and relax, all right?"

"I just… need to do something."

Her friend eyed her, annoyed. For a woman who had given birth not quite twenty-four hours ago, Christina had a peculiar energy—like she couldn't sit still—and Heather wondered if she shouldn't just let her friend wait on her to burn some of it off. God knew *she* didn't have much energy. Her shower and a fresh set of clothes had revived her some, but her chat with Aaron had depleted that significantly.

"Fine. I'm going to go take a shower with Jeremiah while you do whatever it is you need to do."

"I'll lay fresh towels on the bed for you."

Heather nodded and strode down the hall to the spare bedroom at the end of it. She found Jeremiah sitting on the edge of the primly made queen bed. He was awake but barely, and he looked utterly exhausted except for the glimmer of a smile playing about his lips.

"What are you smiling about?" she asked, stripping out of her tank top.

"Just listening to you and Christina. She's as stubborn as you are, and it's easy to see why you're such good friends."

"Damn her," she muttered fondly. "We're here to help her not to make more work for her. We do *not* need her to play gracious hostess. Anyhow, how about that shower?"

"Mmm. Shower."

"Come on, sleepyhead. Shower, then bed. Maybe a little somethin'-something' in between."

"I would love to take you up on that, but I just don't have the energy, baby girl."

Heather tilted her head to the side and the corner of her mouth twitched into a faint smile. "Baby girl?"

"That's what you get for calling me old man. But I won't use it again if you don't like it."

"No… I do, actually. I like it a lot. It's what Morgan says to Garcia on Criminal Minds, and I always liked the way he said it… and the way you said it. Like you adore me and want to keep me safe."

"I don't know if I'll ever deserve you, but I *do* adore you, and I *do* want to keep you safe."

She chewed on her lip. "You adore me?"

"Mmm-hmm."

"I don't think any man has ever said that to me. I've gotten the *I love yous* and the *you're beautifuls* but I don't remember the word *adore* ever coming up. It's…. I like it."

"In that case, let me say it again. I adore you."

She took his hands and pulled him up. It took more effort than she liked for him to stand, and when she hooked her arms around his neck, he leaned into her. It wasn't the physical strain of the day that had so thoroughly worn him down, she knew; he worked far harder on a regular basis than he had today. And it wasn't the lack of sleep, either.

This past day and night had been an emotional roller coaster for her and she'd had only her head-spinning conversation with Christina and the birth of her newest nephew to contend with, so she could only imagine what he was going through with that on top of this thing with his cousin. Or what looked to him like his cousin. That in itself was another layer of stress.

A deer head with a bullet between the eyes....

Jeremiah hitting that deer sixteen years ago was the event that had brought Zach's entire empire crashing down.

How could Aaron not see that it was a threat? It was plain as day to her.

Because she had no answers for him, she kissed him, and the way their bodies seemed to melt together stole her breath. He might be ready to drop, but maybe he *would* be able to summon the energy to make love to her. The anticipation ignited a fire in the core of her being, and she tightened her arms around him and arched her body against his, asking for more. When she tugged his T-shirt loose from his jeans, he let her pull it over his head.

Atta boy.

Releasing him, she unhooked her bra and shimmied out of her jean shorts before turning her attention to his belt. With that out of the way, she slid his jeans down his legs and then his boxers and finally let her panties fall to the floor.

"Come on, lover," she whispered huskily. "Let's steam up the bathroom."

He laughed softly and followed her into the three-quarter bath attached to the guest room. She turned on the water and adjusted the temperature, then shoved him into the shower. They let out echoing groans as the hot water slid over them, and she grinned, claiming his mouth with blatant demand.

With shocking intensity, he responded in kind, digging his fingers into her hips and hoisting her off the ground. She gasped as he pinned her against the cold tile wall and went after her neck, alternately kissing her and raking his teeth over her skin. She sank her fingers into the meat of his back and curled her other hand around a fistful of his hair, staking her claim on him.

Then it was his turn to claim her.

He thrust into her, and she let out a gasp. The hesitation she'd noted the first time they'd made love in the allotment cabin was long gone, and the confidence and attentiveness to her unspoken demands was thrilling. Waves of pleasure coursed through her as her body begged for more and more. She couldn't get enough of him and of the way he seemed to know exactly what she wanted even before she did.

Good lord, the way he made love….

He might not be as experienced as some of the men she'd dated, but he did something for her that none of them had. He didn't just make love to her body—he made love to her heart.

Let me say it again. I adore you.

As the orgasm rocked through her, a thought hit her brain with such splendid force that she nearly cried out.

She believed him. And it was the most powerful thing she'd ever felt.

In the afterglow as steam filled the shower stall and the water continued to stream over them, she had an answer to the question that had arisen this morning. She didn't need to be terrified that she would be willing to have a kid or two if he wanted them. She had finally found a man who gave her the support and sense of security she craved, and that was an incredible thing.

"I adore you, too," she whispered.

The smile he gave in answer was beautiful.

With the water turning cool, she helped him scrub down, careful to keep her hands mostly to herself because she doubted he'd be up for a second round. She wasn't, and she hadn't even done the brunt of the work.

As promised, Christina had left clean towels on the bed for them, and Heather's face heated even though she was pretty sure her friend had expected a little fun time in the shower. At least they'd been quiet and not *too* obvious.

She dried off quickly, slipped into her PJ boxer shorts and a tank top. Pressing a quick kiss to Jeremiah's cheek, she stepped out of their room to bid Christina goodnight and make her friend promise to call on them if she needed anything. That odd surge of energy seemed to have spent itself, and she found Christina not-quite-asleep in one of the recliners in the living room.

"Go to bed, woman," Heather whispered so as not to wake the newborn sleeping in her friend's arms.

"Not quite ready yet," Christina mumbled.

"Bullshit. And if you're going to be a stubborn snot and stay up, I'm going to have to stay up with you. And I am *so* tired."

Christina regarded her with a flat but amused expression. "That's a cheap shot."

"Yeah, but it's going to work, isn't it."

Yawning, Christina laughed. "Yeah, it is. Good night, sweetie. Thank you for everything last night and today. If I hadn't had you and Jeremiah there with me…."

Heather leaned down and hugged her friend. "I'm glad we were there, too. G'night, Chris."

She lingered in the living room until Christina rose from the recliner and headed off to her bedroom, turning off lights as she went. Certain her friend was just as tired as she and Jeremiah were—more so, probably, even if she wouldn't admit it—she returned to the spare bedroom.

Jeremiah was in bed, lying on his stomach, and for a moment, she thought he was asleep already, but then he lifted his head and smiled tiredly over his shoulder at her.

She didn't like the shadows in his eyes, and she didn't have to ask why they were there. Flipping the light in the bathroom off and plunging them into darkness, she crawled onto the bed and slid between the cool sheets, gravitating toward the heat of his body despite the warm evening.

"Thinking about Zach again?"

She couldn't see it, but she felt him nod. Idly, she skimmed her fingers over his back. "What can I do? How can I help you?"

He rolled onto his side and pulled her into his arms, then let out a ragged breath. "Tell me I'm not crazy. Tell me this isn't all just in my head."

She didn't immediately answer, replaying her conversation with Aaron before they'd woken Jeremiah and what he'd said after. There was so much about this whole situation that reminded her of JP. She hadn't even been close to the center of that insanity, but even all these years removed, she had no trouble recalling how he'd toyed with

Luke and June. Jeremiah hadn't received threatening letters or chilling phone calls, but Zach wasn't a single-minded madman. He was a skilled and cunning criminal mastermind, and he wouldn't leave a trail like that.

Propping herself up on her elbow, she gazed down at him, and as her eyes adjusted to the dark, she could make out the outlines of his face. He was frowning, as she'd expected, so she kissed him lightly, brushing her fingertips along his jaw and over his brow.

"I can't see how all this is connected to Zach any more than Aaron can… but I don't think it's all in your head," she said slowly. "And that scares me."

Eleven

"THAT WAS A GREAT SESSION today, Jess. That last run was flawless. You and Cisco are going to take home the blue together at your next rodeo."

Heather turned Rain loose in the pasture with Jessie's gelding and Jinx and pulled the girl against her side in a one-armed hug.

"Thanks, Heather. I should've asked Dad and Grandma to beg you to coach me from the start. Ugh. Jen just… doesn't know how to teach me, I guess. She's a great barrel racer, but yeah. Something just didn't click."

"I may have one up on her from my job. Training horses is as much training the riders as the horse, you know, and if I wasn't as good at that part of the job as the rest of it…. Well, Ty wouldn't have made me his partner."

"I get that. I really do."

"All right, kiddo. I need to drag Jeremiah out of the

shop so we aren't late for dinner with my family, and you need to head home for dinner, too. I'll see you in a few days."

"Yep. Bye, Heather."

"See ya."

Heather watched the girl walk across the yard to the main house before picking up her tack and hauling it into the barn. She needed to thank the Hammonds again for letting her board her horses here. It was so nice to be able to just show up and have her horse already here and not have to endure her family or argue with them about why she needed *her* horse for *her* job when they decided to take her horse without asking.

With her lesson over for the day and everything picked up and stowed, she headed for the shop. In the week since Randall Cochran's arrest, everything had been quiet, and other than the first couple nights, when Jeremiah had stayed with her at Curtis and Christina's until the Brown clan had returned from Curtis's embarrassing final fight, he had continued his stay in the allotment cabin. She didn't like that, but he was adamant about staying up there, certain more trouble was on its way. Of course, that same gut certainty that this—whatever it was—wasn't over was exactly why she didn't want him staying up there alone, but at least he had spent most of his free time down here in the valley working on another portable office. And at least Austin or one of the others checked on him regularly when he was up at the allotment.

As usual, when she walked into the shop, he was so focused screwing the metal roofing sheets in place that he didn't mark her arrival. Murph did, though, and as soon as she stepped through the shop's man door, the Australian shepherd scrambled out from under the trailer and raced over to greet her. The days of his shy hesitation were *long* gone, and she was all too happy to reward his trust with a full-body rub down.

"I hate to interrupt because you look like you're in the zone up there," she called up to Jeremiah, "but we're already cutting it close."

He glanced up and smiled. "Oh, hey. Is it that time already?"

"Yeah," she sighed, "it's that time. Let's get this over with, shall we?"

"We don't have to do this, you know."

"I know, but Mom invited you to dinner so she and everyone can get to know you. Christina's been singing your praises since they got home, and I think they're finally getting the message you're not just a fling. So maybe it'll be okay."

"In other words, you feel obligated to go."

"That, too."

He drove the last screw in on the piece of metal roofing he was installing, and then he sat up there, straddling the peak of the roof in a way that couldn't be remotely comfortable, for almost a minute with his brows drawn deeply together.

"What's wrong?"

"I don't know if it's a good idea to go tonight."

"Why not? We've been planning this for five days."

"I know, it's just... Randall's still swearing he didn't kill the cows, and Aaron believes him, and he's certain Randall knows who did and is protecting whoever it is, but—"

"He's protecting Zach, you mean."

Jeremiah pressed his mouth into a flat line. "Yes."

"Has the ballistics test come back yet?"

"No. There's still a backlog and dead cows aren't a priority, so they probably won't be able to get to it for a couple more weeks."

"That's not what's bugging you," she surmised.

He shook his head. "Why hasn't Zach done anything? What's he waiting for?"

"Maybe he's waiting to see if Randall is going to squeal. If he doesn't… Zach is safe. Right? There's nothing else connecting him to any of this."

There was another option, but she didn't say it because she didn't believe it and neither did Jeremiah.

Maybe Zach really isn't *behind it all. Maybe this really was no more than a ridiculous coincidence.*

"Come on. Dinner with my family is sure to distract you."

He snorted. "While that's probably true, if they say something nasty to you, I don't know if I'll be able to keep a handle on myself."

"Maybe that's exactly what my family needs—a good old-fashioned, harsh judgment from the guy who spent time behind bars." She laughed. "Think about it, Jere. They see you as this big-time criminal, and if you have a better sense of common courtesy than they do, maybe they'll see that, hey, they really are assholes."

"I doubt it. They'll probably just think I'm an even bigger one for daring to judge them."

"You're probably right. But come on. Let's just get it

over with, and if they create drama, we'll leave and come back here and work on your office."

Grudgingly, he gave in, and she suspected hunger had more to do with it than her assurances. She didn't like the strain on his face, so she slipped her arms around him when he walked past her to put his drill away.

"Hey," she murmured. "It'll be okay. One way or another."

Nodding, he let her go, and she stepped in to help him clean up. The idea of hiding out in the shop with him and working on his latest office was certainly far more appealing than dinner with her family, but she couldn't ignore her curiosity. Christina's support of her relationship with Jeremiah was a new figure in the equation, and Curtis may have turned into a self-centered jackass in the last six years who didn't do nearly enough to help his wife, but he loved her, and Heather hoped he would listen to her.

Jeremiah asked to stop by the bunkhouse so he could at least change and wash his face, and she was tempted to decline. So what if he had a little grime on his face? It would do her family well to be reminded that he routinely worked his ass off.

"Mom'll care more if we're late than if you're a little dirty," Heather retorted.

"I don't care. I've gotta drop Murph off and feed him, anyhow. It'll take me two minutes."

"Fine."

She volunteered to feed Murphy while he changed and washed his face, and as it turned out, it took him *exactly* two minutes. Since the plan was to come back to the shop after dinner to work together on his office, they left his truck parked in front of the bunkhouse and took hers.

When she pulled up in front of her parents' house, she opened her door to get out but hesitated when he didn't move to do the same. He drummed his thumbs on his thighs and stared through the windshield, clearly agitated. She wished she knew if he was still dwelling on his own troubles or if he was nervous about spending more than a handful of minutes with her entire family. Both, most likely.

"You all right?" she asked.

He nodded, but it was a lie.

"If it's bugging you that much, I'll go in and tell Mom we need to reschedule."

"No, we're here now."

Finally, he shoved his door open and climbed out of her truck. He waited for her to join him before heading for the front door of her parents' house. As she'd expected, since they were a few minutes late, everyone was already gathered around the dining room table except her mother, Brianna and Brock's wife, Anna, who were in the kitchen putting the finishing touches on dinner. All the kids were still playing out in the yard except, of course, for Curtis and Christina's newborn baby boy, who was asleep in his mother's arms. Christina had given him the name of Jeremiah's brother—Joseph—both as an act of rebellion and as a way of marking her gratitude, but only Heather and Jeremiah knew that. Curtis and the rest of the Brown family would flip their lids if they knew.

Her brothers and father greeted Jeremiah with cool politeness, but Christina welcomed him warmly with a hug that irritated her husband. Heather held her eldest brother's gaze, silently daring him to say something. He didn't take the bait, and when she let her eyes drift over the rest of his face, she grimaced. The cuts on his cheek and through his eyebrow, the black eye, and the split lip from his fight were healing well, but they were still blatant reminders of just how thoroughly he'd lost. She'd heard, of course, that the fight had been embarrassingly one-sided and that the ref had stopped it barely halfway through, but the sight of his face when he and the rest of the family had returned home on Sunday had shocked her. It still did.

"Oh, Jeremiah, welcome," Lily greeted as she brought in a large platter of baked chicken. "Thank you for coming."

"Thank you for the invitation."

If his words were a tad clipped and his smile a little forced, no one but Heather noticed.

"We wanted a chance to thank you for assisting Christina while we were away."

"It was my pleasure, Mrs. Brown. I'm glad Heather and I were here to help."

Without being asked if the women needed assistance, Jeremiah followed them into the kitchen and started carrying out dishes. Heather's lip curled at the incongruous mixture of surprise and disdain on her mother's face, but she hid it by jumping in to help, too.

The kids were called in, Joseph was transferred to the swing, and with the entire family seated at the table, Brian said grace. After that, the clatter of ten adults and six children digging in filled the room. Talk at the table revolved mostly around Curtis's fight, the new baby, and the ranch, and as the meal dragged on, Heather's annoyance grew. Aside from the occasional question for Jeremiah about how the Hammonds ran things on the Lazy H, they more or less *ignored* him, and while he seemed perfectly happy with that, she wondered how her family expected to get to know him better if they didn't bother to ask him anything about himself.

After everyone finished eating, Heather got up to help Anna and Lily clear the remnants away and prepare dessert—cake and ice cream to celebrate Joseph's arrival.

"Jeremiah seems very nice," Anna remarked as she sliced the cake.

"Yes, very polite," Lily echoed. "But nice and polite only go so far in a relationship."

The comment instantly set Heather on edge. "What's that supposed to mean?"

"Well, I just don't see this lasting, my darling."

"Do tell why it won't, Mother."

"Don't get snippy with me. I'm just saying that he's a ranch hand, and it's hard work for not a lot of money. How would he support you if he got hurt? Which happens often. There's a reason there aren't too many old ranch hands."

"He doesn't have to support me, and I don't expect him to. I have a good job, and if something happened that he couldn't work, I make more than enough to support us both."

"And I'm sure that seems like a wonderful notion to you, but he'll resent you. Men need to feel like men, to provide for their families. How will he feel when he can't support you and your children?"

"What *children*? How many times do I have to tell you I don't want any before you get it through your head? Jesus, Mother. You seriously need to update your worldviews."

Lily let out an exaggerated sigh and started scooping ice cream onto plates with the slices of cake. "I had hoped being present for the birth of your nephew would change your mind, make you see sense."

"Make me see sense…."

She had no response to that one. All she could do was stare dumbly at her mother.

"Look at how happy Christina and Curtis are to have little Joseph. Don't you want that for yourself?"

Happy. Right. Christina was so happy that she called Curtis every foul name I've ever heard and invented some new ones.

And Curtis? He barely seemed to notice his new son. The joyous novelty of babies that had radiated from him after Sebastian's birth had long ago faded, and a new baby wasn't anything special. Been there, done that.

"What do you think, Jeremiah? Would you be happy with a woman who refused to give you children?"

Heather glanced toward the door between the kitchen and dining room, and saw Jeremiah freeze mid step with a wide-eyed, deer-in-the-headlights expression. He recovered quickly, though.

"To be completely honest, I haven't thought about it much. I'm alive and I have a good job and a beautiful woman I adore, so I already have more than I ever thought I would. If that's all life has in store for me, it's more than enough."

"So you don't want children?"

He shrugged. "If Heather wanted one or two, I'd be all right with that, but I don't think she does, and that's fine, too. I'm sure of one thing, though—your daughter knows her own mind, and trying to force her into your notion of womanhood is a waste of time. Besides, she's an amazing woman just the way she is, and I wouldn't change anything about her."

Heather almost cheered when he spun on his heel and marched out of the kitchen without giving her mother a chance to retort. Lily's beached-fish impersonation was comical, as were Anna's downcast eyes and the blush of embarrassment blossoming across her pretty face.

"What can I say?" she said with a shrug. "The man gets me."

"Don't be so sure of that," Lily said. "He says that now, but he'll change his mind."

Maybe, but she doubted it. Being happy with what he had came too naturally to Jeremiah. Saying he would be content if what he had now was all he would ever have wasn't just lip service. It was who he was.

And, oh, the relief of that statement! She might've accepted that she would be willing to have a kid or two if he wanted them, but to know that it wasn't some burning desire for him, either, and that he would put her desires first....

No one had *ever* done that. Not to the extent he did.

It was a heady thing to realize, and it left her a little dizzy.

Taking a few plates, she wandered into the dining room and passed them out. She knew she should go back into the kitchen and help her mother and Anna bring out the rest, but she couldn't bring herself to do it and instead sank into her chair beside Jeremiah. Absently, he stroked his hand across her back as he answered Christina's questions about the office he was building. Heather listened passively, but her mind was stuck on the conversation in the kitchen. Wow.

The melodic clinging of a fork against glass snapped her out of her thoughts, and she glanced up to see Todd standing beside Brianna… and looking far too pleased with himself. Heather shifted her gaze to her sister and noted the matching smugness on Brianna's face. The delightful, tingling relief fizzled, and a vague premonition of what was coming dragged her back down to earth.

"Since everyone is gathered together tonight—" Todd began.

Not exactly a rarity, Heather mused.

"—we thought it would be a good time to announce…."

He glanced so obviously at his wife that Heather couldn't help but roll her eyes.

"We're expecting!" Brianna finished.

Jubilant congratulations were offered, but Heather didn't join in. Neither did Jeremiah, and when she looked at him, his attention was on Christina. Following his gaze to her friend, she was shocked to see Christina regarding Todd and Brianna with unveiled shock and indignation.

Suddenly, anger flared, red hot. What was the point of Brianna and Todd announcing that *tonight* when the family had gathered to celebrate Joseph's birth and to get to know Jeremiah? Was it to point out in a new and more insidious way how Heather was failing their family? Or was it Brianna's way of jealously stealing the spotlight from Christina?

Heather glared at her sister, who was positively wallowing in the attention. *Yeah, that's it, isn't it? Little bitch.*

Some days, she really hated her family.

"Are you and Christina still planning to have another baby after Joseph?" she heard Lily ask Curtis.

"Yes, but I don't think I want to wait so long this time because I think we might like to have another after that," Curtis replied. "I think I'd like to start trying again this fall, even."

Christina slammed her glass down on the table, sloshing water all over.

Absolute silence reigned over the table. Every pair of eyes was trained on Curtis's wife. No doubt everyone was shocked that the outburst had come from her and not Heather. Christina didn't have outbursts. She was quiet and polite at all times even when she—apparently, judging by what she'd revealed to Heather last week—wanted to scream.

"I *beg* your pardon?" she snarled. "I gave birth *a week ago* and you're already talking about getting me pregnant *again*?" She lunged to her feet. "Go to hell."

"Babe, why are you upset? I thought we agreed—"

"No, *you've* talked about this, Curtis, and *you* decided by yourself that we're going to have more kids. But guess what. We aren't. Because I am done."

"Babe—"

"*No*. I… am… *done*. No more. I didn't want three kids. I definitely don't want four, and I sure as *hell* don't want *five*. I am sick and tired of having my life dictated to me, of having almost no help from you in raising the children we already have." She walked to the front door and grabbed her purse off the coat hook. Turning back to her husband, she spat, "You want more kids, find yourself a new wife."

Christina slammed the door behind her.

For almost a minute, everyone was too shocked to speak. Curtis stared blankly at his wife's empty chair. Heather slid her hand under the table, seeking Jeremiah's hand, and twined her fingers with his. He turned his face to her and forced a smile.

"This is your fault," Lily said coldly. "Somehow, I know it is."

It took Heather a moment to comprehend that her mother was talking to her. "Excuse me? How is this *my* fault?"

Heather opened her mouth to further defend herself, to repeat every heartbreaking and infuriating word Christina had said to her before she'd gone into labor, but she didn't get the chance.

"Stop," Jeremiah said in a low voice that demanded obedience. The muscle in his jaw twitched, and the battle to maintain a grip on his temper raged brightly in his eyes. "You will not speak that way to Heather in front of me."

"I appreciate you wanting to defend Heather, but she is *my* daughter, and—"

"Yes, she *is* your daughter. And I shouldn't *have* to defend her. Or Christina."

"Leave my wife out of this," Curtis said. "She is none of your concern."

"Actually, she is. You want to know why? Because I was right here in this house when she went into labor with her husband hundreds of miles away."

Curtis leaned forward in his chair. "Who do you think you are to—"

Jeremiah stood abruptly, almost knocking his chair over in his haste, and braced his hands on the table. Anger vibrated from him, and even a blind man wouldn't miss his struggle to keep a grip on his temper. He was the smallest man at the table, but the others all leaned back.

"I'm the man who stepped up when you were too busy getting your face pulverized. I'm the man who carried *your* wife out to Heather's truck because the contraction was so bad she couldn't walk and we didn't have time to wait it out. I'm the man who drove her to the hospital where I held her hand and listened to her cry and curse your name."

"You had no right to be there with my wife."

Heather started to rebut that, but again, Jeremiah beat her to it.

"You're right. It's not my job to comfort *your* wife— that's *your* job. *My* job is to make sure Heather has what she needs, and what she needed that night was for me to be there for her friend. Your wife is hurting and exhausted, and you can't be bothered to see it and to listen to her. You'll lose her if you don't start… and you'll deserve to." Jeremiah straightened, pulling his head back with a condescending sneer that was entirely incongruous with the kind, tolerant man Heather knew, and turned to Brock. "I suppose I shouldn't be surprised. A family who says it's better they hurt their own than let someone else hurt them is seriously screwed up."

He bent to kiss Heather's cheek, and the raw fury radiating from him made her shiver.

"I'm sorry, baby girl, but I have to go. I can't handle this right now."

She nodded but couldn't find her voice to tell him

she was right behind him.

"Mrs. Brown, thank you for dinner—it was excellent. I wish I could say the same for the company."

He started for the door, but Brock sprang out of his chair to intercept him.

"Brock, don't do it," Curtis warned. "Just let him go."

"No. I'm not going to let this piece of shit disrespect my family."

"Your family disrespects itself," Jeremiah snapped.

He brushed Brock off the first time, but when Brock grabbed his shoulder again, harder, and yanked him around, he landed a lightning-fast punch to Brock's cheek, and her brother crumpled to the floor, half-dazed. Jeremiah didn't wait for anyone else to react, and before anyone realized what had just happened, he was out the door and gone.

Again, stunned silence claimed the room. The explosion of self-righteous anger Heather expected didn't materialize. Instead, Brian laughed.

"The boy can hit, I'll give him that. Maybe next time you won't be in such a rush to pick a fight with him, eh, Brock?

Her brother cursed under his breath as he rose clumsily from the floor and returned to his chair.

"Rung your bell a bit, didn't he. You see, Curtis, if you'd landed a few punches like that, you wouldn't have lost your match."

"You're *laughing* about this, Brian?" Lily gasped. "He assaulted your son!"

"The man defended himself, Lily. I may not like him, but I can respect that."

"I cannot believe you, Brian Brown. He—"

"Oh, shut up, Mother!" Heather snapped. "Maybe if you shut your mouth for one damned minute and actually listened to understand instead of listening to lecture, you might see that he is absolutely right. This family is fucked up, and if Christina decides to divorce Curtis's self-centered, worthless ass, I'll help her do it. Good night."

She didn't give her mother or any of the others a chance to respond. She followed Jeremiah out into the cool, damp evening, slamming the door behind her with a satisfying crack. Typical Brown family dinner—it wasn't a success unless someone left angry or crying. But at least this time, they'd all heard something they need to hear, and not only from her this time.

* * *

The walk back to the shop from the Browns' house did little to cool Jeremiah's temper, and it took every shred of willpower he possessed to resist yanking open the door and hurling it closed behind him. He sat heavily on the back end of the trailer in the doorway, and for several minutes, he stared blankly at the tool bench, conscious only of each aching throb of his hand that perfectly matched the rhythm of the anger pulsing through him.

He let out a wordless bellow, then curled over his knees with his arms wrapped tightly around his head because that seemed to be the only way to hold himself together. His body trembled with the flashfire wrath triggered by Heather's mother's insensitive remark, and no matter how he tried to subvert it, it raged on.

What he'd said needed to be said, but he shouldn't have lost his temper like that. He shouldn't have hit Brock, and he sure as hell shouldn't have walked out and left

Heather to fend off her family's cruelty alone. But if he hadn't left when he had, he was certain it would've been far worse.

He didn't imagine he'd be getting any more invitations to dinner at the Browns' house, and that was fine by him, but he hated that he'd put Heather in the middle of it all. She already had enough problems of her own with them, and the last thing she needed was him creating more.

He was still curled into that tight ball when the man door of the shop opened. He didn't have to look up to know it was Heather; he sensed her presence as clearly as he might the warmth of the sun beaming down on him.

"Hey," she said softly as she joined him.

She squeezed herself in between him and the doorframe, nudging him over to make room for herself without a hint of politeness. At any other time, he might've laughed.

"Are you okay?"

He shook his head. No point in trying to lie because it was glaringly obvious that he was *not* remotely okay.

"Yeah, I didn't think so."

"I'm sorry."

"For what? Saying what they needed to hear or for hitting my brother? Because you shouldn't be sorry for either. Dad was impressed by that punch."

She certainly meant that to cheer him up, but it just made him feel even worse. He shouldn't have lost control like that.

Anger slipped into bleak despair, and he massaged his hand again and flexed his fingers. He couldn't recall his hand being this sore after he'd punched Aaron all those years ago. Of course, he wasn't a numb and dumb kid anymore, and maybe thirty-three wasn't exactly *old*, but it was old enough to feel the aches and pains more. Plus, he knew *how* to hit hard now thanks to Henry's determined lessons.

Heather tucked her arms around him, but he couldn't reciprocate her affection. "This isn't you, so stop thinking it is. Everyone has a shorter fuse when they're stressed, and as far as that goes, you kept a pretty tight rein on yourself."

"Sure doesn't feel like it."

"No, but it definitely *looked* like it. You walked away. So… thank you."

He finally uncurled his arms from around his head and winced at the ache in his neck. Hesitantly, he turned his head toward Heather, afraid despite her words that he'd see condemnation in her eyes. "Thank me? For *what*? I ruined dinner with your family and I punched your brother. Is he all right?"

"He's fine. He'll probably have a pretty bruise on his cheek to match Curtis's, but dammit, Jere, you didn't ruin dinner. Mom and Curtis did that." She let out a breath. "Poor Christina."

"Is she all right? I assume you stopped by your place to check on her before you came here. At least, I hope you did."

"I did. She was still fuming. For the time being, at least."

"You should probably go over there and be with her."

"Ainsley's over there right now, and they both understand that I need to be here with you for a few minutes to make sure *you* are okay."

Dragging his hands over his face, he sat up a little straighter. He wasn't okay, and he wasn't going to be until whatever game Zach was playing was over, but at least he didn't feel like he was going to explode anymore. That was something.

Heather rested her head on his shoulder, and he tipped his head against hers and sighed. They sat like that for a long time, without saying a word, and gradually, the simple pleasure of being near her lessened his turbulent emotions until he was almost calm again.

"Better?" she asked.

When he nodded, it was the truth. He even managed a smile for her, and she answered with one of her own.

"There's my Jeremiah."

"Your Jeremiah?"

"Mmm-hmm. Mine."

She was quiet for a while again, and then she sat up. "Where's Murph?"

"Still at the bunkhouse. I didn't want to scare him."

"Ah, Jere…. Don't let my family do this to you."

"It's not just them. It's not even *mostly* them—they were just the trigger that set off the bomb."

"Don't let Zach do this to you, either. Don't let *anyone* do this to you. And, yes, I am fully aware of how much easier it is to say that than it is to do it. I have the scar on my wrist to prove that, remember? Which brings me back to… thank you. For standing up to my family for Christina and me. I told her what you said on her behalf, and she wanted me to tell you it means a lot to her. And you're right. It's not right that we needed defending, and I'm sorry it had to be you, but we both appreciate it."

He nodded, suddenly too tired to form the words to respond. After another minute passed in silence, he found enough energy to speak. "I don't like losing my temper. That's not who I am anymore."

"I know it isn't, and to quote Aaron, I don't think it was ever who you are. And maybe one of these days, if we tell you that enough, you'll finally believe it."

"I doubt it."

"Okay, you gotta pull yourself out of this. I can only do this whole sweet and considerate girlfriend thing for so long before the self-pity gets on my nerves."

He couldn't help but laugh at that. "Thanks."

"You're welcome. I—"

A knock on the man door of the shop interrupted whatever Heather was going to add, and Jeremiah looked toward it with a frown. Who would be knocking? Austin and the Hammonds wouldn't bother—they'd come right in. Maybe it was Christina and Ainsley coming to fetch Heather back to her cabin for a best friends' conference.

"Who…?" Heather asked.

Their question was answered half a second later when the door opened a fraction and Curtis poked his head inside.

"Ah," he said. "You *are* here, Heather. Christina said you were, but, uh…."

"What do you want, Curtis?" Heather asked flatly.

Her brother slipped inside the shop and closed the door behind himself, his expression reminding Jeremiah of his dog's when he'd first adopted him.

"I need the key to your cabin," Curtis said gently, eying his sister like he expected her to rip his head off if he spoke any louder.

Speaking of beaten dogs….

"Christina locked the door and won't let me in," Curtis added.

"I thought you said she told you I was here."

"She screamed it through the door."

"Yeah… I'm not going to help you. You just want a quick resolution so you don't have to deal with a brand new baby by yourself tonight."

The man ducked his head sheepishly, and Heather folded her arms across her chest and scowled at her brother.

"Here's what's going to happen, Curtis. You're going to go home and take care of your kids and give your wife a night to stew and cool off. And while you're doing that, you're going to think long and hard about how much you love her and don't want to lose her. Then you're going to come up with at least two dozen ideas for how you can show her. Making dinner and doing the dishes for her tomorrow night would be a great start. There you go. I gave you one idea. That leaves you with only twenty-three more to come up with."

"You'd really help her divorce me?" Curtis asked uncertainly.

"You bet your ass I would. So I suggest you man up and become the partner you promised her you would be."

Jeremiah glanced between brother and sister, and pride for Heather swelled in his heart, chasing away his dark thoughts. She was an incredible woman, and he hoped he'd get the chance to spend the rest of his life making sure she knew it.

To his surprise, Curtis nodded and opened the door

again.

Heather cleared her throat. "Forgetting something?"

She glanced pointedly between her brother and Jeremiah.

"Heather…" Jeremiah started.

"No," she said. "You stepped up, and he needs to acknowledge that. This is another way he can show his wife he's willing to fight to keep her, which leaves him with twenty-two more to figure out."

The look on Curtis's face said he'd rather do anything but apologize to Jeremiah and thank him for being a friend to his wife, but grudgingly, he did it.

"Thank you for assisting my wife while I was out of town. And you're right. I should've been there with her."

"Yes, you should have," Jeremiah said, in no mood to make it easy on Heather's brother.

"I have to say I'm rather impressed. It took a lot of guts to stand up to me and my family. And that right hook…. That was pretty incredible. Brock never saw it coming."

"Thanks," Jeremiah replied through clenched teeth. The last thing he wanted right now was a reminder of the moment he'd lost control.

"You should've hit him at the Fourth of July barbecue. He can get a little full of himself."

A little? He didn't say it. "It was tempting, but I didn't want to risk you or your dad retaliating. Then again… judging by your face, maybe I was wrong to think I couldn't beat you."

To his surprise, Curtis laughed. "Yeah, everyone thinks I'm the fighter in the family, but it's always been

Heather. She could've taken me any time if she'd ever wanted to. I don't think even Dad could win against her anymore."

He tilted his head and regarded Jeremiah with eyes narrowed, and though he left without saying another word, Jeremiah suspected the man had just realized that he'd majorly underestimated his sister's boyfriend.

"Well, that was interesting," Heather quipped after her brother was gone. "That's the first glimpse of my brother—my *real* brother—I've seen in a long time. Maybe there's a chance for him and Christina after all."

"He *does* seem to want to work things out," Jeremiah agreed. "He had to humble himself to say what he just did and mean it... and I think he did."

"That was pretty amazing, what you did just now. You could've taken the gracious route and told him it was okay, but you didn't. You didn't—what's the word?"

"Validate?"

"Yeah. You didn't validate him. You forced him to recognize that he's been a dick." Heather bumped shoulders with him and grinned. "I love it when this side of you comes out. You're usually so humble and polite that it's even more fun to watch you stand your ground."

Suddenly, she bounced off the trailer and turned to him. "Come on. Let's get to work."

"Shouldn't you head home to be with Christina?"

"In a little bit. Let's get you firmly back in a happier frame of mind first. Christina will understand."

He wasn't in the mood to work on his office, but he appreciated her enthusiasm. And she was probably right. If he muscled through the lingering fog of self-loathing, his love of building would eventually win out. Besides, working with her was always fun. She was a great partner, and he appreciated any excuse to soak up some more of her vibrant spirit.

"So, you finished the roof this afternoon. What's next?" she asked.

"Siding. You up for helping me with some rough sawn? The guy's wife wants it stained a dark green."

"Ooo! That'll be pretty. Nice contrast with the corrugated roofing."

"I thought so."

He set out several pairs of sawhorses and laid out the rough-sawn planks while Heather stirred the stain and located brushes. As they fell into an easy rhythm, the last traces of anger and frustration faded away. Even the doubt that had been festering in his mind all week about whether or not Randall truly had been working for Zach couldn't withstand the simple enjoyment he took from Heather's company. Since he apparently couldn't remember where and when he'd met Randall, there was no point in worrying about it. He couldn't control what his cousin was or wasn't doing, but building and selling this office, treasuring this amazing woman who wouldn't let him wallow in his anxious ponderings, and making a life for himself that he loved and could be proud of.... Those were things he *could* control, so he'd put his energy into them as best he could.

"It's really wonderful that you've started making these offices," Heather remarked. "I know you love the ranch and your job here, but this is something special."

"What do you mean?" he asked absently, mesmerized by the back-and-forth of the brush in his hand and the spread of the deep green stain.

"Well, this is a piece of your dad and your grandparents and your brother, Joe—a natural talent you got from them. When you're working on your offices, they're right here with you."

A genuine smile curved his lips, and it felt good. How many times working on his previous offices had he thought almost exactly that? "Yeah, they are. Sometimes I wonder what would've happened if Joe had had more of a chance to learn the business from them before they died, if he'd been able to hold on to it. I probably never would've gotten tangled up with Zach. Because, even back then, I loved building. Dad was an engineer, but he had a workshop set up in the garage in Huntington Beach, and he used to let me play with his tools and build things with him."

"Aw, what a sweet memory. I bet you loved that."

"Yeah, I did. And after the fire, Joe and I thought we'd eventually take over the construction business from Grandma and Grandpa… but he just didn't have enough time to learn what he needed to know. He had to sell. And then he got royally screwed in the sale, but we were desperate."

Even all these years removed, the memory of the day his brother had told him he wasn't going to be able to hold on to the company their grandparents had spent their lives building was powerful enough to break his heart. He remembered Joe breaking down in tears over it and apologizing that their dream of running it together—with him as the on-the-ground boss and Jeremiah as the brains of the operation since he had a better mind for the logistical end—was gone.

Jeremiah's brush strokes slowed as those memories played through his mind.

Working for the man who'd bought the company was hard; Kirkley had kept Joe on as his crew foreman but had worked him hard, paid him less than he was worth, and dumped the burden of firing lazy or incompetent employees on him, and Joe had hated that the most. He'd been no bigger a man than Jeremiah was now, and most of the men he worked with didn't hesitate to remind him of that.

The paintbrush slipped from his hand and he jerked his head upright, staring at Heather with wide eyes as the memory of a cocky giant of a man arguing with Joe on a job site popped clear in his mind. "Son of a bitch!"

"What?" she asked, concerned. "What's wrong?"

"I know where I met him!"

"Who?"

"Randall Cochran! He worked under Joe for a while after he sold to Dave Kirkley, and Joe had to fire him for coming to work drunk. He was only a couple years older than Joe… but man, he looks so much older now. No wonder I missed it."

"Alcohol will do that to you, I suppose. So how does that connect him to Zach?"

"Joe fired him right after Zach moved up from California!"

"You're certain they know each other?"

"No, but I'm certain they've met because Zach was at the house when Randall stopped by to cuss my brother out for firing him. We had to call the cops to get him to leave. And guess which cop showed up to escort him out?"

"Rogers?"

"Rogers. I'll bet they're both mentioned in the report!"

"If they were, why wouldn't Aaron have found it?"

"He didn't know where to look. He's been focused on more recent records, but that happened twenty years ago. Crap, I've gotta tell Aaron."

"And I should probably head home and spend some time with Christina—see if she's stopped threatening to have my brother castrated yet. Shall we call it a night?"

"Yeah, I think we should." He clasped her face and kissed her soundly. "Thank you! Uh, don't worry about the mess. I'll get it later."

He didn't even bother shutting off the lights on his way out—with the energy pulsing through him, he'd likely come back down to work because there was no way he'd be able to sleep tonight. He kissed Heather again out by their trucks and followed her out to the main road through the valley and all the way to Aspen Creek Road, flashing his lights as he turned right onto the gravel road to Henry's, Aaron's, and Nick's houses. She lifted a hand out the window to wave goodnight, and he could almost hear her laughter.

He skidded to a stop in front of Aaron and Skye's house and bounded up the stairs, taking them three at a time. Without thinking, he pounded on the door with his right hand and was quickly reminded of the events earlier in the morning. He hoped it was only a bruise.

Skye opened the door. "Jeremiah," she said. "I thought you'd still be over at the Browns' or down in the shop."

"Is Aaron home from work yet? I need to talk to

him."

"He's in the shower, but come on in. He should be out in a minute. Everything all right?"

"Fine. Good, I think. I have a connection between Zach and Randall, and I'm hoping it'll help."

"That's fantastic. Well? Don't just stand there. Come in!"

"Oh, right. Sorry."

He followed her inside and sat on the L-shaped couch, declining her offer for something to drink but accepting an ice pack for his hand before she headed back to the bathroom to tell Aaron he was here. Glancing around the open living area, he realized suddenly how quiet it was. Usually, Jessie and Eric and the Hammonds' elderly black Lab Chance were in the living room, filling it with all the happy sounds of family.

"Where are Jess and Eric? And Chance?" he asked when Skye returned.

"Jess is in her room reading, I believe, and I think Chance is in Eric's room playing Godzilla to Eric's Lego city."

As if on cue, the boy's laughter rang out down the hall, followed by Chance's happy barks.

"Typical night in the Hammond household," Skye sighed happily. "Life is good."

Jeremiah pictured himself sitting in the living room of some as-of-yet-unknown house or cabin with Heather and Murph, enjoying a quiet evening together. What he wouldn't give to make that picture a reality not just *for now* but for always.

"Yes, it is," Aaron said, arriving in the living room

clad only in a pair of sweat pants.

Jeremiah averted his gaze when Skye gave her husband a blatant once-over appraisal and wiggled her brows with a devilish grin.

"What brings you by tonight, Jere? I thought you and Heather had a date with her family. And… why do you have an icepack on your hand?"

He repeated the night's events without leaving anything out, and Aaron listened with a concerned frown drawing his brows together, and when Jeremiah was finished, the sheriff examined his hand.

"I don't think anything's broken, but if it's still bugging you tomorrow, go get it X-rayed, all right?" Aaron shook his head. "I was afraid the prick would push you over the edge sooner or later. At least you only hit him once."

"Once was all it took, and I wasn't going to wait around for him to get back up. Anyhow, that's not why I came by. I'm all right—I promise. Heather and I worked in the shop for a while, and that helped. A lot."

"Glad to hear it. So Skye says you figured out a connection between Cochran and Zach?"

"Yeah, I did."

He described the day Joe had had to fire Randall, how the big man had come to their house in a fluster while Zach was over.

"Rogers is the cop who answered the call?"

Jeremiah nodded.

"For once, I'm glad he was involved. He'll have filed the report for sure. I'll look into it tomorrow, and I'll ask Kirkley for Cochran's employment records, too. He'll probably still have them—he's a greedy son of a bitch and treats his guys like crap, but he's meticulous."

"Please, Aaron. Please tell me this will help."

"I don't know if it will or not, but it's something. I know Cochran doesn't want to get nailed for the cattle, too, and maybe this will prompt him to give up whoever did… Zach or maybe someone else working for him."

Impulsively, Jeremiah hugged him, feeling far too much like the scared but grateful kid who had jumped at the chance to turn his life around. Aaron seemed to sense it and returned the embrace, slapping him on the back a few times.

"This is what I needed, Jere. Good job."

Twelve

"CAN WE SWING BY MURDOCH'S before we head to lunch?" Jeremiah asked. "They're having a tool sale."

"All that money burning a hole in your pocket?" Heather teased.

"Maybe a little." He stopped the shopping cart at her truck and lifted the tonneau cover. "But I could really use a bigger compressor, and Murdoch's has a good deal on one right now. Besides, I have two more custom-ordered offices to build, so I figure now would be a good time to invest in my business."

"*Two* more? Wow. Guess my mother won't have to worry about you resenting me for out-earning you."

He eyed her with concern. "I hope you don't think I'd ever resent you for making more money than me. Because if I was the kind of man who had a problem with powerful, independent women, I wouldn't have been attracted to you in the first place."

"Believe me, I know that."

"Good. Your mother actually said that to you?"

She nodded. "Right before she blindsided you with that question about whether you'd be happy with a woman who would 'refuse to give you children'."

Jeremiah let out a guttural sound of disgust.

"So… you really meant what you said to my mother at dinner?" she asked tentatively.

"I wouldn't have said it if I didn't."

Why, after she'd realized and admitted to herself that if he wanted kids she would be willing to have them, was that such a relief? She suspected he'd meant every word he said, but hearing him confirm it somehow took the pressure entirely off. It was one more way in which she was free to be herself with him. It was also a slap in the face to her mother's ever-present nagging voice in the back of her mind whispering that no man would want a woman who didn't want children as if they couldn't be a happy, complete unit with only the two of them. It made her realize that the only two people who could decide what was right for her and Jeremiah… were her and Jeremiah. It was such a simple concept—one that probably seemed like a no-brainer to most people—but she struggled to wrap her head around it.

"Sometimes I feel guilty for not wanting kids." After she said that, her breath came out in a rush. She'd never admitted that before. Not out loud. Not even to herself. "So damned guilty. And selfish."

"Why? Because your mother has pounded it into your head that you *should* want them?"

She nodded. "And because… I feel like I come across like I'm looking down on the women who *do* want kids. But I really don't. I am just so tired of my parents and society saying I'm less of a woman because motherhood doesn't appeal to me."

"You're definitely not less of a woman."

Her lips twitched, but she couldn't quite make herself smile when she was so close to hitting on the heart of why her mother's incessant talks of babies and motherhood hurt her so much. She started to elaborate and explain that having kids just to have kids wasn't enough of a reason for her, but Jeremiah spoke first.

"For the record, your self-awareness is damned sexy."

He was doing more than complimenting her—he was giving her an out from an uncomfortable conversation. With a sigh of relief, she took it. This was undoubtedly something she still needed to talk about and analyze so it couldn't control her anymore, but she'd made enough progress for one day, and she was grateful he recognized that.

"Thank you." She kissed him as she set the last grocery sack in the truck, laughing softly. Recalling what he'd said to her at Christina's house minutes after they'd made love in the shower and the way it had made her feel like the most admired and cherished woman in the world, she said, "I adore you."

"Mmm." He grinned. "You're right. That *is* nice. Better than 'I love you', I think. Deeper and more meaningful somehow."

"Definitely."

They climbed into the truck and left the conversation behind in the Safeway parking lot. She turned right on Montana Street, drove almost to the northern edge of town, and pulled into the Murdoch's parking lot. Murphy, who'd spent most of the trip to town sprawled in the back seat like the king of the four-wheel-drive castle, suddenly appeared between the front seats, his paws braced on the center console as he let out an excited whine.

"Yeah, maybe I'll get you a special treat, too," Jeremiah remarked, ruffling his dog's ears.

Murphy replied with a louder whine.

Heather laughed. "I'd say you're the most spoiled rotten dog I've ever met, but I've known a *lot* of spoiled dogs. Aaron and Skye's black Lab, the Conners' golden retrievers, every dog Nick and Beth have ever owned, Brodie and Celeste's dogs…."

"There are some majorly spoiled dogs in that list," Jeremiah chuckled.

They headed into the ranch supply store hand in hand, but as soon as they stepped inside, Heather released him and headed over to the Montana Silversmith case to look for something special to commemorate Jessie's upcoming rodeo while Jeremiah headed toward the back of the store to drool over tools.

She couldn't decide between a horseshoe necklace and matching earrings or the gorgeously ornate belt buckle with the barrel racer on it. On the one hand, Jess would probably get more wear out of the belt buckle because Heather couldn't recall seeing her wearing much jewelry, but if she won next weekend as Heather believed she would, she'd end up with a better, more meaningful belt buckle.

Just as she stepped away to find an employee to unlock the case for her, her phone rang. She glanced at the screen before she answered and was surprised to see who was calling.

"Hey, Aaron," she greeted. "What's up?"

"Have you guys eaten lunch yet?"

"No, we sidetracked to Murdoch's first. We're heading to Papa T's after this, though."

"I'll meet you there. Fifteen minutes long enough?"

"Should be. What's up?"

"I have some news for Jeremiah."

"All right, I'll go drag him out of the tools. See you in a few."

She ended the call and headed back to the tool section. She found Jeremiah talking with one of the associates, making arrangements to have a compressor and a brad nailer brought up to the front of the store and asking about a couple other pneumatic tools on sale. There was a boyish joy about him that both contrasted and complimented the calculating businesslike inquiries about what brads the store had in stock, and it was fascinating to watch him. He was usually so easygoing that it was easy to forget just how competent he was.

"Find this fascinating?" he asked when the associate stepped away to locate a specific brand and gauge of brads he'd inquired about.

"Not this. You."

He rewarded her with an adorably shy lop-sided smile.

"I hate to cut your frolicking through the tool department short, but Aaron just called. He wants to meet us for lunch, said he has some news for you."

"Good or bad?"

"He didn't say."

He snagged a couple more things off the shelves, flagged the associate down, and started for the front of the store, detouring to the pet section to grab a hedgehog dog toy for Murphy. Heather excused herself for a moment to find someone to help her with that necklace and matching earrings for Jessie.

"Those are beautiful. Who are they for?" Jeremiah asked when she joined him at the register.

"Jess. I wanted to get her something special ahead of her rodeo next weekend. For good luck."

"That's very thoughtful of you." He smiled, took her hand, and pressed his lips to her knuckles, holding her gaze the whole time. "See? Who needs kids when we have nieces and nephews to spoil. How many between us? I have Nick and Beth's three boys, Jessie and Eric, and Noah and Archer."

"And I have Ethan and Blake, Sebastian, Rosalie, and Joseph, and Hannah and Owen, plus another one coming. How many is that?"

"I count fourteen, soon to be fifteen."

"Good lord. How are we supposed to keep track of them?"

"No idea, but you know the best part thing about nieces and nephews?"

"No. What?"

"We get to spoil them rotten and send them home to their parents."

She glanced at the box holding the necklace and

earrings. "I like that. All the fun, none of the hassle."

"Exactly."

They completed their purchases and loaded everything in the back of her truck. With Murphy happily mouthing and squeaking his new hedgehog in the back seat, Heather drove across town to Papa T's.

It was the tail end of the lunch rush, and when they walked into the restaurant, it was packed with diners lingering over their meals. Aaron, dressed handsomely in his brown and tan uniform, waved them over to a table on the left wall, and they made their way carefully between the tables, dancing around the children scampering between the arcade games and their chairs. Heather smiled when one crashed into her, brushing off the startled little girl's apologies.

I love kids. I just don't want any of my own. Why can't my mother understand that?

"Isn't this the same table you and Pearl were sitting at that day?" Jeremiah asked, dropping into the chair across from Aaron and mercifully derailing her train of thought before it had a chance to leave the station.

"I believe it is," Aaron replied.

"What day?" Heather asked.

"The day Aaron offered me a job on the Lazy H instead of rightfully slapping the cuffs on me for a third time." Jeremiah grinned. "Thankfully he saw a hurting kid in need of a second chance instead of a menace to society bound to keep re-offending. He was in uniform that day, too."

Heather lifted a brow. "Is this one of those times you wander off in your head to retrace steps and ponder the quirks of life and fate?"

He chuckled. "Not really. No more than to say this is a fitting spot to talk about the case. That *is* what your news is about, isn't it, Aaron?"

The sheriff nodded. "We have a ballistic match. All three bullets were shot from Cochran's rifle."

"And…?"

"And he sang like a songbird. All I had to do was mention that I knew he lied to me about not knowing Zach Neely. He was rather surprised that I knew exactly how and when and where they'd met and also that I knew he got busted for his DUI in a vehicle registered to Zach six months after that."

Jeremiah's jaw dropped. "You're joking."

"Nope. I was able to make a few more connections between them, thanks to that little piece of information you remembered. Including the fact that they both had memberships to the Devyn Rifle Range over the same period… which led me to discovering that they spent a fair amount of time out there together target shooting. Anyhow, he's claiming Zach shot the cows, says he didn't think anything of lending your cousin his gun after they went out shooting together earlier this summer. Said he figured Zach just wanted to do a little target practice in the hills behind Montana Tech. He says Zach had it for roughly the period between when the heifer was shot and when my buddy at the FWP thinks the calf was shot. Now, Zach has an alibi for the day the heifer was killed—he was at work. And the day the calf was shot, his roommate says they went to a movie that night. There's a corresponding debit from the theater in Butte showing in Zach's checking account."

"The roommate could've used Zach's card."

"We've submitted a request for the surveillance tapes around the time the tickets were purchased. But in the meantime, those alibis make it look like Cochran is lying."

Jeremiah frowned. "But he's maintained this whole time that he didn't shoot the cows."

"Yes… and I believe him. For one, he's not smart enough to come up with a plausible defense and for another, he looked genuinely furious and helpless."

"You talked to him yourself?"

Aaron nodded.

"So what now?"

"We bring in Zach for questioning at the earliest opportunity, probably Friday. Because our friend Randall had more to say. He says Zach may be planning something else—something big. Said killing the deer and leaving it at the cabin was Zach's idea and that Zach had told him to leave the whole deer but Randall didn't want to waste the meat. Which I also believe."

"So the deer *was* meant to be a threat," Heather said flatly.

"Heather…" Jeremiah murmured. "It's okay."

"She's right to be upset, Jere," Aaron said. "And I'm glad to see it, actually. It means she cares about you. But for the record, I never said it *wasn't* a threat."

"Did Randall say anything else?" Jeremiah asked.

Aaron nodded. "Seems your cousin may be planning to retaliate against not only you but me, Rogers, and the county attorney who prosecuted his case."

"Randall said that?"

"No, but he said I should watch my back because

Zach mentioned me and Jeremiah and Rogers and the county attorney enough times to stand out."

"No surprise there," Jeremiah muttered.

"No, not really. Cochran's been helpful, I'll give him that. Now we've just got to be very careful what we ask Zach and how we ask it. I don't like this situation at all, but maybe, if he doesn't think we're on to him, it'll be all right. Somehow." He sat back in his chair and studied Jeremiah for a long time. "That's it. Mostly I wanted you to know so you'll be extra careful. I have no idea what Zach will do. For now, he's still playing the model parolee, and as long as he is and as long as I have nothing concrete proving he shot the cows, there's not much I can do."

"Feels like JP all over again," Heather murmured. "The helplessness."

"It does," Aaron agreed. "And I hate it."

A waitress finally came by to take their orders, and they spent the rest of their meal talking about happier things, mostly Jeremiah's booming portable office business and the tools he'd picked up today and Jessie's upcoming rodeo. Afterwards, she and Jeremiah bid Aaron farewell until dinner with the Hammond clan, something Heather was thoroughly looking forward to. She always enjoyed spending time with Jeremiah's surrogate family; it reminded her of what normal, healthy family relationships looked like and bolstered her growing intolerance for her own family's toxic interactions. And made it easier to see that she wasn't the problem.

They had just one more stop to make before they headed home to the store, and Heather drove across the train tracks running parallel to the street in front of Papa T's to the saddle shop to pick up the show saddle Ty had brought in for repairs on Monday. Jeremiah waited in the truck with Murphy, and she couldn't blame him for needing a few minutes alone to wrap his head around everything Aaron had said.

It was nice to see some progress toward linking Zach to the events of the summer, but it still wasn't enough. As Aaron had said, there was nothing concrete yet, which made the situation scarier. Zach still had the upper hand. What was he planning? Was Randall Cochran telling the truth about Jeremiah's cousin planning something big? Would he really try to kill Jeremiah and Aaron and Steven Rogers and the county attorney?

"I'm sure he's not planning to *thank* them for his lovely stay in the Montana State Prison," she muttered as she walked up the path to the saddle shop.

What else besides murder would satisfy a psychopath's need for revenge?

"Everything okay, Heather?" the young man behind the counter greeted.

Starting, she glanced up and realized she was inside the shop and standing at the counter with the shop's owner regarding her with a welcoming but concerned smile.

"Everything's fine, Jack. Why wouldn't it be?"

"Dunno. But I said hello three times and you didn't seem to hear me."

"Sorry. I may be a little distracted. Is Ty's saddle ready?"

"Yes, ma'am."

She dug out the check Ty had sent with her while she waited and tried not to be dragged back into her ponderings about Jeremiah's cousin and what he was or wasn't up to. Jack hauled the saddle out to her truck for her and thanked her for the payment when he returned.

With that task completed, she hopped back in her truck and glanced over at Jeremiah. The change in him from the time she'd left him to now was remarkable.

"All right. What happened? When I left you, you looked like Aaron told you that you had six months left to live, and now you look almost serene again."

"Aren't you the one who told me I can't let him control me?"

"Something like that, yeah."

"Well, I'm not going to let this get to me. I'm going to keep living my life. And if he shows up looking to make me pay for ratting on him…." He shrugged. "Whatever happens happens. Worrying about it won't stop it."

"I guess you're right. It's still scary, though."

"It is. But fear is poison."

With her hand gripping the steering wheel, she stared at him. "You're absolutely right, but it might take me a little longer to get to where you are right now."

She started to add something else, surprised by the intensity of the thought even though she'd caught the first inkling of it the day Jeremiah had caught Randall Cochran with the poached buck. "I don't want to lose you."

"Then you won't."

"I'm serious, Jere."

"So am I. I'm not going anywhere. I'm yours as long as you want me."

"Unless your psycho cousin gets a hold of you."

"Aaron won't let that happen, and neither will I."

"That's so easy to say, but you've said he's smart. Repeatedly."

"Yeah… and who brought him down last time?"

"You did."

"Yep."

"Don't go getting cocky on me."

"I'm not. But I'm done being afraid of him."

Letting out a breath, she pulled away from the saddle shop and headed toward the Interstate, wishing she could quiet her trembling fear as easily as he had. They didn't talk as she drove out of town, and she was nearly to the spot she'd found him pulled off on the side of the highway on her birthday when she understood the full implication behind her fear and his response to it.

I'm yours as long as you want me, he'd said.

And what if I want you forever?

She didn't dare ask the question. It was too new, too fragile, and even though she knew he would understand, she couldn't share it even with him yet.

Instead, she let out a breath and said, "Well, if you can do it, I guess I can, too."

He took her hand from the gear shift and kissed her knuckles, grinning as he did so. "That's my woman."

* * *

It was a typical, noisy evening in the main house of the Lazy H, and that made it easy to hold to his vow to ignore the fear and focus on living. Heather's admission on the drive home from town made it even easier. That was what he lived for now—the promise that this might last not only a few months or even a few years but for the rest of their lives.

I don't want to lose you.

He still had no idea if this was real or if it would truly last, but he was no longer afraid she'd scorch him with her burn-the-world down fire. He wouldn't say it had cooled and he hoped it never would, but it had turned into a different kind of blaze—the kind of slow, hot fire that fueled her passion for life rather than the explosive inferno that would destroy her and anyone close to her.

To have a woman like her to warm his heart, he was a lucky man.

He watched her playing with Archer, helping him build a gargantuan city out of wooden blocks in the corner of the living room. Caleb and Cade and Eric were hilariously trying to pretend they were too old and too cool to play with the blocks, but Heather was making it look like so much fun that Jeremiah suspected it wouldn't be long before the older boys gave in.

"Someone grab a camera," Henry teased. "That is the dopiest smile I've ever seen."

"Not even close," Jeremiah replied. "You forget we were all present to watch you fall head over heels for Lindsay."

"Dopey's not my style. I was dashing."

"Ha!" Lindsay replied, returning from the kitchen. She sat beside her husband and draped herself around him. "It was your dopey smile that won me over."

"I thought it was my smooth dance moves."

"Mmm," she purred fondly. "Those certainly helped."

"I still think Jere's got me beat in the dopey department," Henry remarked.

"Probably so," Heather said. "I made him wait a lot longer than Lindsay made you wait. He's got more reason to be dopey."

"Gee, thanks," Jeremiah said flatly. "You're as bad as the rest of them."

"She is, so you might want to quit yer bitchin'," Henry retorted. "That means she fits in with this family like the missing piece of our puzzle."

Heather beamed at the compliment. She didn't say it, but Jeremiah suspected Henry's casual comment meant a lot more than he could've ever suspected. She *did* fit in with the Hammonds… far better than she fit in with her own family. Jeremiah knew how good it felt to be welcomed and appreciated when, following his arrest, everyone else he'd met had been more inclined to shun him without bothering to give him the benefit of the doubt.

Tracie and Beth wandered in from the kitchen to join the rest of the family.

"Well, dinner's ready as soon as Aaron gets home," Tracie said, sliding on to her husband's lap.

Jeremiah smiled. The heads of the Hammond clan were now in their late sixties, but their romance showed no signs of slowing down. Between them and their three sons and daughters-in-law, Jeremiah had a very high bar to meet, but it was ridiculously easy to imagine himself flirting shamelessly with Heather in front of the entire family three decades from now.

He wanted that picture to become a reality so much his chest ached.

"There's that dopey smile again," Henry teased. "Seriously. Someone get a camera."

"Oh, leave the poor boy alone," Tracie told him.

"Can't. He might think I didn't love him if I didn't tease him."

"He has a point, Mom," Jeremiah sighed. "I expect it."

Conversation shifted to the ranch and Jessie's upcoming rodeo and Heather's new clients. Eventually, she came over to sit with him on the couch, sandwiched between Nick and Beth and Henry and Lindsay. The kids—even the teenagers—were relegated to the floor, but no one seemed to mind.

Time wore on, and when Aaron still hadn't arrived, talk turned to the possible reasons why he was late. No one was too worried; this wasn't the first time his job had made him late for dinner, and Jeremiah did his best to shrug off the increasingly heavy sense of foreboding.

I will not *be afraid,* he reminded himself.

"I guess we'd better eat without him," Tracie sighed.

The family gathered around the dining room table, and the conversation turned to the football camp coming up. Jeremiah momentarily forgot his concern listening to Will and Noah talk about it. This would be Will's final season, and to hear him and Noah, who'd graduated last summer, bemoaning the end of their glory days was borderline comical.

"What do they know about the glory days ending, eh?" Heather whispered.

"Sadly, more than I do," Jeremiah replied. "I missed out on all that."

"Oh, you poor thing."

"Go ahead and patronize me. I'd rather my glory days

be now and in the future than fading away behind me."

"Good point."

Everyone had finished dinner and was well into Tracie's incredible apple pie when Aaron finally arrived. And the ashen, drawn expression on his face silenced the relaxed chatter. Skye was the first on her feet, and she strode across the dining room and into the kitchen to embrace her husband. Tracie was next.

"What happened?" Skye asked.

Aaron didn't immediately answer. Instead, he clung to his wife with his face buried against her neck.

Jeremiah rose slowly from his chair and stepped quietly into the kitchen. Sensing his presence, Aaron finally looked up.

"You're not going up to the cabin tonight after dinner," the sheriff croaked.

Jeremiah jerked his head back. He couldn't recall ever seeing Aaron so distraught. "Why? What happened?"

"Rogers is dead."

He felt like someone had poured ice water into his veins. "How?"

"Shot dead. Bullet between his eyes like that damned buck. His poor wife found him this afternoon when she returned home from visiting her sister."

"Zach?"

Aaron shook his head. "Couldn't have been. He was at work in Butte when it happened."

"You're positive of that?"

"I have it straight from his boss."

"Then someone Zach knows."

"Rogers made quite a few enemies with the way he

handled his cases," Nick said quietly, joining them in the kitchen. He embraced his brother. "It probably wouldn't be hard for Zach to find someone happy to kill him."

"No, probably not. I know Rogers wasn't the most popular man, and I only have to remember how he treated you and Luke to know why." Aaron pinched his eyes closed. "But who shoots a seventy-six-year-old man already on dialysis for the rest of his life?"

The adults abandoned their half-eaten slices of pie and wandered into the living room, leaving the teenagers to ride herd on the younger kids. Jeremiah pulled Heather into his lap, needing to hold onto her as Aaron's news sank in.

He had no love for Rogers—no one in the Hammond or Conner families did. The former sheriff had handled Nick's arrest pompously and poorly, slapping him in cuffs in front of half the university, and to Jeremiah's knowledge, he'd never apologized even after it was proved Nick had acted in defense of Beth and the assault charge had been dropped. Jeremiah hadn't been in Northstar when JP had killed Mike Thompson and Carol Landers, and he had only met Luke a couple times in passing at school— he'd been a senior when Luke was a freshman but had dropped out shortly after the start of the school year—but he knew Rogers hadn't won any friends in this valley when he'd blamed Luke, however indirectly, for the deaths of his teammate and girlfriend.

He studied Aaron, noted the strain and exhaustion and grief on his surrogate brother's face. Of all of them, Aaron had the most reason to mourn the death of his old boss and rival. Rogers might've been a monumental pain in his backside, but Aaron had worked with the man most of his career. Regardless of whether or not he'd liked the man, his death was a hard blow.

"I should've stayed longer," Aaron said after a while. "But I had to let the deputies take over. God knows Rogers was a pain in my ass—"

"He was a pain in a lot of asses," Henry remarked.

"—but I never would've wished this on him. To die like this...."

Jeremiah waited for the fear to rebound, but it didn't. Instead, anger curled through him, slow-burning and ravenous. Zach might not have pulled the trigger, but he'd found someone to do it for him.

Go ahead, he could hear his cousin whispering. *Try to prove it's me.*

He clenched his jaw. This was Zach all the way, taunting him and reminding him how helpless he was.

Heather tightened her arms around him and let out a breath. "Here we go again."

"He'll make a mistake again," Jeremiah whispered. "That's his one fault—his arrogance. There has to be some way to prove what Randall said—that Zach shot the cows."

An inkling that he was overlooking something tickled his brain, but it eluded him, and the harder he tried to chase it down, the faster it escaped beyond his reach. So he let it go for now, kissed Heather, and focused attention on supporting Aaron. He'd remembered where he'd met Randall, so he was sure this would come to him, too, if he relaxed and coaxed it back.

He just hoped he would remember before Zach moved on to the next step... before someone else died.

Thirteen

"HE LOOKED ME right in the eyes and swore he had nothing to do with Rogers's death," Aaron said, leaning against the kitchen counter in his parents' house. He folded his arms across his chest and stared blankly out the window overlooking the front yard. "He even brought up that he'd been at work—something he knew I've already verified— when Rogers was shot. And when I asked him about shooting the cows and about Cochran saying he'd mentioned Rogers more than a few times, he just… shrugged. Said Cochran was probably trying to shove his crimes off on him because Cochran knows I'm looking for 'any excuse' to bring Zach in. Those were his words."

Jeremiah pressed his mouth into a flat line. "He's playing games with you."

"No shit, Jere."

He glanced sharply at Jeremiah as soon as he said it and opened his mouth to apologize, but Tracie threw the cinnamon roll dough she was rolling out down on the counter, and he winced.

"Aaron Samuel Hammond! That was *way* out of line."

"Yes, it was. I'm sorry, Jere." He raked his hands through his hair and sighed. "This whole thing is really bugging me. Rogers, as much as he drove me nuts and generally treated me like crap most of the time we worked together, deserved better than this. His *wife* deserves better. But even worse than that, I just feel so goddamned helpless. I don't like waiting to see what Zach's going to do next, but that's all I can do. Wait and hope no one else dies."

"Guess I'm not going back up to the cabin this summer," Jeremiah observed.

"No, not unless I get a lucky break. I've got nothing on Zach other than what Cochran's saying, and with the evidence contradicting him, that's not enough to arrest Zach for even the cows. I'm not going to let you stay by yourself in a place where I am damned sure now your cousin has been."

"So… when am I going to be able to get up there to clear out the cabin?"

"What time is Steven's funeral this afternoon?" Tracie asked.

"Not until four," Aaron replied.

"It's a slow day down here, so why don't you boys go up and get it done this morning? Shouldn't take you more than two or three hours, and that'll leave you with plenty of time to get home and showered and changed before you have to head into town, Aaron."

"Yeah," he sighed. "We could do that. Promise you'll make sure everyone saves us some of those cinnamon rolls?"

"You know I will."

"Mind if we stop by Heather's on the way up?" Jeremiah asked. "We were going to work on my office today, and I need to let her know there's been a change in plans."

"You sure you don't want to do that instead?"

"I do, but I need to get my stuff out of the cabin. Even if you catch a break or Zach slips up, we'll be moving the cows down in a few more weeks, anyhow."

"Good point. All right, let's get this done." Aaron leaned down and kissed his mother's cheek. "Love you, Mom."

Jeremiah did the same. "Love you, Mom."

"Love you both. See you in a couple hours."

They headed out to Aaron's truck. Murphy was sprawled in the sunshine in the front yard, but when he saw Jeremiah, he jumped to his feet.

"Not this time, Murph," he said to the dog. "There won't be any room for you once we get everything loaded in the truck. Stay. Oh, don't give me that look."

Murphy laid in the grass with his head on his front paws, staring up at Jeremiah with the whites showing at the bottom of his eyes and gave a practiced and exquisitely pathetic sigh.

"I'm not sure who was the best thing to happen to whom in that relationship," Aaron remarked, nodding his head toward the Aussie.

"It's mutual."

"He's a great dog."

Jeremiah nodded in agreement, and he swore Murphy's expression turned just a tiny bit smug at those words.

Aaron tried to apologize again for snapping at him as he drove away from the house, but Jeremiah wouldn't let him. This whole situation was probably harder on Aaron than on the rest of them. The burden of figuring out how to prove what his instincts were screaming at him was entirely on him, and while he was in the position to do something about it, he couldn't until or unless he had that proof.

It made Jeremiah tired just thinking about how frustrating that must be.

Since he'd made the decision to stop letting fear of Zach govern him, he had been remarkably calm about the whole situation, and it wasn't fun watching Aaron struggle with this.

He tried not to dwell on the fact that this was just one more way Zach was winning. Somehow he'd find a way to make his cousin pay for this and every other pain and frustration he'd inflicted on Jeremiah and the people he cared about since he'd set foot in Montana.

"Too bad you didn't die with your old man," he muttered.

"What'd you say?" Aaron asked.

"Nothing important."

When Aaron pulled up in front of Heather's cabin, she was sitting out on her deck with a cup of coffee. And, damn, in those cutoff jeans, a black tank top, her feet bare, and her rich, dark hair hanging loose around her shoulders, she was incredibly sexy.

"Hey there, baby girl," he greeted as he climbed the stairs.

She grinned. "I still love that. I've been trying to come up with something for you, but so far, nothing's good enough."

"Call me anything you want. Just don't call me late for dinner."

This time she laughed. "Where did you come up with *that*?"

"God only knows where I heard it first. Hey, Aaron and I are heading up to clear out the allotment cabin, so we'll have to wait until this afternoon for our work date."

"I have a better idea. I'll come up and help."

"Sure. If you want."

"Better than sitting at home being bored. I'll meet you boys up there."

Jeremiah nodded and jogged back to Aaron's truck.

When they arrived at the cabin, he stared up at it for a minute, unable to pinpoint why he'd expected it to be any different than it had when he'd left it the day Rogers had been shot. Austin had done the herd checks since that morning with Jeremiah tied up down at the ranch rebuilding a shed that had collapsed after a big aspen had fallen on it during the thunderstorms three nights ago, so Jeremiah hadn't been back up in the past four days.

He was going to miss being up here. Before this summer, he'd liked this cabin well enough, and he had fond memories of previous stays in it and of enjoying the utter peace that came with it, but there were now even better memories attached to the old log structure.

This was where he'd fallen in love with Heather.

No point in denying he was in love with her.

He'd been attracted to her since the first time he'd met her, and he'd suspected for a long time that they could have something incredible together, but it wasn't until he'd finally worked up the courage to invite her out for drinks on her birthday that he'd begun to realize just *how* incredible. They were kindred souls—scarred but still fighting.

"Despite everything, this cabin has been damned good to you this summer, hasn't it?" Aaron observed. For the first time in four days, a smile graced his face.

"Yes, it has."

"Are you thinking of asking her to marry you?"

"I've been thinking about *that* for a long time."

"Not like you are now, I'd say."

Jeremiah chuckled and got out of the truck. Standing beside Aaron, he gazed up at the cabin with his hands in his pockets. "No, not like now. Before, it was a daydream. Now, it's…. It's hard to imagine my life without her in it."

Aaron laughed. "I bet every man who's ever found the love of his life has said those words or something like them."

"Did you?"

"Twice. Both with Erica and with Skye. So don't screw it up because I can tell you from those years between them that being alone after you've tasted real love is agonizing. It's an ache that's always there."

"Way to pile on the pressure, Aaron. Thanks."

Aaron clapped him on the shoulder.

"If you want to get started in there, I'll get the chairs and barbecue loaded and check the stable," Aaron offered.

"Sounds good."

Jeremiah pulled the key out of his pocket and unlocked the door, quickly scanning the interior. Nothing had been disturbed. He got to work packing his clothes and books first. There wasn't much, so it wouldn't take him long, but he'd gotten barely halfway through that task when Heather showed up.

Leaning in the open door of the cabin, she glanced around the interior. "I'm never going to look at this place the same again."

"How did you look at it before?" he asked.

"As nothing more than a dusty old cow camp cabin." She pushed off the door and sauntered over to him, draping her arms around his neck and angling her body against his.

"And now?"

"My own personal heaven."

"Sounds delight—"

She cut him off with a blatantly passionate and demanding kiss that brought his mind right back to that cool, misty morning and making love to her for the first time right here in this cabin on that bunk. Heaven was a fitting description.

"Think we have time for one more round here before it belongs to the Forest Service again and not to us?" she asked huskily, wiggling her brows. "Aaron's busy outside, and I'm sure he'd agree to give us some privacy. We could make it quick."

"Don't tempt me."

She pushed him down onto the bunk and straddled his waist, but instead of tumbling into a deliciously sensuous storm of passion, they broke into laughter. He pulled her head down and kissed her.

Footsteps on the porch alerted him to Aaron's imminent arrival.

"Hey, Jere, I—" The older man stopped short in the doorway, and after a fleeting moment of wide-eyed surprise, he grinned. "Never mind. Carry on."

Laughing too hard to do that, Heather climbed off the bunk and offered her hands to help Jeremiah up. After popping his head briefly out the door to see what Aaron needed—to say he was going to drive over to the Royal R to borrow some tie downs as it appeared someone had borrowed his out of his truck and not put them back—Jeremiah started stripping the blankets and sheets off the foam mattress.

"That'll take him at least fifteen minutes," Heather said, wiggling her brows. "You sure I can't convince you?"

"Baby girl, fifteen minutes is not *nearly* long enough to satisfy either of us."

"I suppose you're right. Anyhow, I'm not in the mood for a quickie. I'm in the mood for an all-dayer."

Jeremiah chuckled. "We may have to settle for an all-nighter."

"You're on, Jere Bear." She curled her lip. "God no, not that. Sorry. That was cheesy as hell. Ugh. I'll think of something."

He didn't bother trying to fold the blankets and sheets perfectly since they were bound for the washer anyhow. After he'd stuffed them in the back seat of Heather's truck, he returned to the cabin and grabbed the bungies from under the bunk. With Heather's help, he rolled the foam mattress, secured it, and hauled it outside.

After he'd dumped it in the bed of the truck, he returned for his suitcases. Heather turned to him with the silver cross dangling from her fingers.

"I never figured you for the religious type," she remarked.

"I'm not. I found…."

Son of a bitch.

"Jere?" she asked.

There had been a lot going on the last couple weeks and he'd had a lot on his mind, but how had the *key* to Zach's involvement in everything that had happened this summer slipped his mind?

"I found it the day I moved into the cabin. I'm pretty sure it's Zach's, but when I found it, I thought it had been planted here. After we met Randall, I thought he was the one that did it. But if he's telling the truth about Zach shooting the cows…."

"How sure are you that this is Zach's?"

"It's plain, but that X there is just like the one he carved into his. *Just* like it. He said…."

He heard the words as clearly in his head as if Zach had just spoken them. He took the necklace from her and studied it with a renewed interest, paying closer attention to the clasp. It wasn't, as he'd thought, undamaged. It appeared to be at a glance, but when he tested it, it didn't stay closed. The spring inside must've broken.

"He said, 'people around here are quick to trust a guy wearing a cross.' He even had a whole philosophy about it, about how it needed to be a simple one like this and not some gaudy blinged-out cross because too many people here associate those with rappers and gangs. At the time, I thought he was being sarcastic, but I guess he was right. It certainly worked like a charm for him. No one ever thought to point the finger at him… until I ratted him out. If he dropped this here….”

“Is there any way to prove beyond a doubt that it's his?”

“I don't know. Maybe, if we get really lucky and he was wearing it in his mugshot or something.”

“With the luck you've had in your life, it's bound to turn around sometime, right? Maybe now's that time.”

He tipped his head back and exhaled. “Wouldn't that be great?”

Of course, knowing his luck, there would be no way to prove the cross was Zach's. It'd fit right in with everything else he and Aaron knew but couldn't prove. He set the necklace on the table and went back to packing, turning now to the kitchen.

When he heard Aaron's truck returning, his heart leapt and he snatched the cross off the table and trotted outside.

“Hey, Aaron!”

The sheriff glanced up as he stepped out of his truck.

“I found something you need—”

Movement to his left caught his attention, and he snapped his mouth closed.

His heart lunged.

The visage had changed some in the past sixteen years, but Jeremiah instantly recognized the slender man with the neatly trimmed dark hair and the terrifyingly cool and soulless hazel eyes so similar in shape to the ones that looked back at him whenever he passed a mirror.

Zach.

And his gun was trained on Aaron.

Time slowed to a crawl.

From the corner of his vision, Jeremiah saw Aaron's gaze shift to follow his at the same time Zach's fingers tightened around the grip of the 9mm. His cousin tipped his head to line up the sights.

"NO!"

Jeremiah leapt off the porch, somehow keeping his feet when he landed on the packed dirt of the road, and sprinted for his cousin. Zach's gaze didn't waver from Aaron. Behind him, Heather screamed his name, but he barely heard her.

The gun fired just as Jeremiah came between Zach and Aaron, but he didn't slow and didn't look back to see if Aaron had ducked for cover, trusting the sheriff's well-trained instincts to save him. He barreled into his cousin, and with his arms locked around Zach's waist, he picked him up and slammed him down onto the hard earth. He grabbed Zach's wrist and wrenched the pistol free from his hand, turning it on his cousin.

"Do it," his cousin spat.

"You should've just killed me instead of trying to mess with my head first."

"What would be the fun in that?"

Jeremiah's hands trembled, and he adjusted his grip on the gun. He rocked back on his heels and rose to his feet, keeping the gun on Zach. His cousin climbed slowly—almost lazily—to his feet and smirked.

"You can't do it, can you."

Just pull the trigger and this all ends right here. Right now.

You'll never have to fear him again.

The world seemed to tilt around him, and he blinked to clear his vision, but that didn't help as a stronger wave of dizziness assaulted him. Why was it suddenly so hard to breathe?

Zach's face split in a demonic grin. "I may not get the cop, but at least I got you."

That didn't make any sense. But then Jeremiah coughed, and hot droplets splattered his chin. His mouth tasted metallic, like blood. Aaron appeared beside him, the .38 he kept in his truck gripped lightly in his steady hands.

"Keep your gun on him, Jere." With his sidearm in one hand, Aaron unbuckled his belt and slipped it free from his jeans. "You make even the tiniest move to run and I will gun you down right here, right now, Zach."

The longer Jeremiah held the gun on Zach, the more his hands shook. His cousin held his gaze with that malicious, smug gleam burning in his eyes while Aaron bound his hands behind his back. What did he have to be smug about? He was on his way back to prison, this time for attempted murder at the very least, and yet… that didn't seem to matter. It was as if he'd already gotten what he wanted and twenty to life behind bars was worth it.

"I win," he said.

"Jere, you all right?" Aaron asked.

He couldn't seem to form the words to answer. The gun slipped from his hand, and he sank to his knees, vaguely aware of a sharply increasing pain in his chest. He glanced down to see a dark red stain spreading on his white T-shirt. He pressed his fingers to it, surprised when they came away wet and red, too.

At least I got you….

Laughter swirled around him, uncontrollable with a triumphantly maniacal edge to it. The meadow and forest and mountains careened wildly.

Agony exploded.

"Jeremiah!" Aaron yelled, jumping around Zach to catch him as he started to fall forward. "Shit!"

He gasped again, clutching at his chest and fighting for breath, but every attempt to draw in air made the pain worse. He stared up at Aaron's terrified face, clinging to the sight of those familiar blue eyes.

"God damn it! Heather, I need the first aid kit. Passenger side of my truck, under the seat."

There was no answer, but the laughter stopped abruptly with the crunch of breaking bone. The cursing that followed ended just as quickly.

"Heather! I need the first aid kit *now*! Jere's shot—in the chest." Aaron repeated the location of the first aid kit and turned back to him, pressing his hand over the gunshot wound. "Stay with me, Jeremiah."

He nodded, but he didn't have the strength or the breath left to answer.

"I already lost Erica like this. You will *not* die in my arms like she did. You hear me, little brother?"

* * *

The insane laughter broke the spell, and Heather strode down the steps, side-stepping Aaron as he leapt to stop her.

Zach tore his gaze from Jeremiah, and he laughed even harder as if he had nothing to fear from her. She caught him square in the nose with a fast jab.

He stopped laughing.

"You fucking bitch!"

A left hook to the mouth shut him up, and a right hook sent him stumbling backwards. She chased him down and got in two more punches—another jab with her left and an uppercut with her right that snapped his head backwards. His eyes rolled back into his head as he crashed to the ground.

"Heather!"

Aaron's sharp bellow jerked her around. With the adrenaline pounding through her, she didn't hear his words, but when her brain put the pieces of the scene before her together—Aaron clutching Jeremiah in his arms with his hand over Jere's chest and a crimson blotch stark against Jere's white T-shirt—she raced to Aaron's truck and located the first aid kit under the passenger seat.

When she returned, her eyes sidetracked to Jeremiah. He was conscious but frighteningly pale and his breathing was far too fast and shallow. Fine droplets of blood speckled his lips and chin. Terror like she'd never known gripped her.

"Heather!"

Aaron's voice yanked her attention to his face.

"I need you to look in the first aid kit and see if there's something plastic—like maybe cellophane wrap on the bandages. I need that and the medical tape. Then I need you to get out some gauze sponges and the scissors. You'll have to cut his shirt off him, and when I lift my hand away, I need you to mop up the blood around the wound so I can tape the plastic over it."

"Why—?"

"I think the bullet hit his lung—I can feel the wound sucking as he breathes. I need to stop air from getting into his chest and crushing his lung."

She popped open the first aid kit and located the items Aaron requested, focusing on his step-by-step instructions to keep her hands from shaking. They were surprisingly steady as she cut Jeremiah's T-shirt open, and she exhaled. She could do this. She'd seen plenty of blood in her life, had patched up injured horses and herself. This was no different.

Except that this was Jeremiah and he was dying.

She ripped that thought out of her head before it had time to take root and glanced away, searching for any distraction. Her gaze landed on Zach still lying prone in the dirt where he'd fallen.

"I knocked him out," she uttered. "Zach."

"Great. I really don't give a damn about him right now," Aaron said. "Are you ready for this?"

She had no idea what to expect when he took his hand off the wound and lifted what was left of Jeremiah's ruined shirt away from it… and there wasn't much to see. Just a lot of blood. Too much blood. Marred by the occasional air bubble, it oozed like a sluggish red river from the tiny hole in Jeremiah's chest. At least it wasn't a gushing torrent. That was good, right?

"Focus, Heather."

Nodding, she wiped around the wound as best she could, trying to ignore the tears seeping down the sides of Jeremiah's head as he glanced between her and Aaron with a building panic flashing in his eyes.

"Shh, little brother," Aaron murmured. "I bet it hurts

like hell now, doesn't it? No, don't try to talk. Just stay as still as you can, all right? Stay with us, Jere. We're not going to let you die. Not today. Not after you've survived so much already. And not when life is really getting good."

He glanced at Heather when he said that last bit, and the emotion in his eyes—fear and hope entwined—centered her. She could do this. She had to. Because she'd finally found the man she could spend the rest of her life with and she would *not* lose him. Not until they were old and gray and ready to greet death on their terms, like old friends because they'd both already had a brush with it.

Aaron kept talking while she worked, and when she had the wound as dry as it was going to get while it was still bleeding, he said in the same soothing voice he'd used with Jeremiah, "Okay, Heather. Grab those alcohol pads now, alternating with gauze sponges as you need."

With that done, Aaron laid the plastic over the wound and asked her to tape it in place.

"That'll have to hold you until the pros can get here," Aaron murmured to Jeremiah. "All right, Heather, now I need you to go over to the Royal R and call for a life flight. The GPS coordinates for the cabin are in the center console of my truck, on the Forest Service map. Tell the dispatcher what happened, tell them Sheriff Aaron Hammond is on scene but needs backup. Then call my mother at the main house and have her send Henry or Nick up. Got all that?"

He rattled off a few more instructions for her and then sent her off.

She didn't want to leave Jeremiah, but he was in good hands with Aaron.

The next forty-five minutes were the longest of her

life.

The local Northstar EMTs and Henry had arrived at the cabin before she made it back from the Royal R, and one of Aaron's deputies showed up seconds after she did. Because she would only be in the way if she tried to go to Jeremiah, she sat on the steps of the cabin and watched and hoped. Aaron's deputy checked Zach over while the EMTs were working on Jeremiah—his nose was broken and it appeared he had a concussion as well. That gave Heather a modicum of satisfaction.

Finally, the sound of an approaching helicopter filled the meadow, echoing and re-echoing off the mountain and forest. The cattle, who'd been grazing on the lush alpine grasses as if nothing was out of the ordinary, scattered as the life-flight helicopter landed on the soft, spongy ground. Heather shielded her eyes from the wall of dust and pine needles kicked up off the road by the wind its blades created.

She jumped off the steps and ran with Aaron across the soft, uneven meadow to say goodbye-for-now to Jeremiah as he was carried out to the chopper.

"See you in Missoula in a couple hours," she yelled over the din, her voice cracking. "Hang in there, Jere. Okay?"

He nodded, but his eyes were closed and she heard one of the EMT's say "…fading in and out of consciousness now…" so she had no idea if he'd heard her.

"You can't leave me now. You said you wouldn't leave me!" she called louder as they lifted him into the helicopter. "Remember that? I'm holding you to it because I love you, dammit."

His eyelids flickered open for a moment.

No, that wasn't enough. *More than I love you.* "I adore you. You hear that, Jere?"

This time, his eyes opened all the way and locked on hers. He'd heard her.

Then he was beyond her sight in the helicopter and it was taking off and she was clinging to Aaron in the hurricane howling around her. Long after she could no longer hear the helicopter, she held on to Aaron. He was the only thing holding her up as comprehension of everything that had happened in the last hour crashed down on her.

"He'll be okay," Aaron murmured, hugging her tightly. "He's a fighter."

With her face buried against Aaron's shoulder, she cried as she had not allowed herself to cry since the night she'd cut her wrist. She might've felt as alone now as she had that night, if it weren't for the feel of Aaron's firm chest and his strong arms around her. Then Henry was hugging her, too, and she drew in a ragged breath to stop the tears.

She would *not* act like Jeremiah was already dead or give in for a second more to the fear that he wouldn't win this fight.

"Stay strong, little sis," Henry whispered. "Your hands all right? Because Zach's face sure isn't."

She lifted hands and inspected them, but it was hard to tell what injuries she'd sustained with all the dried blood. Aaron asked Henry to help her wash them off while he talked to his deputy. She held her hands under the pump around the side of the cabin while Henry lifted the handle and brought it down repeatedly until frigid water sloshed out. The breath hissed between her teeth, but the cold water numbed the ache in her hands as she scrubbed them clean.

There were a couple minor cuts on the knuckles of her left hand, most likely from Zach's teeth. Her right hand was okay… except that there was a vivid bruise forming around the two outside knuckles and it hurt a lot worse than her left hand did. She flexed her fingers, and a sharp pain shot through the outside edge of her hand.

She looked up at Henry, expecting some wise crack or other about giving Zach his just desserts, but for once, he wasn't in a joking mood. She wished he was.

"Say something," she said. "Please. Some smartass remark. Anything."

"Remind me never to get into a fight with you." He took her hands and examined them. "Left hand seems okay. But it looks like you might have a boxer's fracture on your right."

"I'll get it looked at when we get to Missoula."

Nodding, he tipped his head toward the road where Aaron and his deputy now had Zach secured in the deputy's SUV. When they reached him, Aaron immediately embraced Heather again and then his brother.

Glancing between them, he asked, "You all right?"

"Fine," Henry replied. "What the hell happened? All Heather could say was Jeremiah had been shot by his dickhead cousin."

"More or less. But actually, he jumped in front of the gun. Zach was aiming at me," Aaron said. "He started to say he had something I needed to see, and then Zach steps out of the woods there beyond the pump…."

Heather stepped away, and Aaron's words faded

behind her. She walked over to the spot where Jeremiah had pile-driven his cousin into the ground, ignoring the scattered drops of blood as she searched the dirt for a glint of silver.

There it was, mostly buried just to the right of where Zach had landed the first time. Jeremiah must've dropped it when he'd wrestled the gun from his cousin. She lifted it gently and blew the dust from it. It gleamed brightly—innocently—in the brilliant late morning sunlight. She walked back to the Hammond twins and handed it to Aaron.

"This is Zach's. Jeremiah said he found it when he first moved into the cabin."

Aaron nodded. "He's positive?"

"Mostly, but he said it'd take a miracle to prove it was Zach's."

"Well, we need a miracle right now, but not that one. Hen, can you let everyone know what's going on? Heather and I need to leave for Missoula. I don't want Jere to wake up without family there."

"Sure thing, bro," Henry replied. "We'll be right behind you. If he wakes up before we get there, give him our love."

Heather latched on to that. Jeremiah *would* wake up again. With a burning ferocity, she refused to believe there was any other possibility, as if that alone was enough to keep him alive.

Fourteen

THE THREE-AND-A-HALF-HOUR RIDE from Northstar to Missoula was excruciating. The miles and minutes dragged by even though Aaron drove faster than the already generous speed limit. Her right hand ached annoyingly, and she wished she'd taken Aaron up on his offer to stop at a gas station to pick up a bottle of ibuprofen or to make an ice pack, but the pain was nothing compared to the memories and scenarios that played through her mind. Aaron called the hospital several times throughout their drive for updates, running it through the Bluetooth in his truck so she could hear it, too, so they knew when Jeremiah had landed, but since then, every call had yielded the same answer—he was in surgery and there was no update.

No news is good news, she reminded herself. *If he'd died, they would tell us.*

At the hospital, Aaron went to check for news on Jeremiah while Heather had her hand checked. By the time the doctors finished poking and prodding and X-raying her right hand and determining that she did indeed have a boxer's fracture, she was frantic. It couldn't have taken more than an hour for the exam, but being so close to Jeremiah without a word about how he was doing was a lesson in balancing precariously on the edge of hysteria.

Just as the doctor was immobilizing her hand in a boxer's splint, a nurse showed Aaron into the room.

"Any news on Jeremiah?"

He shook his head. "Nothing yet."

"But he's been in surgery almost three hours."

"The nurses I talked to said it could take up to six. Maybe more."

Finally noticing that he had neon pink tape wrapped around his left elbow, she asked, "What's that?"

"Donated blood. Don't know if they'll be able to screen it in time to help Jeremiah, but if nothing else, it'll replace some of what they're using on him."

"You're the same blood type?"

Aaron nodded. "Me, Hen, Nick, Dad—we all are."

Why was that such a comforting thought?

Because they're his family. He has people who love him— people he has to stay alive for.

As soon as the doctor released her, she walked to Aaron and hugged him.

The doctor gave her instructions to care for her hand, but she didn't pay any attention. This wasn't her first boxer's fracture; she'd live. Aaron walked with her to the receptionist's desk to finish filling out the paperwork she hadn't had time to complete before she'd been taken into the exam room. Writing with her fourth and fifth fingers immobilized by the splint pushed her to the brink of an explosion, so Aaron took the pen and clipboard and filled in her information as she gave it to him.

"How the hell are you so calm right now?"

"I'm not," he replied, handing the clipboard to the receptionist. "I've just had training and a lot of experience shoving everything deep down until I'm free to give in to it. Ask Skye. She's had to deal with me losing it at home after a bad day numerous times."

They headed toward the waiting room of the ER where a trauma surgeon was currently doing his or her best to save Jeremiah's life, and Heather tried to shove the worry down but failed miserably. She sat in the chair next to Aaron, leaning against him, and closed her eyes, focusing on her breathing. She'd never had much patience for meditating, but she *had* to calm down or she'd send herself into a nervous breakdown before the night was over, and that wouldn't do anyone any good.

Somehow, she managed to exhaust herself into a half-conscious state. A familiar contemporary rock song played faintly from somewhere nearby, and for a moment, she listened—it was one of her favorites. But then the lyrics filtered into her brain, bringing her back to full consciousness as their meaning sank in. The song was about a woman laying her lover in the ground, and an image flashed in her mind. In it, she was standing beside an open grave, surrounded by the Hammonds and many other familiar Northstar faces, and staring at a sleek oak casket bedecked with a huge bouquet of flowers.

No no no no. NO!

She jerked upright with fresh tears burned her eyes. "Whoever is playing that song, please stop," she croaked. "Please."

Why would her imagination *do* that to her? A tear slipped free when she pinched her eyes closed, and she let out a small squeak. The song played on, burning that image deeper into her mind. No… Jeremiah would be okay. That scene would *not* come to pass.

She opened her eyes again and glanced around, trying to locate the source of the song. "Please…. I can't…."

Across the room, a woman about her age hastily poked at the screen of her smartphone, silencing the song, and stared at her with wide eyes.

"I'm sorry," Heather whispered.

Aaron wrapped his arm around her and hugged her.

"I'm sorry," she said again, not sure whom she was apologizing to.

"It's okay, little sis. Go ahead and fall apart now so you can pull yourself back together by the time he wakes up."

By the time he wakes up….

Aaron sounded so sure that would happen, but dammit, they hadn't heard *anything*.

"Aaron? Heather?"

They rose together at Tracie's call. Aaron's mother ran to them, wrapping her arms around them both. Henry, Nick, and Skye were right behind her. Tracie spent at least two full minutes checking her son over to make sure Henry hadn't lied to him and that Aaron was safe and unhurt. Then she released him and hugged Heather, nearly crushing her. The love in that embrace….

Heather shuddered and glanced over Tracie's shoulder at the others as they came in close, silently reaffirming their familial bonds.

"Any news on Jeremiah?" Nick asked.

Aaron shook his head. "Still in surgery."

"But he's alive."

He nodded. When Skye embraced her husband, Heather saw him buckle for the first time.

"I should've listened to him," he whispered.

"Don't do this to yourself, Aaron," Skye said, clasping his face and forcing him to look at her. "You did everything you could within the bounds of the law."

"Did I?"

"Yes, you did."

"God… when he fell…. It was like Erica all over again."

"I know, my love. But it isn't. Jeremiah's still with us, and he's going to *stay* with us."

Feeling like she was intruding on their private conversation, Heather turned away. Aaron had been the steady shoulder she'd needed to lean on, and the least she could do in return was give him a few moments with his wife to—as he'd said—fall apart so he could pull himself back together by the time Jeremiah needed them.

"How's the hand?" Henry asked.

"You were right—boxer's fracture on the fifth metacarpal. It hurts, but they gave me some ibuprofen, and it's helping. Wish it'd help with worrying about Jeremiah, too."

"Nothing but good news is going to help with that, I'm afraid. But take heart, little sis. The house fire couldn't kill him, the deer he hit the night Aaron arrested him couldn't kill him, and jail didn't kill him. This bullet isn't going to kill him, either."

She nodded, hoping with every beat of her heart that he was right. Then she tilted her head. "Little sis? That's the second time you've said that today, and Aaron just said it a couple minutes ago, too."

"Well, you are, aren't you? Maybe not *officially* yet, but as far as I'm concerned, you're my honorary little sister now. And you were before this happened. And you will be even if you and Jeremiah don't stay together."

"Thank you." She exhaled. "I really need that right now."

He hugged her, and she almost started crying again.

"Anyhow, Christina and Curtis should be here in a bit."

Oh, God. Her family. She hadn't given them a second's thought throughout this whole ordeal, and the thought of facing her brother right now threatened to overwhelm her. Then again… he *had* been pretty decent since the night Christina had walked out threatening to leave him. And she could really use her best friend's company right now.

"They're coming?"

"Curtis didn't seem too keen on it, but I don't think Christina gave him a choice."

"I'm going to take Aaron to get some coffee," Skye announced. "Heather, can I get you something?"

"Um… I could use a bottle of water. Thanks."

Heather hunched over her knees, staring at the doors into the ER for a moment before she buried her face in her hands. Tracie sat beside her, rubbing her back, and without meaning to, Heather leaned toward her. The older woman didn't say anything, and Heather marveled at her strength. Jeremiah might not be her son by blood, but he was her son in every other way, and this must be so incredibly hard on her, but she had love and strength enough in reserve to comfort Heather. Tracie didn't say anything, but she didn't have to. Her presence was enough.

Henry and Nick spoke quietly nearby, shifting restlessly between gratitude that Aaron was unhurt and fear for Jeremiah. After Aaron and Skye returned and handed Heather an ice-cold bottle of water, they joined Nick and Henry, and Aaron described everything that had happened in detail.

Heather clamped her hands over her ears. Being there had been bad enough, and it would undoubtedly haunt her dreams for a long time without hearing it all repeated again.

She lifted her eyes to the big clock on the far wall. Why was the second hand moving so slowly?

She took a long drink of her water, screwed the cap on and off and on again, and then spent two minutes tapping her fingers against the bottle. Then it was back to watching the clock's hands. A few people came with minor emergencies, and even the woman who'd been playing the song on her phone was able to take her loved one home. Heather watched them all go, her anxiety rising with each one that walked out the door as she bounced between disbelief and numb terror.

Rapid footfalls echoed in the waiting area, approaching.

"Heather!"

She rose and turned toward the doors just in time for Christina to slam into her and wrap her in a tight hug. Curtis was a dozen paces behind his wife, looking harried and drawn.

"Thank God you're okay," Christina sighed. "How's Jeremiah?"

"Don't know yet. He's still in surgery. He's been in surgery for hours. Four now? Five? I've lost track."

Curtis reached them and didn't wait for Christina to step away before he hugged Heather. "I'm so sorry, Sis. He'll be okay, though, right?"

"I don't…." She drew in a shuddering breath and let it out slowly. "I don't know. But he'd better be."

"Whatever I might think about him, he makes you happy, and that's what matters. Of course, he's starting to grow on me, too. He has a good heart."

"He does." Heather looked up at her brother. "Thank you."

"I should warn you. Mom's—"

"Heather!"

She winced at the shrill note in her mother's voice.

"—here," Curtis finished. "Sorry, Sis."

"I do *not* need her stressing me out any more than I already am," Heather muttered.

"I know, but she wouldn't let us leave her at home. Not even to watch the kids—she asked Anna to take them."

Lily reached her then and threw her arms around Heather's neck. "Oh, thank God my baby girl is okay!"

"I'm fine, Mother."

"I was so worried. We've been trying to call you for hours, but it keeps going to voicemail."

"I'm sorry. My cell phone's in my truck, which is still parked up at the allotment cabin. Everything happened so fast—it was crazy—I didn't even think to grab it."

Her mother hugged her again. "I'm just so glad you're okay."

"More or less. I'd be a lot better if someone would just tell us how Jere is."

Heather wandered back to her seat and perched on the edge of it with her hands folded in her lap. Aaron, Skye, and Henry moved to the other side of Tracie so Heather's family could sit with her. Christina quickly took the chair to her left and folded her hands around Heather's. Curtis sat beside his wife, leaving the chair to Heather's right for Lily.

Just like that, she was back to waiting.

For a little while, she was glad to have her mother and Curtis and Christina here with her. Especially Christina. The heat of her friend's hand in hers and the weight of Christina's head on her shoulder was an anchor that kept her from being swept away by fear. But gradually the agitation radiating from her mother began to wear on her. For a while, Heather ignored it. But the longer she let it go unremarked, the more it grated on her. Realizing Lily hadn't once asked about Jeremiah, Heather turned to her mother.

"Why did you come? I'm sure Henry told you I was okay."

"I had to make sure for myself."

Out of habit, she reached to comb her right hand through her hair and was suddenly reminded that her hand was in a split. She frowned at it and dropped her hand back into her lap.

"What's wrong with your hand?"

"Boxer's fracture. It's fine."

"How on earth did you get a boxer's fracture?"

"How do you think? Punching someone."

"Aaron said it was pretty impressive," Henry remarked to Curtis. "Said your sister knocked Zach out with just five hits."

Curtis reached behind his wife and gave Heather's shoulder a squeeze. "Well done, Sis. How'd you do it?"

"The same combination you were never fast enough to master."

He chuckled, and for the first time since this morning, she smiled. "I'm glad you're here, Curtis." She hugged her friend. "And of course I'm glad you came, Christina. So glad."

"Hey, Jeremiah's my friend." Christina let out a breath, her face pale. "I still can't believe it."

"Neither can I."

Lily bolted to her feet. "All right, this has gone on long enough. We're going home now, Heather. Go get your things out of Sheriff Hammond's truck."

"I beg your pardon?"

Surely her mother wasn't asking—no, *telling*—her to leave the hospital right now.

"I know you think he's a good man," Lily continued, "and I love that you are so willing to look for the good in people, but now it's time for you to end this foolishness."

Her brain refused to process those words. They were just too absurd, even for her mother. "What foolishness?"

"This! All of this. Before *you* end up in the hospital, too. I will *not* stand by any longer and watch you throw your life away. I will not lose my daughter to this… this…."

Her mother gestured around the waiting room and at the Hammonds, who regarded her first with shock and then with revulsion and anger. Unlike Lily Brown, however, they were too gracious to give voice to it. Heather's gaze locked on them, and Tracie and Aaron both gave her a subtle nod.

Without a word, she understood their message. This was her battle to fight, and they believed she was more than capable of waging it on her own… that she *needed* to fight it herself. But they had her back just as Jeremiah had had her back since their first date on her birthday.

"I'm not leaving Jeremiah," she said, rising slowly and glaring down at her mother. "Not now. Not *ever.*"

"Look what he's dragged you into!"

"How *dare* you."

Even to her ears, her voice sounded low, deadly, and from the corner of her vision, she saw smug pride infiltrate the Hammonds' expressions, but her mother scowled at her, oblivious. She jabbed her finger toward the doors into the ER.

"He is in there fighting for his *life!*" She stared her mother down, her lip curled in disgust, and when Lily opened her mouth to retort, she said, "No."

Something in her voice must've hit the right nerve because her mother jerked back like she'd been slapped.

"Not another word. You are done talking. You're going to listen now."

Wide-eyed, her mother responded with silence. For once.

"For *years*, I have picked men I thought would please you. Men that fit *your* ideals of what a good man is. And not one of them gave me the courage to open up about the night I contemplated killing myself."

Lily flinched.

"You want to know who gave me the courage to open up about it? Go ahead and guess. That's right. Jeremiah." She loosened the laces of her wrist band and yanked it off. She'd never wear it again. When she held her hand up and turned the inside of her wrist to her mother, breath sucked through Lily's teeth. "I did that when I was seventeen—the night I broke Brock's nose. The night my entire family left me alone to cry myself out in the barn with my horse because they blamed me entirely for the fight without giving me even half a chance to defend myself. Jeremiah was the first person I told the whole truth to… because, instead of tearing me down like you do, he built me up and loved me for who I am, flaws and all."

Her body quivered with a lifetime of pent-up rage.

"Heather, please."

She held her mother's gaze, daring her to contradict any of it. When anger ignited in Lily's eyes, she tensed, ready for the fight.

"This will end right now. You see what that boy is doing to you? He's got you so tied up in knots that you can't even see what he is."

"No, it's *you* who can't see. He's in that operating room because he stepped in front of a bullet meant for Aaron. He was willing to sacrifice his life to save his brother's."

"Aaron isn't his brother."

"Like hell I'm not," Aaron snapped.

"All that and you *still* question his heart." A strange calm washed over her—the same serenity she usually found only when she was alone with Jeremiah. There was a line she'd been waiting for her mother to cross, and that was it. When she spoke again, it was with a level voice. "I am done with you. You hear me? You, Dad, Brock, Brianna—I am fucking done with you all."

"Heather, please don't do this. Please, come home."

She didn't respond. Instead, she returned to her chair, picked up her water bottle, and took a long drink. Her mother's increasingly tearful pleas fell on deaf ears, and finally, Curtis excused himself to escort his mother out to the car. She expected him to return, but minutes passed, and he still hadn't come back. Then Christina's cell phone dinged with a new text message.

"He took her to a hotel," she said. "She's hysterical, so he's going to sit with her for a little while."

"I really don't give a damn. But it's good of him to put up with her. Tell him I'm sorry for putting him in that position."

"I will do no such thing," Christina retorted. "He still has a lot to make up for."

Heather's lips quirked.

A doctor stepped through the doors to the ER, but she'd seen so many come and go that she didn't pay the woman any attention.

"Sheriff Hammond?"

Everyone rose and turned to the door, gathering together as they waited anxiously for the report. The doctor looked tired but…. Heather couldn't quite decide. Relieved?

Pleased? That had to mean good news, right?

Aaron stood and gestured for the doctor to join them.

"He's out of surgery. He was lucky—the bullet just barely missed his heart. It went through his left lung and lodged in a rib, but it was a fairly straight shot, and we were able to remove the bullet. I assume you'll need it as evidence, Sheriff?"

"Yes, ma'am," Aaron replied.

"He may need another transfusion or two before this is all over, and we've got him on the ventilator to regulate his breathing and make sure that lung stays inflated. He's also got a chest tube in place to drain off the excess air and fluids in his chest cavity."

"Is he awake?"

"No, and we're going to keep him sedated while he's on the ventilator."

"How long will he be on that?" Tracie asked.

"We're going to see how he does tonight before we make that call, but hopefully only overnight."

"He's going to be all right, though?" Heather asked.

The doctor smiled, and it was the most beautiful thing she'd ever seen. There was so much hope in that smile. "He's not out of danger yet, but I'm optimistic."

Suddenly, her legs couldn't hold her, and she leaned heavily on the person closest to her—Henry.

He slipped an arm around her shoulders and squeezed. "See? I told you this wouldn't kill him, little sis. He's got too much to live for."

"Heather? Why don't you go in to see him first," Aaron suggested. "I need to talk to the doctor for a few minutes, and then I'll be right behind you."

Christina gave her a hug as she left the group and followed the doctor's directions to the ICU room Jeremiah had been moved to. A nurse was just stepping outside when she reached it, and he smiled brightly as he held the door open with a chipper *come on in.*

The room was mostly dark; the lights were off and the heavy curtains were drawn across the window. There was another nurse at Jeremiah's bedside, jotting notes on her clipboard, but Heather paid her little attention. Her gaze was drawn to the man in the bed.

The crisp sterility of the blankets on the bed and the hospital gown were a sharp contrast to the blood-soaked T-shirt she'd cut off him hours ago. She shuddered when she took in all the tubes and wires—the ventilator, the chest tube, the IV, and the various monitors. They and the beeping of the machines drove home even harder than the blood just how close he'd come to death and reminded her that he still wasn't too far from it.

"I'll leave you alone with him," the second nurse said when she'd finished her task. She slipped quietly from the room and closed the door.

Heather pulled a chair over and sat lightly in it. Tentatively, she slipped her hand around Jeremiah's. What she wouldn't give to see his beautiful, kind eyes open and crinkle at the corners as he smiled at her....

"Hey," she whispered. "Glad you're still with us."

There was no response, and even though she hadn't expected one, the silence was agonizing. Her eyes burned, and she didn't bother trying to fight it. The tears fell, streaming silently down her cheeks as she stroked

Jeremiah's hand with her thumb. His skin was cool, but there was enough warmth in it to reassure her.

"That's right. You have to stick around for a long time because I need you." A lyric came to mind from the song she'd asked the woman in the waiting room to stop playing, and a sob escaped her. "The angels can't have you yet."

Fifteen

AWARENESS CAME SLOWLY. Small details filtered through the comfortable, murky darkness—the beeping first, then quiet voices he couldn't make out. Little by little, consciousness returned, and with it came the bigger details. Why was his throat so raw and why did his body feel so sluggish? As the pieces came together, fragments of memory returned. A helicopter. Paramedics and doctors and nurses. Blood. Pain. Aaron telling him he couldn't die in his arms like his first wife had. Heather telling him that he couldn't leave her because she loved him and adored him.

Heather.

He smiled. Or rather, tried to. He didn't have the energy to do more than make his lips twitch.

He opened his eyes, and when his surroundings came

into focus, he was unsurprised but disoriented to find himself in a hospital room hooked up to an IV and various monitors… and what the hell was sticking out the side of his chest? He lifted his head to look but was distracted when he saw Heather with her chair pulled over beside him, her head pillowed on one arm and a paperback copy of *The Hunger Games* lying beside her with her left hand holding it open. Her cherished face was slackened by sleep, but the faint frown indicated it was a light, fitful respite.

His gaze shifted to the table beside the bed, and this time, he managed a full smile. Rather than the usual flowers and balloons, the table held a stack of new books—all titles he'd been wanting to read.

Too tired to keep his eyes open long, he let them close again and redirected his limited energy to knitting the fragmented memories together. He was able to come up with an incomplete and distorted but comprehensible understanding of what had happened.

His fears had come true. Zach had found him.

And he had survived.

He was a little worse for wear, obviously, but he was alive.

"He should be waking up soon," an unfamiliar, feminine voice said quietly. "I'm confident he's past the worst. His pulse is strong, and his blood pressure's almost back up to normal again after that last transfusion this morning—thank you for donating, by the way."

"It's the least I could do," Aaron replied. "The *very* least."

"The chest tube will probably come out tomorrow."

"Excellent news."

"Indeed. Everything is looking great, Sheriff Hammond. You and Ms. Brown did an excellent job with that temporary patch. He's lucky you were there."

"No, I'm lucky *he* was there."

Feeling movement on the bed, Jeremiah opened his eyes.

The surprise widening Heather's sleepy blue eyes shifted into a startling relief.

"Hey, angel," she murmured. "Welcome back."

"Hi, baby girl," he croaked. "What is wrong with my throat?"

"Look who's awake," Aaron remarked, joining Heather at his bedside.

"Your throat and vocal chords will probably be sore for a day or so from the endotracheal tube," the doctor said. "Frustrating, I'm sure, but perfectly normal."

The doctor gave him a brief overview the extent of his injuries, but his mind was still too foggy to make sense of even that simple explanation.

With a sympathetic smile, the doctor added, "I'll give you all the details of your surgery and recovery later, when you're more lucid and have had time to visit with your family. The most important part is that everything looks great, and I expect you'll recover fully in no time."

"Thanks, Doc," he rasped.

"My pleasure. I'm sure you have a lot of questions to ask your family, but try to rest your voice and let them do the talking."

Jeremiah nodded in agreement.

"I'll be back to check on you in a little while."

After the doctor left the room, Aaron sat beside him

on the bed, careful not to sit on his leg or any of the tubes or wires that seemed to be running everywhere. The older man stared at him for a long time without speaking, and then let his gaze wander over the medical equipment surrounding him. When their gazes met again, Jeremiah was shocked to see tears in Aaron's eyes.

"I've never been so scared in my life," the sheriff said. "Not even when Erica died. I didn't have time to be scared then. I had *way* too much time to be scared yesterday, though."

"*Way* too much time," Heather agreed.

"Almost seven hours from the time you were shot to the time Dr. Cruz came out to tell us you were out of surgery. And I don't think anyone in that waiting room has ever been as relieved as we all were when she told us she was optimistic you'd survive."

"And I don't think any of us slept last night," Heather remarked. "I didn't."

She glanced at Aaron, who shook his head.

Jeremiah tapped Aaron's watch.

"It's almost noon," Aaron replied. "You've been out for twenty-four hours."

He closed his eyes. He'd lost a full rotation of the earth.

"How are you feeling?" Heather asked hesitantly.

"Tired. Out of it."

"No kidding." She gave a sniff of laughter. "I meant… how's the pain?"

He opened his eyes again and frowned. His chest hurt, mostly on the left side, but it was with a strange detachment that he felt it. The doctor undoubtedly had him on some serious pain meds. "Tolerable."

"Good."

"Zach?" he asked.

"In jail," Aaron replied. "Don't worry about him. Worry about healing."

"I'm done worrying about Zach."

"Good. Because he'll be going away for life. There's not a jury in this state that will find him not guilty even if he doesn't enter a guilty plea." Aaron gripped his shoulder for a moment with bright relief and affection in his eyes. "You up for seeing everyone else?"

"Everyone?"

"Well, Mom, Skye, Henry, and Nick. Dad, Linds, Beth, and Austin are at home with the kids and Murphy, holding down the fort. We didn't figure the kids needed to be here until we were sure…."

Aaron didn't finish the thought, but he didn't need to. Jeremiah got the message. *Until we were sure you were going to make it.*

Clearing his throat, he added, "Curtis and Christina are here, too. Do you want me to send them in a couple at a time or can you handle all of us at once?"

"Maybe all at once," Jeremiah croaked. "Don't know how long I can stay awake."

Nodding, Aaron left him alone with Heather. The room was lit only by the sliver of bright sunlight streaming through the gap between the heavy curtains, but it was plenty bright enough for him to see the dark circles under her eyes and the shifting tides of fear and affection and relief in them.

"Sorry I scared you."

She nodded in acknowledgement, pinching her lips between her teeth.

He reached for her hand. When he encountered a splint, his brows furrowed. "Your hand?"

Her expression shifted into a devilish grin. "I broke it on your cousin's face."

"How bad?"

"His face or my hand?"

He laughed lightly and instantly regretted it.

"Yeah, don't laugh. Sorry. My hand's not bad. His face…. Not sure. I broke his nose, though, and the EMTs were pretty sure he had a concussion, but that could've happened when you plowed into him—I think he smacked his head on the ground. How much do you remember?"

"Bits and pieces. Not very clear right now."

"That's probably for the best." She shook her head. "That's a good thing you did. He would've killed Aaron. But don't you *ever* do anything so stupid like jumping in front of a loaded gun again."

She held his gaze for a long time without speaking again, and his heart ached as tears filled her eyes.

"I'm sorry," he whispered.

"Don't be. I didn't fully realize until you were lying on the ground in Aaron's arms with b-blood pouring out of your ch-chest that I don't want to live without you. I love you, d-dammit."

He had never wanted to hug someone in his life as badly as he did now. He wished he could wrap her in his arms until the tears stopped and promise her he'd never leave her again.

One corner of his mouth twitched. "You love me?"

"More than that, I adore you. That's more than love, right?"

He nodded.

"You're the right man for me, angel, and I want to spend the rest of my life with you. How could I not when you bring out the best in me and make me feel wanted and, well, *adored* just as I am? Who wouldn't want a man like that?"

Was this the pain meds talking? Surely she hadn't just said…. "Is this your way of saying you want to marry me?"

She laughed softly. "I guess it is. And with my track record, you ought to know how I feel about that kind of commitment."

He smiled and fought the laugh that threatened. "Please don't make me laugh. It hurts."

"Sorry."

He searched her eyes for what felt like at least a minute for any sign that she was joking, although his groggy brain couldn't think of a reason why she would tease him with his wildest dream come true. Hospital bedsides were the place for honest, deeply felt confessions, not light-hearted teasing.

"This is real?"

"This is real, angel." She leaned forward and kissed him lightly. "You're something special, and I'd be a fool to ever let you go."

Aaron returned with the members of the Hammond family who'd made the drive to the hospital—he didn't even know which one he was at—with Heather's brother and sister-in-law right behind them, preventing him from asking Heather again if she really meant what she'd said. He would've thought nothing could drive that wonderful idea from his head, but with his energy so low, he didn't have enough to focus on more than one thought at a time, and with Tracie crying over him and Henry wholly serious for once in his life as he expressed his gratitude that Jeremiah had pulled through, his energy was drawn to them. They took turns talking, sensing perhaps that he wasn't awake enough to process several people talking at once. Tracie tried to apologize for smothering him, but he shook his head and smiled. It was more incredible than he could say to be a part of her family.

Heather was silent while the others talked, but she didn't let go of his hand.

Curtis didn't say much other than to add to the chorus of "we're glad you're alive", but he sensed whatever animosity or feelings of ill will Heather's brother had ever held for him were a thing of the past. There was no condescension or impatience in Curtis's gaze. Only the same relief that was in everyone else's. When Jeremiah asked what had changed his mind, he shrugged.

"Heather's right," Curtis said. He turned his gaze on his sister. "You're good for her. That's all I ever needed to know, and I'm sorry it took me so long to figure that out. The rest of the family will come around eventually."

Christina snorted. "After what your mother said to Aaron yesterday, I doubt Heather will give them a chance to."

"She's here, too?" Jeremiah asked. "What'd she say?"

"She said Aaron isn't your brother," Christina replied. "And he made it quite clear you are."

"In blood now, too," Henry muttered, scowling.

"Sorry, Heather. I don't think I'll ever forgive your mother for that one. Or any of what she said about my little brother."

"Neither will I," Heather replied.

The chill in her voice shocked him, and he tried to sit up, but Aaron pressed down on his shoulders. That he was too weak to resist *at all* sent an instinctive rush of panic shuddering through him.

"Easy, angel," Heather murmured.

"What *happened?*"

"What do you think? My mother ran her mouth like she always does… and I've had enough. I told her I wanted her and Dad and Brock and Brianna out of my life."

"Only she wasn't nearly so polite," Christina remarked.

"I'm sorry, Heather, I never—"

"Aren't you the one who told me I shouldn't put up with their shit?"

He nodded.

"Well, this is the only way that I won't have to. And that is *not* your fault in any way, shape, or form. They are poison to me. All right? So let's not talk about that anymore. Because it stresses me out, and judging by your heart monitor, me being stressed stresses *you* out, and we all need you to relax and rest and get better. Got it?"

"Yes, ma'am."

Two nurses swarmed into the room, alerted by the increase in his heart rate. Everyone fell silent while they checked him over, giving his visitors less than friendly looks. Satisfied he wasn't in danger, they left the room again, and if he was feeling stronger, he might've laughed at the sheepish expressions on nearly every face gathered around him. But his energy was dwindling; sluggishness trickled through him, leaving him ever weaker and making his limbs leaden.

He wanted to stay awake to soak up the love that filled the room because it was more powerful than the pain and exhaustion, and he knew if he could let it seep into him, he'd be healed in no time, but his body slackened with frightening speed, utterly spent.

"I'm sorry," he murmured. His eyelids, too heavy now to hold open, slid closed. "But I'm done. More later?"

"Lots more later," Tracie replied. She kissed his forehead and brushed her hand back through his hair. "See you again in a little while. I love you, Jeremiah."

"Love you, too," he mumbled.

The others expressed similar sentiments, and by the time they had all filed out of the room, he was teetering on the edge of sleep. Only Heather remained; he didn't need to see her or hear her breathing to know it. He'd recognize her incredible, fiery spirit anywhere without sight or sound or smell or touch or taste. She was in his heart, now and always, and she was what had kept it beating even when death had beckoned.

* * *

After a week in the stuffy hospital, the perfect summer air blowing on his face through the open window of Aaron's truck was heavenly. Jeremiah had spent most of the ride home from Missoula resting with his eyes closed and his head propped against the headrest—not quite awake but not quite sleeping, either—enamored with the fresh air laden with the warm scents of late summer in the mountains.

He would never take the simple pleasure of this clean, wild air for granted again.

Heather laid her hand on his thigh. "Still doing okay?"

"Not okay. Great. I'm not sure I ever realized how wonderful the air smells up here."

"It's pretty amazing. How are you feeling otherwise? The bumps and turns aren't bugging you too much, are they?"

He opened an eye to locate her left hand and squeezed it. "I'm fine, Heather, really. A little sore, especially the ribs, and tired, but I actually feel pretty good. I promise."

"All right, Jere," Aaron said, slowing the truck. "Are you *sure* you want to do this?"

"Positive."

The sheriff turned off the scenic byway onto the dirt road to the allotment cabin, driving far slower than he normally would to avoid jarring Jeremiah on the potholes. He parked in front of the cabin but left the truck running—this wouldn't take long.

Gingerly, Jeremiah opened the door and stepped outside into the brilliant afternoon. The meadow was as gorgeous and as unspoiled as ever, sprinkled with wildflowers and dotted with Lazy H cattle, and above it, the granite dome of Comet Mountain gleamed against a vivid cobalt sky with only a few patches of tired snow remaining. The cabin sat quietly at the edge of the forest, and he climbed the steps. It was locked and they didn't have the key, so he could only peer in through the windows. While he'd been in the hospital, the Hammonds had finished clearing his things out of it. He'd worried that seeing the cabin vacant again would somehow reduce the strength of the memories he and Heather had made in it, but they swirled around him with delightfully sweet intensity.

The other thing he'd dreaded—that what had happened here would somehow taint those memories— also proved to be a baseless fear. He still struggled to recall the details of everything that had happened after the bullet had hit him, and maybe that lack of clarity made it possible to survey the scene with a surprising serenity, but he doubted it.

Zach had come here to kill him and Aaron, and he'd failed.

The fear that had gripped him since Zach's release from prison was gone. Deciding that he would no longer let it control him had significantly reduced it, but it wasn't until he stepped out onto this porch and saw his cousin walk out of the trees with his gun aimed at Aaron that it had truly vanished. In that moment, love of his brother had shattered it, destroying it once and for all.

Acutely aware of his injuries, he descended the stairs with delicate steps and trod out to the place where he'd tackled Zach. Funny that he hadn't immediately realized he was shot.

"Jere, I don't think this is a good idea," Heather said, still standing beside Aaron's truck, hugging herself.

"Sure it is. Doc Cruz said I'm fine to take short walks."

"That's not what I'm talking about."

"I need to do this," he replied. "I need to face what

happened and reclaim this place."

Heather and Aaron joined him after that and listened as he described what he remembered, filling in the gaps for him. He especially liked the parts where Heather knocked Zach out and Aaron's deputy was none-too-gentle loading him in his SUV. Judging by the pallor of their faces and the haunted looks in both their eyes, Jeremiah figured they needed to reclaim this spot even more than he did.

"What happens now?" he asked.

"Zach's expected to plead guilty at the pre-trial hearing tomorrow morning. You remember me saying I wanted an airtight case against him?"

Jeremiah nodded.

"Well, we've got one. For you *and* for Rogers."

"I thought Zach was at work when Rogers was killed."

"His boss has been covering for him this whole time."

As soon as Aaron said it, Jeremiah nearly slapped his palm to his forehead. How had he not once thought to question the boss's innocence in all this? Having an employer willing to lie and provide alibis for him would've been one of Zach's top priorities, and he had an incredible talent for charming and manipulating people into doing whatever he wanted them to… and making sure once he had them that they understood what would happen if they didn't cooperate. "Why didn't I think he might be?"

"I keep trying to tell you—you're a good man. You always have been. That goodness is so ingrained in you that you can't actually see the world the way Zach does, no matter how adept you are at reading his invisible trails."

He wasn't quite convinced Aaron was right, so he filed the praise away. "What convinced the boss to talk?"

"The same nine-millimeter Zach shot you with…" Aaron had to pause to clear his throat. "…was the same gun that fired the bullet that killed Rogers, and it belonged to his boss, who, as you can imagine, wasn't willing to face the death penalty for Zach. Apparently, money and loyalty and fear of retaliation only go so far when one's life is on the line. Ain't ballistic forensics great?"

"And the cows?"

"That part's not *quite* as airtight as I'd like—we have several witnesses stating that that cross you found in the cabin is in fact Zach's—but it doesn't matter. He'll plead guilty and be sentenced to two life terms to be served consecutively."

Zach's words echoed in his mind. *I win.*

Jeremiah shook his head. "I almost—*almost*—want to go to his pre-trial hearing. But he knows I'm alive, right?"

"He does. And is none too happy about it."

"Good. That's enough then, that he knows he lost."

Taking Heather's hand, he pulled her gently against his still-healing left side and wrapped an arm around her shoulder. Then he grabbed Aaron's hand and brought him in close, too. They stood like that for a long time, silent, letting the memories of the events of the summer flow through and around them and then… together, they let go. He felt the tension slip from their bodies, and as it did, they all tipped their faces toward the brilliant August sun.

Smiling, Jeremiah said, "See? We all needed this."

"All right," Aaron laughed. "You were right again. But if we're all satisfied that Zach will never haunt us here, we need to get home. Murphy has been absolutely beside himself without you, and Mom and Dad want us all down to the main house. They—we—have a surprise or two for you."

"A surprise? What is it?"

"That was the lamest attempt at sleuthing out an answer I've ever heard."

"What can I say? I'm wounded."

"Yeah, that's only going to work for a few weeks, and then you're back to work part time on your portable offices. You've got orders backing up."

"I do?"

"Yep. Five now, I think?"

"Wow. You going to help me with them, baby girl?"

"You bet," Heather replied.

Aaron headed back to his truck, but Jeremiah lingered behind with Heather.

Turning to her, he frowned. "You all right?"

"Yeah. Just… basking in the knowledge of how amazing you are. You almost died right here only a week ago, and yet here you are, smiling and joking like it's no big deal."

"It isn't. I survived, it's a gorgeous day, the woman I love is right here by my side, and I have my whole life ahead of me to love her the way she deserves to be loved—wholly, adoringly, and unconditionally."

"I can't believe it took me so long to see what a rare gem you are," she murmured. "Better late than never."

He took her face in his hands and kissed her gently. He wanted to kiss her more deeply, but he didn't dare; that would only make him want more than he could give right now. He *was* still healing, after all. Without letting go of her hand, he started toward Aaron's truck.

As Aaron drove down to the main house on the Lazy H, Jeremiah resumed his earlier occupation of appreciating the breeze coming in the open window. The air was so sweet and soft that he chuckled. *No wonder Murph likes window surfing.*

The thought brought a refreshed longing. Every member of his family had been to Missoula to visit him in the hospital, but he hadn't seen Murph since he and Aaron had headed up to the allotment cabin to clear it out, and as the week had progressed, he'd missed the Australian shepherd's companionship more and more until missing him was a worse ache than the healing lung and ribs.

He was mildly surprised to see Curtis and Christina's car and Ainsley's SUV parked among the Hammond family's vehicles. He also spotted Luke Conner's black Dodge and his parents' pickup. There was also a 1978 Ford that looked like his truck… but didn't. Instead of rust-spotted cream and brown, this truck was a flawless gleaming metallic root beer.

"That isn't…" he started, staring at it.

"Your truck?" Aaron finished for him. "Yes, it is. I'm glad Henry was able to get it back home in time."

"My truck? Seriously? How'd you know?"

"Heather said you'd talked about having it painted that color."

"I hope I did okay picking the color," she said. "I didn't realize there was more than one shade of root beer paint. The guy at the body shop gave me half a dozen to pick from. This one seemed the most like you."

"Okay? It's *perfect*." He turned abruptly to her. "Wait. You've been in Missoula with me the whole time. When did you...?"

"Before Rogers was killed. We all thought it would be a good birthday present. Because we *know* how much you love that truck."

"I do." He hugged her tightly, uncaring when his chest complained. "Thank you. So much."

She beamed at him. "Well, go on. I know you want to reunite with her."

He stumbled out of Aaron's truck as soon as his brother parked it and wandered over to his own. He let his hand hover over the hood for a moment, inspecting the paint job. It was, as he'd thought upon first glance, flawless. Whoever had done the paint had also finished the bodywork he hadn't had a chance to get to yet. With Heather's comment in mind, he slid his hand over the hood, making a show of hugging his truck.

"So, that's the first surprise," Aaron remarked. "Come on around back, and we'll get to the rest."

With Heather's arm around his waist, he followed Aaron to the backyard where a banner saying *Welcome Home, Jeremiah* had been strung between two posts. Tracie had her smoker going full force with June and Beth and Lindsay helping.

Excited whining and barking drew his attention to one of the picnic tables; Murph sat on the table with Austin holding his leash as a precaution. The dog wiggled uncontrollably in his excitement, and Jeremiah let go of Heather to greet his dog.

The leash proved unnecessary; Murph seemed to

sense that he wasn't himself and kept his rear end planted on the table. Jeremiah was glad not to have to bend over to give his dog some long overdue loves. He buried his hands and his face in the dog's soft, freshly groomed fur and was rewarded with anxious kisses all over every inch of his neck that Murph could reach.

"Damn, I missed you," he whispered. "Good dog."

Murph whimpered in reply.

"How bad was he?" Jeremiah asked Austin when Murph finally stopped licking him.

"Bad. But don't let him fool you. We've all been spoiling him in your absence."

"I'm sure you have been."

After that, it was time for everyone to greet him and welcome him home. It wasn't *quite* a hero's welcome, as everyone seemed hesitant to talk about what had happened, and he was grateful for that. He was no more a hero than anyone else here; he knew with a certainty that any one of them would've done the same thing he had in the same situation. Luke *had* done the same thing, if he'd heard the correct story of what had happened up at Sawtooth Lake all those years ago.

"Saved by a tree root," June's son joked when Jeremiah asked him to clarify. "And I'll take that concussion over your bullet to the lung any day."

Next it was Curtis and Christina's turn. Curtis embraced him lightly. Christina was a bit more enthusiastic, but she was careful not to hurt him.

Jeremiah groaned inwardly. He couldn't wait to be past *that*. He didn't like feeling so fragile, and he was certain that he'd be going stir crazy from sitting around so much by the time he was allowed to return to even part-time work. Thank God for that stack of books everyone had brought him.

"I'm surprised Mom isn't here trying to crash the party," Heather said to her brother.

"Don't count on her doing that anymore," Curtis replied. "She's pretty humbled after what you said… and after I refused to be her go between."

"Oh? Give me the dirt."

"Not much to tell. She asked me to convince you to talk to her. I told her no."

She wrapped her arms tightly around her brother's neck. "Thank you, Curtis. I'm sorry she's trying to put you in the middle. But I just can't deal with her anymore. Or Dad or Brock or Brianna."

"I get it, Sis. I do. You know, at first I thought you were being a little unfair, but I gotta say… it's been nice to spend time with you and see a side of you I'm not sure I've ever really seen."

"Yeah? What side is that?"

"The happy one."

Heather looked at Jeremiah and smiled. "I'm definitely happy."

Tracie, who'd had her hands full with the pulled pork, was the last to welcome him home and also the only one who cried. She tried to fight it, swiping at her eyes, but the tears fell, anyhow. "I'm sorry, Jeremiah. I promised myself I wouldn't, but I can't help it. It is just so good to have you home again. I know it's only been a week, but this family has had a hole in it without you here, and now that you're back… we're whole again."

"You have no idea how much that means to me, Mom."

"Anyhow, let's get your surprises out of the way because I'm sure you're ready for some home-cooked food."

He almost groaned at the promise of tasting his first bite of something that wasn't boring hospital food, and it appeared Tracie had gone all out with the barbecue. "Oh, yeah."

"All right!" she called. "Let's get some things out of the way so this boy can eat!"

Her declaration was met with cheers and laughter, and Jeremiah soaked it up.

"You've already seen your truck, right?"

He nodded and kissed Heather's cheek.

"The next one is a bit bigger."

"Bigger than having my truck painted? Is that possible?"

"Wait and see, little brother," Henry remarked, grinning.

John handed him a hand-drawn map, and it took him a minute to figure out what it was—Aspen Creek Road with Henry's, Aaron's, and Nick's houses marked on it. But there was another spot marked, between Aaron's and Nick's homes. He looked up at John.

"What is this?"

"A newly leveled home site," he replied. "More specifically, the home site where you and Heather will build your house."

"I can't."

"You can and you will. You're family, Jeremiah. And

before you get to thinking we just came up with this after all this happened, we didn't. Tracie and I have been talking about this for a long time. Ask Nick. He's the one who picked the spot—right there next to the creek in that little aspen grove."

Jeremiah knew the spot well—it was his favorite on Aspen Creek Road.

He opened his mouth to thank them, but another thought interrupted. John had said it was for him and Heather. "Hold on a second…."

"I think he's caught on to us, John," Heather remarked.

"I didn't imagine you saying you wanted to marry me. That wasn't the pain meds talking."

"No." She ducked her head shyly. "But I didn't think you'd remember it."

"I'd have to be dead to forget it."

When she and half the people gathered flinched, he offered them a sheepish smile.

"Sorry. Bad choice of words."

"Hey, it's good you can joke about it," Henry remarked.

Aaron nodded. "It just might take some of us a little longer to get to that point."

"I'll try to remember that." Jeremiah slipped his arms around Heather. "Anyhow, back to this idea of you wanting to marry me… yes."

"Yes what?" Heather asked, frowning.

"Yes, I'll marry you. Though there is an issue of who buys the ring. Since you asked, does that mean I get a pretty sparkly ring to broadcast to the world that I'm taken?"

"Actually, we have a solution," Tracie said. "Love, would you do the honors?"

Nodding, John disappeared into the house for a moment. When he returned, he held a small box reverently in the palm of his hand. He took Jeremiah's hand and set the little box in it.

"What's this?" Jeremiah asked, opening it.

"It's the ring I proposed to Tracie with."

He started to say he couldn't take it, but he couldn't make his mouth form the words. It was too perfect—a square-cut diamond set low in a sturdy yellow-gold band—and he wanted to see it on Heather's hand too much. He hugged John and Tracie together and thanked them.

"Glad you're not going to try to argue us out of this, too."

He shook his head and turned to Heather as he plucked the ring from its cushion. "You're sure this is what you want?"

She only nodded and held out her hand.

As he slid the ring onto her finger, he marveled at how *right* it looked. It was sturdy enough to withstand the abuse it was sure to endure in her line of work but unmistakably feminine—just as Heather was. As she kissed him, their friends and family cheered. He tucked his arms around her and rested his forehead against hers.

"Any ideas about *when* you want to get married?" he asked.

"Next summer—August third. I *think* it's a Sunday."

"That's oddly specific."

"It's the one-year anniversary of the day you got shot."

He lifted a brow at her. "*Now* who has the morbid sense of humor?"

"It's not morbid. It's… making the anniversary of the day you almost died the first day of our life together as husband and wife. Overwriting a horrible memory with a good one. You seem to like connections like that—the quirks of life and fate, as you say. What do you think? Perfect or a horrible idea?"

"Perfect. Now, we're absolutely sure I haven't died and gone to heaven?" he asked. "Right? I mean, surely life can't be *this* incredible."

This time, even though it was a terrible joke, she laughed. "I adore you. Getting tired of hearing that yet, angel?"

Grinning against her lips as he kissed her again, he whispered, "I'll *never* get tired of hearing it, baby girl."

Epilogue

HEATHER HAD BARELY STEPPED through the front door when the phone rang. Dropping her bag on the floor she raced to answer it, glancing briefly at the caller ID as she grabbed the cordless. Murphy pranced around her feet and she reached down to pet him.

"Hi, Tracie," she greeted breathlessly.

"Ah, you're home at last! How'd everything go?"

"Fantastic. As easy as we could hope for."

"Glad to hear it. How'd Murphy react to that new baby?"

"He is absolutely smitten with her."

"Where's Jeremiah?"

"Bringing Ellie in. I can't wait for you to meet her, Tracie. She has the most beautiful blue eyes."

"Just like her big brother."

The phone beeped in her ear. "Hey, can I call you back in a minute? Christina and Curtis are calling."

"Don't worry about that. I'll just come up, if that's all right. I can't wait to meet my new granddaughter."

"We'll see you in a few," Heather laughed and switched the phone over. "Hi, Chris."

"Actually, it's Curtis. Chris is outside with the kids. I'm just calling to see if you guys are home yet. Obviously you are. Are you feeling up for a visit or would you rather we gave you a couple hours to get adjusted?"

"No, come on over."

"Um… Mom and Dad wanted to know if they'll get to meet the newest member of your family."

Heather let out a breath. Once she'd gotten over her guilt for cutting most of her family out of her life, she had found a new rhythm and a blissful peace without their constant negativity. She'd already broken her promise to herself and invited her parents to her and Jeremiah's wedding reception not quite a month ago. Her mother had initially been upset Heather hadn't invited them to the wedding, too—proving why Heather had been right to exclude her from the ceremony—but at least she'd *sort of* apologized for all the pain she'd put her daughter through over the course of her life.

She hadn't talked to Brock or Brianna at all in the last year—not even to meet Brianna and Todd's new daughter.

Her relationship with her father was easier. Part of her still resented that it had taken Jeremiah getting shot to convince Brian he was a good man, but at least he'd been friendly in the last year. It irritated her mother to no end that Heather had welcomed him back into her life, but he was willing to abide by Heather's wishes. Lily wasn't, and at this point, Heather doubted she ever would be. Which was fine with her. Her new life was quite comfortable and enjoyable just the way it was.

"Heather?" Curtis asked. "If it's taking that long to make a decision, the answer's probably no. Go ahead and say it. She'll just have to accept it."

He had a point, but… she was curious.

"Yes, Mom can come meet her," she replied finally, "but not today. Dad can come with you if he wants."

"I think he'll wait until you say Mom can come meet your little girl. All right, Chris and I will be over in a bit."

"You're going to bring the kids, right?"

"Of course. Joseph is dying to see his Un Juh."

Heather smiled, remembering Christina's remark that Joseph would have a stronger bond with Jeremiah than with his own father. It hadn't *quite* come true, but Jeremiah was easily one of Joseph's favorite people, and he definitely had a special bond with the little boy. "See you then."

She ended the call and set the cordless back in its cradle, wondering what was taking Jeremiah so long. When she and Murph stepped out onto the porch of their new home—a beautiful two-story affair with a stunning view of the Lazy H Ranch—she saw *exactly* what had delayed Jeremiah. Tracie was here already, ooing and awing over her new granddaughter.

Was I on the phone with Curtis that *long?*

With Ellie tucked in her arm, Tracie embraced Heather. "You're so right. She *does* have the most beautiful blue eyes."

As if the twelve-week-old Aussie pup understood

every word, she licked Tracie's face enthusiastically, eliciting a girlish giggle from the matriarch of the Hammond clan. Heather ruffled the little girl's ears.

"I thought you wanted the mom," Tracie said. "What changed?"

"We did," Jeremiah replied, "but she's going to an even better home—she's going to be a therapy dog for a little girl with autism. It was a good week for this family of rescue Aussies. Both of Ellie's littermates got adopted, too."

"Wonderful. What did the rescue people think of Murph?"

"They adored him, naturally." Jeremiah squatted to give his dog loves, laughing when Murphy was more concerned with sniffing his new sister. "And he was too enamored with Ellie and her pretty mama to be his usual shy self. Needless to say, the folks at the rescue didn't have any concerns about what kind of life Ellie would have here."

"I bet not."

"Come on in, Mom. No point in standing out here sweating."

"I will, but I have something out in my car for you. Here."

Tracie handed Ellie to Heather and trotted out to her car, returning moments later with an external hard drive. "Skye finished going through all your wedding photos, and now she needs you to pick which ones you want made into prints." Tracie glanced around their house, which they'd moved into only a month ago—right before their wedding. "Because you need some pictures to make this place look lived in."

"We do indeed," Heather agreed. "Would it be too

much to ask to get some copies of some of the pictures you have of Jeremiah with your family?"

"It absolutely would not be."

Noticing that Murphy had been staring at her for some time now, Heather gave in and set Ellie on the floor with him. They immediately started playing, and she was impressed again by how gentle he was with her. He was just a good dog, all the way around. Glancing at Jeremiah as he made his way back into the living room with their shiny new MacBook Pro, she smiled. Like owner, like dog—just good. Or was it the other way around?

They streamed the photos of their wedding to the Apple TV so everyone could see, and as they browsed, Heather had a hard time deciding which ones she wanted made into prints. The one of their first kiss as husband and wife was a definite must-have, but otherwise, they were all so good and captured their love for each other so elegantly that she had no idea how they were supposed to choose. There were a few Skye had taken of Jeremiah and the doctor and nurses who had saved his life, and maybe it was weird, but Heather wanted a print of one of them—a reminder of how special each day with him was just in case she ever started to take him for granted.

At some point, Curtis and Christina showed up with their three kids, and they had to start over. As the humans talked photos and the dogs played, Heather glanced around her. This was what life was supposed to be all about.

Leaning against Jeremiah and sharing him with little Joseph, she beamed at him. "I'm so glad you offered to salvage my birthday last year."

He kissed the top of her head. "Me, too."

Suzie O'Connell

She took him by the chin and kissed him soundly. "Took you long enough."

* * * *

About the Author

Suzie O'Connell is the *USA Today* bestselling author of the Northstar romances. The series is the product of a love affair with Southwestern Montana that began with a two-week adventure at her stepsister's rustic cabin in her teens. That love affair shows no sign of abating.

She has been writing stories for as long as she can remember, and her love of writing and of Montana pushed her to earn a Bachelor of Arts in Literature and Writing from the University of Montana-Western. What else would you expect from a self-professed mountain-loving nerd?

When she isn't writing, you'll probably find Suzie in the mountains with a camera in hand and enjoying the beauty of Montana with her husband Mark, their daughter Maddie, and their golden retrievers Reilly and Angus.

Find Suzie online at www.suzieoconnell.com